THE PALACE OF LAUGHTER

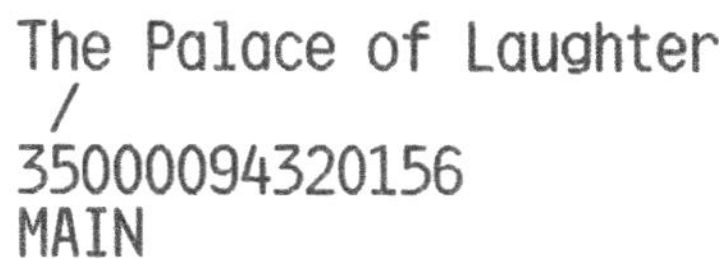

THE WEDNESDAY TALES ~ NO. 1

JON BERKELEY

ILLUSTRATED BY BRANDON DORMAN

THE JULIE ANDREWS COLLECTION
HARPERCOLLINS*PUBLISHERS*

The Palace of Laughter: The Wednesday Tales No. 1

For information address HarperCollins Children's Books, a division of HarperCollins Publishers, 1350 Avenue of the Americas, New York, NY 10019.
www.harperchildrens.com

Library of Congress Cataloging-in-Publication Data
Berkeley, Jon.
The Palace of Laughter / Jon Berkeley.— 1st ed.
p. cm. — (the Wednesday tales ; no. 1) (The Julie Andrews collection)
Summary: Orphaned eleven-year-old Miles Wednesday and his companion, a Song Angel named Little, are helped by a talking tiger as they set off to find a missing Storm Angel and Miles's beloved stuffed bear, ending up in a peculiar circus where the audience cannot stop laughing.
ISBN-10: 0-06-075507-5 (trade bdg.)
ISBN-13: 978-0-06-075507-2 (trade bdg.)
ISBN-10: 0-06-075508-3 (lib. bdg.)
ISBN-13: 978-0-06-075508-9 (lib. bdg.)
[1. Adventure and adventurers—Fiction. 2. Circus—Fiction. 3. Angels—Fiction. 4. Orphans—Fiction. 5. Tigers—Fiction.] I. Title. II. Series.
PZ7.B45255Pal 2006 2005022801
[Fic]—dc22 CIP
AC

Typography by Christopher Stengel
1 2 3 4 5 6 7 8 9 10

First Edition

This one's for Orna,
who makes the magic happen round here

CONTENTS

One: A Boy in a Barrel 1

Two: A Bag of Bones 11

Three: The Tiny Acrobat 20

Four: The Null 30

Five: A Black Hole 41

Six: Lady Partridge 60

Seven: Falling Through Thunder 75

Eight: The Silver Ticket 90

Nine: The Council of Cats 97

Ten: The Surly Hen 107

Eleven: Tangerine 124

Twelve: Sunflower and Stormcloud 132

Thirteen: Varippuli 145

Fourteen: Baltinglass of Araby 158

Fifteen: Apple Jelly 168

Sixteen: Big Laughing Head 181

Seventeen: Halfheads 188

Eighteen: Boneyard 202

Nineteen: Pigball 218

Twenty: A Nest of Ants 227

Twenty-one: A Mouthful of Nails 251

Twenty-two: Back to Front and Inside Out 264

Twenty-three: Top Hat and Sandbag 274

Twenty-four: Silverpoint 283

Twenty-five: A Box of Stars 294

Twenty-six: The Electric Boy 304

Twenty-seven: Providence 314

Twenty-eight: Chief Genghis 331

Twenty-nine: Fish to Fry 344

Thirty: Many a Slip 357

Thirty-one: Tin Can't 373

Thirty-two: String 388

Thirty-three: Little 395

Thirty-four: *The Larde Weekly Herald* 416

THE PALACE OF LAUGHTER

CHAPTER ONE
A BOY IN A BARREL

On a blustery October night the Circus Oscuro came to town. It was clear from the start that this was no ordinary circus. It did not roll into town with fanfares and cartwheeling clowns. No one handed out flyers or announced the show through squawking loudspeakers. Instead, the circus came in the dead of night, when all the townspeople were asleep. Its wagons crept and rumbled down the winding road and across the old stone bridge while the town's fat mayor, who normally had to give his permission before anyone could set up as much as a fruit stall, was snoring in his bed. The circus wagons turned in to the long field at the bottom of the hill that overlooked the town of Larde, and creaked to a halt in neat rows with barely a sound.

From the wagons and trucks a strange crew emerged into the moonlight—great muscled men with sun-darkened faces, a tattooed giantess with a booming voice who could lift three of the men at once, small wiry boys dragging coils of rope and buckets of sawdust. They began to set up their enormous tent there and then by the light of flickering lanterns, with the wind whipping at the stripy canvas and cracking the ropes across the men's hairy arms. Their shouts and curses were snatched from their throats by the wind and flung up over the hill. Two elephants were led from one of the wagons and set to work, lifting wooden poles into place and pushing them upright with their stubbly foreheads. Acrobats ran up the swaying poles like monkeys, fixing ropes and leaping from point to point as though they were only inches from the ground, gripping lanterns in their strong teeth. A thin man on stilts 20 feet high checked blocks and pulleys and shouted orders to the men below. Slowly the huge tent rose from the grassy field like a great beast awakening, and still the townspeople slept, and the fat mayor's snores ruffled his walrus mustache and rumbled through his wife's dreams.

There was just one witness to the arrival of the circus. A small boy, huddled in a large wooden barrel high on the side of the hill, watched the raising of the big top, awakened from his sleep by the shouts of the circus people and the occasional trumpeting of the elephants. The boy's name was Miles, and the barrel was his home.

Now if you are picturing a shivering boy standing knee-deep in slimy rainwater in an upright barrel, you will need to turn that picture sideways and let the water run out for a start. This barrel lay on its side under a low-spreading pine tree, which provided shelter from the wind and the rain. It was an enormous barrel that had once held a fine vintage wine, and Miles could almost stand upright in it, although he was nearly eleven. It was dry and warm inside. In the barrel was an old mattress that had been thrown out by Piven, the baker, and which still gave out a cloud of fine flour when you sat on it. A candle stub in a fat bottle served as a lamp, and an old biscuit tin with the paint worn off as a larder.

Miles had lived in his barrel on the side of the hill since escaping (for the seventh time) from Pinchbucket House, the county orphanage. He shared his wooden home with a small stuffed bear named Tangerine, no larger than a tall man's hand. When Tangerine wasn't out and about with his owner, he lived in a deep pocket of the old overcoat that Miles used as a blanket. Some of Tangerine's stuffing had escaped, which made him a little floppy. His fur, which had once been the color of a tangerine, was now a kind of orangey gray. His mouth wore a crooked smile, and although he never said a word, he was a good listener.

Under a silver moon Miles, curled up in the mouth of his barrel, watched as the circus tent grew fatter and taller and the thick ropes that anchored it grew tauter. The hypnotic ringing of sledgehammers on iron pegs and the snatches of strange music that floated from the trailers made his eyes heavy and his head nod with sleep. He pulled the old overcoat tighter around him, and closed his eyes for a moment.

When he opened them again he did not know how much time had passed, but everything seemed strangely still. Not an owl's hoot or mouse's rustle broke the silence, and the pine tree stood silently, undisturbed by the faintest breeze. Miles rubbed his eyes and looked out to see if work on the circus tent had ceased, but his eye was caught by something that had not been there before. A large shape crouched in the grass not twenty paces from where he sat in the mouth of his barrel. A shape with a huge head, enormous paws and a long striped tail. It was a fully grown Bengal tiger, stretched out motionless except for the tip of his tail, which twitched from side to side in the silvery grass.

The tiger was so close Miles could almost count his whiskers. His inky stripes seemed to shift and breathe as the thin clouds swept across the moon. Miles held his breath. It was no use crying out; no one would hear him. He had never been face to face with a tiger before, but he was pretty sure that to the magnificent striped beast who sat a stone's throw from his barrel, he must look like a sandwich whose bread had fallen off.

The tiger yawned, his teeth like yellow knives in the red cave of his mouth, and gave a loud but oddly human sigh that made his whiskers shiver. His massive head turned and he stared directly at Miles with his amber eyes. The world turned and the grass grew, and still the tiger regarded the boy silently. Although he had never seen a tiger before, Miles found his gaze strangely familiar, like an echo of a dream often visited and always forgotten. He could feel his heart thumping, and realized that he had not taken a breath since the tiger had appeared.

"Most people run," said the tiger at last, in a deep smooth voice. He flicked the tip of his tail.

Miles said nothing for a moment. Obviously the tiger could not really have spoken to him. Everyone knows that tigers can't talk. Except for the tiger himself it seems, who was waiting for an answer.

"I have nowhere to run to," said Miles, his voice barely above a whisper. "So if you are going to eat me," he added after a moment, "please make it quick."

The tiger gazed at the skinny boy, wrapped in an oversized overcoat and curled up in the mouth of a barrel. "Now that you mention it," he said, "I do get a little peckish at this time of the morning, but you wouldn't make much of a snack."

"You're right about that," said Miles in a slightly stronger voice. "I am very thin, and . . . and my feet smell terrible! I don't think you'd like them at all, unless you like strong cheese."

The tiger made a rumbling noise, which might have been a chuckle, or the sound of an empty stomach. "I've eaten far fouler things than you, tub boy," he said. "I once ate a health and safety inspector, clipboard, bowler hat and all. I had stomach cramps for a week."

"D-didn't that get you into terrible trouble?" asked Miles.

"On the contrary," rumbled the tiger. "I was given a week off from performances, and a whole wagon to myself."

He got to his feet and stretched himself, five hundred pounds of teeth and muscle rippling in the moonlight. "All this talk of food is making me hungry after all," he said, taking a step toward the barrel and fixing Miles with his steady gaze. "And one can't be too choosy when there's only one item on the menu."

Miles shrank down into the overcoat, trying to look stringy and unappetizing. He had often wished he were anywhere but inside a wooden barrel on the side of a hill, but it had to be better than being inside a large tiger's stomach. He groped desperately behind him on the untidy floor of the barrel. His fingers closed on the stub of a candle. No good. He dropped it and groped again, finding one of his threadbare socks. "Maybe I can stink him to death," he thought as the tiger padded closer. He was only a few whisker lengths away now. His hot musty breath warmed the boy's face, and his eyes burned like cold fire, but Miles could not look away. The tiger stopped, the rising sun giving him a halo of fur the color of flame.

"You can stop scrabbling, little tub boy," he said.

"There are some hungers too deep to be satisfied by skin and bones." His nose twitched slightly. "Besides," he said, "I never had a taste for circus people."

"What do you mean?" asked Miles, the words barely escaping his dry throat.

"What I say," said the tiger. "I can smell the circus in you, though you don't look like you could even stand on your head."

"I can't," said Miles, "and I've never even been to a circus."

"Believe what you will," said the tiger, and he turned slowly and began to pad down the grassy slope without a backward glance. The circus was quiet now, its people hidden in their wagons as the town began to stretch and wake in the dawn. The only sound from below was the faint cracking of the long black pennant that fluttered from the peak of the big top, and the squeaking of a rusty wheelbarrow in which a tiny man carried large slabs of red meat between the animal cages, shoving them through the bars with a stout pole and whistling softly to himself.

Miles rubbed his eyes, which smarted from lack of sleep. He shook his head and looked down the hill, but the tiger was nowhere to be seen, and the wheelbarrow sat empty and unattended in the shadow of the farthest wagon.

• • ● • •

Miles woke again when the morning sun was already high in the sky. He was stiff from sleeping curled up in the mouth of his barrel, and his hungry stomach grumbled. He looked down to the bottom of the hill, half expecting to see nothing but an empty field, but there it was, the enormous black and red tent with its rows of silent wagons. "At least that part wasn't a dream," he said to Tangerine, whose head poked from the overcoat pocket. Tangerine just smiled.

In the daylight Miles could see more clearly what a strange circus it was. The wagons were painted in dark and lurid colors, with patterns that were spiky and tangled. Their wooden wheels were studded with iron hobnails. The largest wagon was decorated with an enormous clown's face, his eyes and black-lipped mouth wide open in a silent laugh, and his electric-blue hair standing out from his head, like a hungry crocodile that had been struck by lightning. There was a painted scroll beneath the clown's head, and Miles squinted as he read the letters. "The Great Cortado," said the scroll. The name was somehow ominous. *The Great Cortado.* He shivered in the thin sunlight.

The two elephants were tethered to a tree at the

edge of the field, where they stood patiently resting from their labors of the night before. Other beasts could be half seen in their cages. Several monkeys screeched insults at the haughty camels next door. Another wagon housed a pair of zebras whose stripes blended with the shadows of the bars, so that you could only see them when they moved. A long scaly tail hung through the bars of one cage almost to the ground. Miles searched for any sign of a tiger.

There was one wagon set apart from the others in a corner of the field. It was painted entirely in red, except for black frames on the door and on the tiny barred windows. The door was fitted with three strong bolts, each with a padlock the size of a man's fist. The dogs that ran in circles, barking at the flapping canvas and stealing scraps of meat that had dropped from the cages, steered well clear of the corner where the red wagon stood. It seemed a strange sort of housing for a tiger.

"As soon as it gets dark," said Miles to Tangerine, "we're going to sneak into that circus, and we're going to find that tiger, if he really exists."

CHAPTER TWO
A BAG OF BONES

Miles Wednesday, barrel-dwelling, unwashed and tiger-visited, made his way through the narrow streets of Larde until he reached the warm smelly butcher's shop in Sausage Lane. Haunch the butcher was chopping ribs with a shiny cleaver, flipping them over on his worn wooden block behind the marble counter and grumbling to his customers as he chopped. He saw Miles in the doorway and scowled.

"You again," he said in his big bassoon voice. "It's no good scrounging off me. I've got nothing for you."

"I'm not scrounging," said Miles. "I'm looking for

work. You must have something you need doing."

The butcher grunted and went back to his chopping and complaining, while the women queuing for his paper parcels of meat clucked sympathetically. Miles waited patiently, his arms folded and his feet planted wide in the doorway, making it difficult for the butcher to ignore him.

"Well don't just stand there," he growled eventually, as he handed a packet of sausages to a big square woman with a head scarf knotted under her chin. "Out the back with you and get scrubbing. And mind you make a good job of it or you'll feel the toe of my boot."

Miles slipped through the forest of women in their scratchy woolen coats, out into the butcher's yard, where halved carcasses swung from steel hooks, and the smell of old blood made it hard to breathe. He filled the wooden pail with soapy water and began to scrub the cracked tiles with a worn brush. The water was cold and his hands were soon red and raw, but he scrubbed and dunked and scrubbed again. The last time he had cleaned out Haunch's yard he had been paid with a dozen leftover sausages. He could almost smell them now, sizzling plumply on the end of a stick, the drops of fat hissing on his little campfire under the pine tree on the side of the hill.

As he scrubbed the smelly yard he thought about the tiger. Its steady gaze burned so clear in his memory that a couple of times he glanced over his shoulder, half expecting to see the huge beast stretched out in the corner, watching him. His head buzzed with the strange sounds of the circus, and when his hunger made him dizzy, the patterns in front of his eyes were spiky and tangled like the decorations on the wagons. He could not wait for nightfall, when he would sneak into the circus and look for the tiger's cage, just to see if he was real. Darkness seemed a long time away, and he scrubbed even harder, as though it would make time pass more quickly.

A burst of laughter came from the butcher's crowded shop, the cackling of the customers like a flock of geese startled by the distant thunder of the big man's guffaw. Miles edged toward the back door to see what was happening. Laughter had been strictly banned in Pinchbucket House, and it always made him curious. The butcher was wiping his eye with the corner of his apron. "There's not enough laughter in this world," he said, and he brought his chopper down hard on a chunk of meat. His customers nodded and sighed, their shoulders sagging and the tiredness returning to their faces. Miles went back to work.

By the time he had finished, the floor tiles were gleaming, and the pail had been emptied of water and filled with the big blue-knuckled bones that had littered the yard. Haunch came to the door and scowled at the scrubbed floor, as though it were knee-deep in rotting meat.

"Hmff," he grunted.

"I'd like my sausages please," said Miles. His stomach was rumbling at the thought.

"No sausages," grunted the butcher. "Sold out of sausages. Sold out of everything. You can have some bones."

"Bones?" said Miles "I can't eat bones!"

"Boil 'em up. Make soup," said the butcher. "Bones is all I got." He shook open a paper bag and scooped a few handfuls of bones from the wooden pail, rolling the top of the bag shut and thrusting it into Miles's arms. "Hold it underneath," growled the butcher, "else them bones will fall out the bottom."

As Miles left the butcher's shop, his bag of bones clutched in his numb fingers, the butcher called after him. "Shouldn't of never left that orphanage. You'd've got properly fed there."

"I'd have got properly poisoned there," Miles shouted back over his shoulder, "if I'd stayed much longer."

A pale sun hung low in the afternoon sky, and the sound of barking dogs carried on the breeze from the city pound. The smell of the butcher's bones seeped from the soggy brown bag, making Miles turn his head to the side just to breathe clean air. "I can't make soup from these," he thought. "Even Mrs. Pinchbucket's gruel would be better than that." He stopped for a moment, shifting the weight of the bag in his aching arms.

A smile crept over the boy's face. If you knew Miles well (which few people did) you would have recognized that smile as the one that always appeared on his face when a plan was hatching in the back of his mind. The smile grew wider, and he turned to head for the pound, following the noisy barking of the mongrels of Larde.

The city pound was a narrow yard beside the police station, surrounded by a high red-bricked wall. Right now it was full of shaggy, limping, drooling dogs, the result of Mayor Doggett's annual roundup of the town's stray mongrels. The order had been telephoned to Sergeant Bramley, who had listened with his little raisin eyes screwed up in his porridgy face. Sergeant Bramley and his two trusty constables had dropped their official duties (searching the newspapers for evidence of crimes, especially in the crossword clues, and making hot sweet tea in a battered tin pot in case of emergencies), and had marched out purposefully into the street with a large net on a pole, and two big cloth sacks.

The sergeant and his constables, who worked in a crack team of three, had rounded up the dogs of Larde and taken them into custody for the Good of Public Health. They knew the mayor's fickle attention would soon turn elsewhere, and the dogs could be quietly released "back into the wild," as Constable Wigge put it, and in any case it made a change from the crossword.

The barking grew louder as Miles approached the pound. Thirty mongrels and more were in full throat at the sound of his footsteps and the reek of tasty bones carried on the breeze. Miles laid the bag carefully outside the pound, leaving the smell to creep over the high wall, and climbed the worn stone steps of the police station next door.

The police station was small and cluttered and stuffy. It contained two old wooden desks, an ancient typewriter with several keys missing, a cast-iron potbellied stove, three very unhappy policemen and a little old woman with a green umbrella. The end of the umbrella was a dangerous metal spike, and its owner was waving this under Sergeant Bramley's shapeless nose. She was yelling at him angrily, but what she could be yelling about it was impossible to tell. The pokey office was so full of the din of barking dogs that there was no room for any other sound. Indeed the old woman might have been barking herself and no one would have been any the wiser.

Sergeant Bramley had his hand cupped behind his good ear. He was trying to lean close to hear the old woman's words without getting the point of her umbrella up his nose at the same time. He turned and bawled something at Constable Wigge, but Constable Wigge could hear nothing, as his ears were plugged with soft wax from the candle on his desk. He was frowning at the crossword, trying to think of a seven-letter word beginning with "B" and meaning "dog speech."

Constable Flap, who had once done a short course in lipreading in *Modern Constable* magazine and could read the sergeant's flabby lips like a large-print book, leaped from his seat instead, and opened the side door that led into the pound. The noise of the dogs was deafening. Constable Flap opened his mouth and yelled "QUI-ET!" but his mouth was small and his voice was reedy, and the dogs ignored him completely. He shut the door again and flopped back, defeated, into his chair.

Miles climbed onto a stool beside the high counter, where he found a yellow pencil stub and some squares of paper. He thought for a moment, then wrote carefully with the neat letters that his friend Lady Partridge—who lived up a tree—had taught him:

I CAN STUP THE DOGGS BARKENG

He slid the note over to the sergeant. The old lady was still shouting at the top of her voice, despite the barking of the dogs, and the sergeant's glasses were flecked with old-lady spit. He removed them from his nose and wiped them with his handkerchief. He read the note twice, then turned it over to see if there was more.

He squinted at Miles for a moment, then he reached into his pocket and held up a silver coin. Miles nodded and left the police station, being careful to close the door behind him. He picked up the bag of bones and selected the biggest one. This he wrapped in paper torn from the bag and wedged it into his pocket. Then he began to toss the rest of the bones, as quickly as he could, over the wall. The barking turned to snarling and yelping as the dogs fought and nipped and shoved, then one by one they fell silent, until the only sound was the crunching and cracking of dog teeth on butcher bones, and the occasional growl as a dog warned his bone not to try any funny business.

Back inside the police station the silence seemed almost as deafening as the barking had been. Constable Wigge had removed the candle wax from his ears and was writing in his crossword, his tongue sticking out with the effort: B-A-R-K-I-N-G. The sergeant stood and stared, his pudgy fingers still holding the coin in the air. Miles climbed onto the stool, plucked the money from his fingers, said thank you, and jumped down again. The old lady jabbed Sergeant Bramley in the chest with the point of her umbrella.

"Well?" she shrieked. "What are you going to do about it?"

"About what?" asked Sergeant Bramley.

CHAPTER THREE
THE TINY ACROBAT

Miles Wednesday, wind-swayed, bread and cheese in hand, sat in the fork of a tall tree outside Pinchbucket House. He had bought his dinner with the sergeant's shilling, but it was not yet dark enough to sneak into the circus. With time to kill, his feet had found their way through the familiar lanes to the grimy building that had once been his home.

Pinchbucket House was a squat gray building with row upon row of small, mean windows. Steam belched from basement-level gratings, creating a permanent fog around the lower floors. Any children of Larde or the surrounding area who had the misfortune to lose their parents would sooner or later find themselves hauled to the doorstep of Pinchbucket House. Once inside those gray metal doors, they would have their hair shaved off (Mrs. Pinchbucket sold it to the wigmaker in Calvo Lane), and their nice clothes (if they had any) exchanged for a set of worn and faded pajamas. Anything of value in their pockets would end up in the locked tin box under Mrs. Pinchbucket's rickety iron bed.

In return the child would be given a name taken from the day on which he arrived, and set to work in the sweltering laundry that steamed and rumbled all day long in the basement of Pinchbucket House. The only child in the whole building who was not named after a day of the week was Hettie November. She had been found, half frozen in a cardboard box on the orphanage steps, while Mrs. Pinchbucket was in the hospital having a stubborn trace of generosity removed. Her husband, Fowler Pinchbucket, who could not tell one day from another, had put the child in the boiler room to thaw out and forgotten all about her, until one of the older girls heard her whimpering and rescued her from the sooty basement. Miles himself had been brought there as a baby, and could remember no other home.

From his perch in the tree Miles had a clear view through the lit windows at all the little Fridays, Mondays, Saturdays and Tuesdays who sat in shaven-headed rows at the two long tables that stretched the length of the dining hall. Mrs. Pinchbucket, as thin and dry as a pencil, stalked between the tables, rapping her knuckles on the skull of any child who was not spooning gruel into his or her mouth as fast as possible. Miles imagined he had a powerful catapult and a smooth stone in his hand, and squinted through one eye. Mrs. Pinchbucket's nose, like a pink shark's fin dividing her sour face, made a tempting target.

Fowler Pinchbucket was kneeling by a square hole in the wall, a screwdriver between his crooked teeth. A tangle of brown and black wires stuck out of the hole, and Fowler frowned stupidly as he looked at them. Fowler fixed everything in Pinchbucket House to save money, and once something had been fixed by Fowler the Growler it was never the same again.

Miles had finished his bread and cheese and was about to climb down from the tree, when Fowler Pinchbucket reached a decision on his electrical problem. He grabbed a thick black wire and a crumbling brown one with his hard square fingers and twisted them together. There was a loud bang and all the lights in the orphanage went out. The lumpish silhouette of Fowler Pinchbucket flew backward through the dining hall in a shower of sparks.

As the lights flickered back on, a singed figure could be seen rising unsteadily to his feet. His hair stood out from his head like blackened corkscrews, and wisps of blue smoke escaped from the collar and cuffs of his shredded shirt. One of his shoes had landed upside down in Ruben Monday's soup bowl, the other was steaming in the mop bucket. He swayed on his stockinged feet for a moment or two, squinting at Mrs. Pinchbucket as though trying to remember who she was.

At the sight of the singed Fowler Pinchbucket the children burst into laughter, and the sound seemed to fill the drab dining room with warmth. Now you might remember that laughter was strictly forbidden in Pinchbucket House, and at the sight of the laughing orphans Fowler's face turned even blacker. He took a wild swipe at the nearest table, knocking a small child clean off the wooden bench and smashing a couple of plates. At the other end of the table Mrs. Pinchbucket boxed a few ears for good measure. The laughter died at once, leaving only the ceaseless clanking and belching from the laundry below, and the scraping of benches as the children scrambled to their feet, ready to be marched to their dormitory.

Miles sat in the fork of the tree a moment longer, feeling the same knot in his stomach that had awoken him every cold morning in Pinchbucket House. He pictured himself now, bursting in through the gray doors on the back of a magnificent tiger, leaping the stairs in a couple of bounds and prowling into the dining hall, where the tiger would swallow the Pinchbuckets whole, to the cheers and whoops of the orphans.

He thought of his barrel on the side of the hill, where he would curl up later that night with only a stuffed bear and the hooting of the owls for company, and quickly turned his mind to the circus instead. Dusk was falling, and he had an appointment to keep. He scrambled down the tree, and his feet skipped on the worn paving stones as he trotted down the hill toward Beggar's Gate, feeling the weight of the bone that he had kept for the tiger swinging in his jacket as he ran.

The strange smells of animals from foreign lands drifted through the narrow streets at the edge of town. The townspeople were making their way in a steady stream toward the circus, which was dressed in a million red and yellow lights. They pushed and jostled, and their children pulled eagerly on their hands as they followed the jangly music and the rolling of drums. Brightly colored posters were tied to every lamppost. Some showed daring trapeze artists flying through painted air; from others the proud face of a tiger snarled, his great paws raised in menace. Miles joined the crowds, hoping to slip in unnoticed among them, but at the circus entrance he spotted Constable Flap standing on tip-toes to shout in the ear of the tattooed giantess, who loomed over the policeman as she collected the tickets at the turnstile. Miles remembered Constable Flap's Special Ear Pinch Arrest Method, which he had also learned from a short course in *Modern Constable* magazine, and decided to find another way into the circus.

He made his way around the edge of the moonlit field, where the outer trailers squatted silently in pools of darkness. Miles slipped in among the wagons, looking for anything that might betray the presence of a tiger. As he darted between the shadows he saw two men walking toward him, deep in conversation. One was a dwarf wearing a shiny round helmet decorated with flames. The other was a big square man with a high old-fashioned collar and a bowler hat. His huge bloated belly hung out between his suspenders, and the ends of his trousers stopped several inches short of his ankles, as though he were expecting a flood.

"Now look here, Mr. Genghis," the dwarf was saying. "I need a proper flying suit for this stunt."

The big-bellied man gave a wheezy laugh. "A flying suit, is it? We ain't shooting you to the moon, you pocket-sized prima donna."

"You can laugh," said the dwarf testily, "but last show I was blown clean out of my trousers by the gunpowder, and it's no fun sailing over five 'undred people in your second-best underwear."

Miles ducked down just in time and slipped under the canvas of the circus tent where a missing rope left it flapping loosely in the breeze. He found himself under banked rows of wooden seats, his boots squelching slightly in the trampled mud. The orchestra had struck up for the start of the show, and Miles moved forward quietly, crouching down as he came to the lower benches nearest the ring.

Looking for a clear view through a forest of ankles, he caught a glimpse of the elephants that he had seen the night before. They wore ornate blankets with swinging tassles now, and a man in shiny knee-length boots was cracking a whip and shouting commands at them in an unfamiliar tongue. Miles could only see the bottom half of the elephants, their wrinkled knees bending as they performed some trick that he could not see. The crowd applauded, and the shiny-booted man bellowed something more at the elephants. Their big round feet began to trot around the ring. A clown's baggy trousers and battered boots appeared, the feet leaping high as he ran in front of the elephants. The townspeople laughed and clapped some more.

As Miles hunkered down to watch, a generous scoop of ice cream dropped through a gap between the benches and fell straight down the back of his shirt collar. His gasp was drowned out by a child's wail from the seat above him. The upside-down, ice cream–smeared face of a small girl appeared below the bench. Her eyes widened when she saw Miles. "Give me back my ice cream," she yelled at him. Several voices shushed her. She shouted louder.

"Mum—a mucky boy has my ice cream! Dad! There's an escaped ice cream thief under the seats!" As Miles scrambled away in the gloom a few more heads appeared below the level of the seats and peered about, like ducks foraging for river weeds.

If you've ever had to crawl through cold mud with

half a pound of strawberry-vanilla ice cream creeping down your spine, you will know why Miles felt that his first visit to a circus was not going according to plan. As soon as he had put a safe distance between himself and the scene of the crime, he sat down in the muddy grass below the banked backsides of the people of Larde, and removed his shirt and jacket. He rolled the sodden shirt into a ball and crammed it into his remaining jacket pocket, then put his jacket back on and buttoned it up tight.

He turned back to face the ring, and found himself a gap between a pair of pin-striped trousers and some very tall high heels, which gave him a clearer view of the performance.

The elephants and the clown had gone, and in the center of the sawdust-carpeted ring sat a large frosted white ball. Balancing on the ball was a colored pyramid, and on top of the pyramid wobbled a cube, and on top of the cube another frosted ball, and on this ball a steel table was balanced on its side, and as Miles craned forward, he could see more and more shapes piled up in a teetering tower that stretched up almost to the pointed roof of the circus tent.

At the very top of this precarious tower stood a tiny girl in a sparkling white outfit. Thirty feet from the ground she balanced on tiny feet, with her arms outstretched and her head held high. No one watching dared to draw a breath. Every eye in the tent was fixed on the little girl, who looked no more than six years old. Her short blond hair was tucked behind her ears, and though she was lit by a spotlight she seemed to give off a soft glow of her own. To Miles she looked like a magical creature, more like a dream than the tiger he had dreamed of the night before. As he watched, transfixed, he saw her glance down at the crowd far below her, and Miles was sure that she looked straight at him, hidden in the gloom between the ankles of the people of Larde.

And then it happened—the tower began to fall. A ball halfway up began to wobble off the pyramid that supported it; the cylinder on top of the ball tipped the other way, and the whole fabulous balancing act came undone in slow motion and began to cascade to the ground. The crowd gasped in horror as the tiny girl began to fall to earth, her eyes wide with fright, and neither net nor cushion to catch her.

CHAPTER FOUR
THE NULL

Miles Wednesday, ice-cream-chilled and mucky-booted, saw the tiny acrobat fall from the toppling tower. Before he knew what he was doing, he was scrambling through the gap between the bench and the walkway as though he could catch her in his arms, but as he clambered over the seat in front of him the crowd gave another gasp, this time in wonder. Halfway to the ground the girl's fall had suddenly slowed. A pair of delicate pearly wings sprouted from her shoulders, fluttering minutely as she floated gently to the ground.

Her feet touched down so lightly that they left

no mark in the sawdust. Her wings folded and tucked themselves away, and a tiny smile crossed her face as the last of the colored shapes crashed to the ground around her and bounced to a standstill. In the stunned silence she looked directly at Miles, who was suspended half in and half out of the darkness. She looked into his face with her clear blue eyes and gave him a tiny bow, before being scooped from her feet and set on a beautiful piebald horse, which carried her proudly from the ring and through the star-strewn velvet curtains at the back.

Forgetting altogether that he was not supposed to be there, Miles picked himself up from the dusty planking, and stared at the swinging curtain through which the horse and his rider had disappeared. He was not the only one. At the other end of the curtain stood the ringmaster, a small neat man in red trousers and high black boots, and he too was staring after the tiny acrobat, stroking his blue chin beneath his enormous mustache and frowning to himself.

Some of the townsfolk broke into halfhearted applause, but others were confused and angry.

"Shouldn't be allowed to give people frights like that," said a woman with a fur collar.

"Nearly gave me a heart attack," said another.

"If you ask me she's far too young to be performing dangerous stunts," said her husband. "You can be sure they're breaking some law putting her up there. Probably breaking a dozen of them."

"It's all done with mirrors," said a man in the row behind. "You'll find she never left the ground in the first place, if I'm any judge."

"I prefer the clowns, anyway," said the first woman. "I get enough of balancing just doing me finances of a Monday."

Miles was about to say that it was the most magical thing he had ever seen, but he never got the chance to speak. A hand gripped his collar tightly from behind. He twisted around to see the man with the enormous belly and too-short trousers glowering down at him.

"Got your ticket, then?" said Genghis, giving his collar a shake for good measure. His voice was high and wheezy like a broken whistle.

"Lost it," said Miles, looking him in the eye.

"Cobblers!" said the man. "You never came in the front door at all, you little weasel, but that's the way you're going out." His swollen purple nose stuck out between his battered bowler hat and his stiff white collar, and he smelled of stale cigar smoke. He marched Miles toward the entrance, the boy stumbling as he tried to keep up. When they reached the flap of the tent, Genghis grasped the seat of Miles's pants with his free hand and tossed him through the air like a sack of coal. He landed in the mud with a splash, and picked himself up just in time to avoid the toe of Genghis's boot.

"Next time I see your dirty face around here I'll feed you to *The Null*," said Genghis as he turned on his heel and went back into the tent.

Miles headed for the exit, but as soon as he was sure the fat-bellied man had disappeared, he doubled back and began to slip between the wagons again. The second half of the circus show had started, with a clashing of cymbals and banging of gongs, and he was still determined to search for a tiger's cage. He peered into a wagon with barred sides. A reptilian eye stared at him unblinking from the smelly darkness. "Not that one," he whispered to Tangerine, and crept on. Cage after cage he visited, some empty and some occupied. The zebras he had seen that morning stamped and whinnied. The next wagon contained long-necked wooly animals he had never seen before. The last one in the row was full of parrots and macaws, who screeched insults at him in several languages.

A little distance away he spotted a single red

wagon standing apart from the others. It was the one he had seen that morning, the one that even the dogs steered clear of. Making sure he was not watched, he ran lightly across the grass and slipped into the shadows beneath the red wagon. He took from his pocket the bone that he had kept for the tiger, and unwrapped it carefully. He wondered what would happen if he dropped it in through the small barred window above his head.

Miles did not know that this decision, along with the bone itself, was about to be taken out of his hands. The creature that lurked in the wagon above him was no tiger, nor anything that had been given a name. It was known only as "The Null," a word that means "nothing." It was a dark and terrifying beast, the sort of being that haunts the deepest corners of your blackest nightmares. The Null was large and squat and hairy and immensely strong, with red-rimmed eyes and bone-crushing teeth. Some said it was a kind of ape, or even a yeti from the unexplored reaches of the Himalayas. Others whispered that it had once been a man, turned into a monster by powerful witchcraft. Whatever was the truth, few had ever seen The Null face to face, for it could be neither tamed nor trained. The last man to try had ended up in Saint Bonifacio's

Hospital for the Unhinged, and had not spoken a coherent word for seven years.

As Miles removed the last shred of soggy paper from the bone, an immense knotty black arm swung down from the small barred window, snatched the heavy bone in its clawed hand, and withdrew with it into the darkness.

Crack! The Null's mighty jaws split the bone with ease, and it slobbered and gulped as it sucked the marrow from inside. Its great teeth ground the bone to splinters in seconds, and a belch like a blast on a tuba made the wagon dance on its iron springs. Miles crouched, trembling, under the monster's cage. He had no idea what kind of creature lurked in the wagon above him, but it was not the tiger he had expected, and he knew that if it once got hold of him it could crack his skull like a boiled egg.

Miles Wednesday, bone-bereft and shaken, crouched behind the wooden spokes of the red wagon. He was afraid to leave his hiding place, and just as afraid to stay in it. As he huddled out of reach (he hoped) of the monster's hairy grasp, he saw two figures emerge from the back of the circus tent, one large and one small. The bigger one, a black shadow with a bowler hat and an unmistakable belly, was pushing in front of him the tiny acrobat from the toppling tower. Her hands were tied behind her back. The moonlight shone in her hair and winked from her sparkling outfit. Genghis opened a small wagon with a key from the large ring hanging on his belt. He lifted the girl, threw her bodily into the wagon and locked the door. He turned and stumped over to the Great Cortado's trailer with its crazed clown's face, and disappeared inside.

"It's time we got out of here," whispered Miles to Tangerine.

Tangerine said nothing, but Miles knew what he was thinking.

"If they catch us, we'll be fed to The Null," he said. Still Tangerine kept silent.

"We *can't* get her out," he hissed, beginning to feel annoyed. "The door is locked, and there are bars on the windows. Besides," he said, forgetting to whisper now, "it's none of our business."

At the sound of his voice the red wagon tilted on its creaking iron springs. The Null's hairy claw appeared and began to grope between the spokes of the wheel. It had enjoyed its starter, and was looking for the main course. A curved yellow nail scraped Miles's bare ankle, and with that he was out from under the wagon like a greyhound from a trap and flying across the muddy grass. In his panic he headed for the cover of the nearest wagon, and only when he reached it did he realize it was the small one in which the tiny acrobat was imprisoned. He groaned quietly.

"Who's there?" came a small voice from the barred window.

"Me," said Miles.

"Can you get me out of here, Me?" said the voice.

"Not Me, Miles," said Miles.

"Who's Miles?" asked the voice.

"I am," said Miles. "And I can't get you out. The door is locked."

"Then you'll need the key," said the girl.

"Genghis has the key," said Miles.

There was a shuffling sound from inside the trailer, and the top half of the little girl's face appeared in the window, peeping over the wooden sill.

"Oh!" she said in surprise. "It's you! You tried to save me when I fell."

Miles blushed in the darkness.

"I'm glad it's you," said the tiny acrobat. "You are very brave. I'm sure you can get the key and let me out."

Miles sighed, and looked up at the girl. She looked small and frightened in the darkness of the wagon.

"What's your name?" he asked.

She hesitated for a moment, then said, "Little."

"All right, Little," said Miles. "I'll try to get the key. Get down from the window and stay quiet."

Little nodded. Her face stayed at the window.

The large wagon that Genghis had entered stood a short way from the one where Little was locked up. It was a dark midnight blue, edged with silver decorations that curled and twisted like thorn bushes. The door to the wagon stood ajar, and a dim red light and the sound of muttered conversation escaped from inside. Miles crept forward and hid himself beside the wooden steps. His heart was beating like a drum.

A man's voice came from inside the wagon. "The older one is going down a storm at the Palace of Laughter. His trick with the firebolts works a treat, though I still haven't figured out how it's done."

"You reckon we can trust him?" asked Genghis's reedy voice.

"As long as we keep his little sister here at the circus, he'll do as he's told."

"What about her then . . . that business with the wings?"

There was a long silence, followed by a cloud of smoke that curled out through the half-open door and was whipped away by the breeze.

"There's more to that little one than meets the eye," said the first man finally. "We'll have to get to the bottom of this before someone gets too curious, and the sooner the better. See that she gets some sleepwater with her supper tonight."

Miles raised himself up quietly and risked a glance over the top step. Through the gap in the doorway he could see a slice of the wagon's interior. The two men sat in leather armchairs, their faces out of sight, their legs stretched beneath a black marble table that stood in the center of the thick red carpet. Big Belly's too-short trousers revealed lemon yellow socks peeping over the necks of his boots. Miles recognized the other man as the ringmaster by his black knee-length boots and red trousers with the yellow stripe. Lazy plumes of cigar smoke drifted back and forth in the dim red light, as though each man were trying to outsmoke the other.

An ebony carving of the laughing clown's face hung on the trailer wall, just inside the door. A mirror was set in the clown's wide-open mouth, and below it was a row of hooks. An enormous key ring, carrying at least forty heavy keys, hung from the nearest hook. Miles felt his heart beat even faster. He had just made up his mind to run up the steps as quietly as he could, when Genghis leaned forward and placed his empty glass on the table. Miles froze.

"Well," said Genghis, squinting through the smoke at a large pocket watch, "show's just about over." He put his cigar butt in his mouth and sank back out of sight, in order to make the biggest smoke cloud he could manage by way of a finale.

The orchestra in the circus tent reached a crescendo that sounded like several angry cats doing battle with a buffalo in a hotel kitchen. Miles seized his chance. He ran up the wooden steps of the Great Cortado's luxurious wagon and reached for the heavy keys that dangled from the hook. As he did so he glanced in the ebony-framed mirror, and found himself looking straight into the eyes of the Great Cortado himself.

CHAPTER FIVE

A BLACK HOLE

Miles Wednesday, mud-caked and red-handed, stared at the Great Cortado through a cloud of cigar smoke and an ebony clown's mouth. At first glance, the only thing great about the ringmaster was his mustache. It was a fine, thick mustache that swept outward from his face like wings and curled up to two needle-sharp points. It far outmustached Mayor Doggett's droopy whiskers. By contrast, everything else about the Great Cortado was small. He had a small round head like a marble, with hair slicked back and curling behind his ears. His delicate red lips held a fat cigar, and blue smoke curled from the nostrils of his neat button nose. He looked almost like a child with a blue chin and false mustache, but his pale eyes seemed to overflow with wisdom and humor.

Genghis hoisted himself from his armchair with a grunt, and the Great Cortado spoke.

"We have a visitor, Genghis," he said. "Bring him inside."

Miles froze for a second. His gaze was still held through the mirror by the Great Cortado's clear gray eyes. Had Cortado guessed what he had been reaching for? Should he grab the keys and make a run for it? But by the time these thoughts had flashed through his mind it was too late; Genghis had reached him in two strides. He grabbed his arm and hauled him roughly into the trailer.

"Genghis, please!" said the Great Cortado, with a smile in his voice. "Is that any way to treat a guest?"

Genghis released his grip, but not before giving Miles a hard pinch. "Not sure if 'guest' is the word for this 'un," he said sullenly. "I've already turfed him out of the show once tonight. Caught him sneaking around under the seats. Told me he'd lost his ticket, the little weasel."

"Is that so?" said the Great Cortado, his eyes wrinkling with amusement. Miles felt himself relax a little under the small man's steady gaze. "Perhaps you would go and see the punters off, Genghis, while I find out from this lad why he is so drawn to our circus that he is undeterred by the mere lack of a ticket."

Genghis shot Miles a dirty look and clumped down the trailer steps. The Great Cortado stubbed out his cigar and waved Miles into the empty chair. Miles felt scruffy and out of place in these comfortable surroundings. He sank down into the soft leather upholstery, and held the collar of his jacket closed so that Cortado could not see that he wore it over his bare skin.

"Well," said the Great Cortado at length. "Do you have a name?"

"Yes," said Miles.

There was a moment's silence, then the Great Cortado laughed. "Would you like to tell it to me, or is it top secret?"

"It's Selim," said Miles at once. He was not sure why he said this, although he knew from his spelling lessons with Lady Partridge that Selim was his own name spelled backward. "Perhaps it was that mirror," he thought, "that made me think back to front."

"Tell me, Selim," said the Great Cortado, "what did you think of our circus? Was it worth watching from under the seats?"

"I didn't see much of it, to be honest," said Miles. "And I was hoping there would be a tiger."

"A tiger?" The Great Cortado took another cigar from the box on the table, and tapped it twice on the lid. His clear gray eyes fixed their gaze on Miles. "Why a tiger, Selim?"

"There's one on your poster," said Miles. He did not think it wise to tell the Great Cortado of his moonlit conversation with a tiger the night before.

"So there is," said Cortado, "so there is. But that's an old poster, and a traditional design. There has not been a tiger in this circus for many years."

"Maybe you should get one, since you still have one on the poster. If I'd bought a ticket, I would have been disappointed."

The Great Cortado's face cooled, and the smile disappeared from his eyes. "There are not many people who would speak to the Great Cortado like that," he said quietly. "I wonder is it courage or foolishness that makes you so bold?"

"Maybe it's a bit of both, Mr. Cortado," said Miles.

"Perhaps it is," said the Great Cortado. He lit the cigar that he had been turning over in his fingers. "In which case," he said, "you would have precisely the qualities needed in a circus performer."

"That's what I wanted to talk to you about," said Miles. He was becoming anxious about Little, waiting for him in the locked trailer, and an idea was beginning to form in his head.

"I thought it might be," said Cortado. He leaned forward in his seat. "Let me show you something that might change your mind." He unbuttoned his shirt, and opened it to reveal a long white scar that stretched diagonally across his chest and abdomen, from collarbone to hip. The skin around the scar was puckered and bore the traces of large clumsy stitches. "This," he said, "is the mark of a tiger, a tiger that I adopted from another circus and cared for as though he were my own. This is how he repaid me." He buttoned his shirt again. "The circus is a dangerous place, my boy, and if it is the life you choose, you had better be strong enough to stay on top. What would your parents have to say about this idea, I wonder?"

"I wouldn't know," said Miles. "I've never met them. I live by myself, and I make my own decisions."

"I see. And in the absence of a tiger to tame, what do you feel you could bring to a show as spectacular as the Circus Oscuro?"

"Oh I wouldn't want to tame any tigers. I was

thinking more of a disappearing act."

"A disappearing act? Is that it? Every nickel and dime show has a disappearing act, Selim."

"Not one like mine. Mine is different."

The Great Cortado raised one eyebrow.

"Mine is completely unexpected," said Miles.

The Great Cortado leaned forward again in his seat, and fixed Miles with his unwavering stare. The smile had returned to his face, but it did not reach his eyes. "Would this act simply consist of you disappearing from my trailer, by any chance?"

"That wouldn't be very spectacular, would it, Mr. Cortado?"

"No it wouldn't," said the Great Cortado. He sat back. "In that case, when will I have the pleasure of seeing this fabulous act?"

"I can show you now, but I will need to go outside and make some preparations."

The ringmaster considered this for a moment, then he said, "You look tired and hungry to me, Selim. So this is what we will do. I will fix you a drink from an old recipe that we circus people guard jealously. I guarantee you it will take care of all your hunger and fatigue. While I do this, you will have a minute or two to make your preparations. But I warn you, I am the Great Cortado, and people who waste my time end up very sorry indeed. This trick of yours had better surprise me."

"I think I can promise that," said Miles.

He stood up and went to the door. A glance in the ebony mirror showed him that the Great Cortado had turned his back and was fixing his special drink at the marble bar in the end of the trailer. Miles lifted the heavy key ring gingerly from the hook and slipped it inside his jacket. His heart was beating so loudly that he was sure the ringmaster would hear it. He went quickly down the steps and ran across the grass to the trailer where Little was being held. The keys clinked together as he took them from his jacket.

"Is that you, Miles?" whispered Little through the keyhole.

"It's me," said Miles. "But I don't know which is the right key. There are a lot of them to try."

"Come to the window and show them to me," said Little. Her face appeared over the sill again. Miles climbed onto the wheel rim and held them up for her to see. She examined them for a moment. "That one," she said. "The one with the twisted stem and the curly end."

Miles put the key in the lock and it turned with ease. Little slipped out through the door. Her wrists were tied behind her back by a long rope, wrapped several times around her waist for good measure, and Miles had left his pocketknife in his barrel. She held a thin blanket behind her back. Miles wrapped it around her to hide her bound wrists and sparkly suit, and she stood on tiptoe on the wooden step to whisper in his ear.

"We have to go quickly," she said. "These are bad, bad people."

The circus show had ended and the crowd began to spill out into the night air, laughing and jostling. Miles could see Genghis tying back the flaps of the tent. The big man barked something at one of the circus boys, who was waiting for the townspeople to go home so that he could search for their loose change under the wooden benches. Genghis turned toward Little's wagon. "Quickly!" said Miles. He pulled Little down into the shadow beneath the wagon and crawled in after her. As they crouched in the darkness, a faint glimmer of light caught his eye. Some sort of ticket lay in the long grass. It shone faintly as he picked it up and slipped it into his pocket with barely a glance. He saw Genghis's windswept ankles appear by the bottom step and stop there.

"Hell's teeth!" hissed Genghis's voice. He ran up

the steps and peered into the empty wagon. The door slammed behind him as he stomped back down the steps. "Now I'm for the high jump," he muttered, as he strode off in the direction of the Great Cortado's wagon.

As soon as he was gone, Miles and Little crept out from under the trailer and slipped into the crowd that was streaming past them toward the exit. A large woman swirled by with a gaggle of small children hanging on to her skirts, and Miles and Little joined them, trotting to keep up. As they passed the Great Cortado's wagon they could hear the ringmaster's raised voice through the curtained windows.

"Then get after them, you great barrel of pork! I want the girl back in her wagon within the hour, or you'll find yourself starring in a disappearing act of your own!"

"What about the boy?"

The Great Cortado spat in disgust. "Give him to The Null."

"*Give* him to The Null? But it'll tear him to pieces!"

"Stop whining, Genghis," barked the ringmaster. "The boy's no use to me, and nobody will miss him. It will be the last time he tries to play games with the Great Cortado."

Genghis emerged from Cortado's trailer, and at the same time the large woman in whose skirts Miles and Little were hiding stopped to pick up one of the children who had tripped and fallen. It took her some time to stop the child's crying, and Miles had to bite his tongue to keep from telling her to hurry up.

As they neared the circus exit they could see a bare-chested fire-eater standing by the ticket box, belching balls of flame over the heads of the departing townspeople. The people ducked to avoid having their hats set on fire, and as they did so, the dwarf with the helmet (who had managed to keep his trousers on this time) was handing them silvery tickets like the one Miles had found under Little's wagon. "Congratulations," he told each one in turn. "Another lucky winner." Beyond the fire-eater Miles could see fat-bellied Genghis, who had stationed himself at the exit and was scanning the children in the crowd for escapees.

"Not that way," said Miles. He steered Little out of the crowd into the shadow of one of the cages. He peered around the back of the wagon, but one of the circus boys stood there, holding a snarling dog on a short lead. The dog strained and growled, and it took all the boy's strength to hold him.

"He's had a splinter in his back paw for weeks,"

whispered Little, "and no one has noticed it. That's why he's so mean."

"How do you know?" asked Miles

The girl looked at him in surprise. "He told me," she said.

Something warm and wet slopped against Miles's ear, making him jump. The llamas had crowded against the door of their cage, and one had stuck his tongue out between the bars. Little giggled. "I think you should let them out," she whispered to Miles. "They want to go for a little gallop."

She nodded at the iron bolt on the cage door. It was unlocked. Miles eased it open and slid the door back. Immediately a woolly mass of llamas leaped out of the cage and charged happily into the shrieking crowd, sending people diving into the mud. One knocked against the fire-eater, who belched an extra-large fireball straight at Genghis's head. Genghis leaned backward in the nick of time, but not quickly enough to save his cigar and the front of his hat brim, which both went up in smoke. He roared and swung a fist at the fire-eater. In the confusion Miles and Little darted behind Genghis and in among the hurrying townspeople on the road. Miles held Little's arm in case she tripped. She seemed to weigh nothing at all.

"Where are we going?" she asked as they ran.

"To see Lady Partridge," said Miles. "She'll know what to do. But first we'll go to my barrel to get my knife and cut that rope off you."

"Why do you keep it in a barrel?" said Little.

"I live in the barrel," said Miles, lifting Little over the ditch and starting up the hill. "It's my home."

"Oh," said Little. "Does Lady Partridge live in a barrel too?"

"Of course not," said Miles. "She lives up a tree."

Little gave a sudden gasp as she twisted her ankle on a loose stone. She sat down on a tussock and grimaced with the pain. Miles pulled up some cold dock leaves and wrapped them around her ankle. "We're nearly at the barrel," he said. "You can rest there for a few minutes before we move on."

He helped her hop up the last part of the slope. She winced with each hop.

"It's a pity you don't have those circus wings on," said Miles. "You could fly the rest of the way."

Little laughed her musical giggle. "You're funny!" she said.

Once inside the barrel he took his pocketknife from under the mattress and cut the rope binding her wrists. "They weren't taking any chances with you, were they?" he said.

"They never tied me up like this before," she said. "I think something bad would have happened tonight, if you hadn't helped me escape."

Miles wrapped her in the overcoat, and she watched him silently as he coiled the rope and put it in his pocket, along with his last apple and his pocketknife. He went to the door of the barrel and looked down the hill to see what was going on below.

"Are they looking for us?" asked Little.

"I don't think so," said Miles. Darkness stole over the field as a cloud covered the moon, leaving the swaying strings of colored bulbs to cast a dim light over the scurrying circus people as they rounded up the last of the reluctant llamas. When the moon emerged again, Miles noticed a knot of people gathered around the red wagon in which The Null was housed. Two boys carried lanterns, and there were several strongmen holding long poles and heavy chains. Two of them held up what appeared to be a net. Genghis stood to one side of the wagon door. It looked as if he were removing the padlocks.

Miles felt the floor of his stomach fall away. "Oh no," he whispered.

"Oh no what?" asked Little.

"It's The Null," said Miles. "I think they're letting it out."

"Oh *no* oh no," said Little. "We have to go now, at once. Far away."

"You can't walk, and I can't go fast enough carrying you," said Miles. "You'll have to stay hidden here, and I'll draw them off."

Little shook her head. "But I . . ." She paused, looking uncertain. "Are you sure I'll be safe here?"

Miles covered her completely with the overcoat. "You'll be fine," he said. "Just keep out of sight, and whatever you do, don't make a sound until I come back for you."

"Be careful," came a muffled voice from under the overcoat.

"Don't worry," said Miles. "I know this hill inside out, and they're strangers, even if they do have a monster with them." He wished he felt as confident as he sounded.

He slipped back down the way they had come, peering through the shifting darkness for any sign of the circus men and their beast. The moon was hidden behind another cloud, and the wind gusted up the hill, flattening the grass and stealing the breath from his mouth. A strong odor like rotten bananas reached his nose, mixed with the stale cigar smell that surrounded Genghis like an invisible fog, and he heard the clink of chains and the nervous shouts of the strongmen. An eerie barking laugh made the hair stand up on his scalp.

He left the path and pushed through the bushes, heading directly away from the barrel. As he half ran, half slithered down the side of the hill, he strained his ears for any sign that the circus men and their beast were following him. He remembered the smaller children he had tried to bring with him on his failed escapes from Pinchbucket House, and the beating they would all receive from Fowler Pinchbucket on their return. Miles had a feeling that Little's fate, if his diversion should fail, would be something far worse. The men's shouts were getting closer now, and he could see the lanterns swinging crazily as the boys who held them clambered over the rocky ground. They had picked up his trail all right, and they were gaining on him.

Deep beneath the town of Larde, an ancient stream flowed through a dark tunnel before emerging through a stone arch below Beggar's Gate. Miles had used this underground stream in two of his failed escape attempts, and it was to the stone mouth of the tunnel that he was headed now, along the slippery bank of the stream. He knew his footprints in the mud would make him easy to follow.

The moon came out again as he reached the tunnel mouth, and as he ducked down into the darkness, he risked a glance over his shoulder. The Null was no more than twenty yards behind him, a hideous shadow that seemed to suck the moonlight into itself like a black hole. It had shaken off the strongmen, and its three stout chains dragged loose behind it from its iron collar. The creature's red mouth opened wide in the blackness and its manic laugh followed Miles into the tunnel.

The tunnel was clammy and pitch black, and cold water soaked Miles as he ran through the shallow stream. The faint moonlight from behind was blocked by the huge beast that splashed through the water on all fours, almost at his heels. A little way up the tunnel was an iron gate, and he knew from his Pinchbucket House escapes numbers three and five that he could just about squeeze himself between the bars. He was struck by the awful thought that he may have grown too big since the last time he tried this, and a moment later he was struck by the bars themselves as he ran full tilt into them in the inky darkness. His head met the iron gate with a loud clang, and he almost fell backward under the feet of his pursuer. With stars exploding in front of his eyes, he stumbled to one side and began to wedge himself into the narrow space between the bars. He breathed in, and turned his head sideways, but it was no good. He was stuck fast.

In the cold darkness, deep below the sleeping town of Larde, The Null hit the center of the gate like a giant hairy cannonball, almost wrenching it free of the crumbling stone walls. The impact buckled the gate, pulling the bars apart slightly and releasing Miles from its rusty grip. He fell through the gate and onto his knees, and began to crawl through the water, his head throbbing. The Null was rattling the bars and screeching with rage. Between its shouts he could hear Genghis's wheezy voice echoing up the tunnel.

"You, Knoblauch and Kartoffel, get in there and see what's going on."

"Not me, sir, I ain't going into the dark with that thing."

"You'd better get in there, you haddock-brained half-wits, or I'll have you boiled in vinegar," shouted Genghis.

"You'd best heat up the vinegar then, sir, 'cause I ain't going in no tunnel with that devil-thing."

There was more shouting and cursing, mixed with The Null's angry gibbering, as Miles felt his way along the left-hand wall, looking for the rusting iron ladder that led up to the drain in Crooked Street. The ache in his head was subsiding, and he felt pleased with himself. The Null would keep them occupied for a while, leaving him to slip back to the barrel, collect Little and bring her to Lady Partridge. She would be safe there, and Lady Partridge would know what to do.

Miles climbed the ladder and pushed at the heavy grating above his head. It was jammed shut with dirt, and he had to work at it with his pocket-knife for some time before the grate would open. He clambered through the opening and crept through the winding alleys, shivering in his thin jacket. He had lost the heavy keys somewhere in the darkness. He kept to the shadows as he passed the circus, dark now except for the glow of lamplight from some of the trailer windows. Somewhere a concertina played a cheerful tune, and there was the sound of laughter and the clinking of bottles. There was no sign of The Null or its reluctant handlers. "It must be back in its wagon by now," he whispered to Tangerine, who was cold and damp too, and not feeling talkative.

When he came within shouting distance of his barrel, he stopped. Something was wrong. He could smell the rotten-banana smell again, and there was harsh laughter coming from the direction of his home. Miles sank down and began to crawl through the long grass, his heart thumping. As he neared the spot where the tiger had sat the night before, the moon emerged from behind a cloud and shone on a terrible scene.

The Null had not been returned to its barred wagon at all. It sat among the smashed ribs of Miles's barrel like the black heart of some ruined animal, tearing chunks from the mattress and stuffing them into its mouth. The strongmen had a tight grip on the chains again, and the boys with the lanterns leaned against the trunk of the pine tree, smoking the cigarette butts that the strongmen had thrown aside. Genghis kicked through the ashes of old campfires, a cigar glowing beneath his singed bowler hat. A handful of gnawed bones lay in the grass next to The Null, and there was no sign of Little anywhere.

CHAPTER SIX

LADY PARTRIDGE

Miles Wednesday, homeless and headstruck, wormed through the long grass in a wide circle around his smashed barrel. His head throbbed from the impact of the iron gate, and fear crawled over his skin like a swarm of icy centipedes. He found a vantage point behind a small twisted bush, and tried to blank out the pictures that ran through his mind of what The Null might have done to Little. The beast had tired of chewing the mattress now and was beating it with a curved rib from the barrel. Tufts of white stuffing rolled up the hill before the breeze.

Genghis blew his nose on a large gray handkerchief that he had pulled from his sleeve. "Knoblauch! Kartoffel! Get that creature to its feet and let's get it back into its box," he said. "And don't let go of it this time." He gave the ashes an angry kick.

"Wasn't our fault, sir," said Knoblauch, his white hair standing up from his scalp like a yard broom. "Monster was 'ungry."

"It hunts better when it's hungry, you bonehead," said Genghis. "But it's supposed to be hunting runaway brats, not flocks of sheep."

"It only ate two, sir."

"Ought to have the beast put down," muttered Kartoffel. "Gives me nightmares, it does."

"Course it does," said Knoblauch. "It's meant to. That's why the boss keeps it, innit? Keep everyone in line."

"Stop flapping your gums and get moving," barked Genghis. "We have to get The Null back into its wagon before the Lardespeople roll out of their beds and find something's been snacking on their mutton."

The strongmen yanked on the chains, and The Null whipped around in the remains of the mattress and gave a cackle that made the hair stand up on Miles's neck. Two of the strongmen pulled it after the retreating figure of Genghis, while another couple hauled from behind, stumbling and slipping as they struggled to keep the creature from mauling the men in front.

Miles waited behind the rock a few minutes more, shivering in his wet clothes. He stared at the bones that lay scattered in the grass. If The Null had been eating sheep, he thought, perhaps it had not devoured Little after all. But if not, where was she? She could not have run away with her twisted ankle. Perhaps she was under what remained of the mattress, squashed flat by the weight of the monster. He crept forward and stood before the mattress, summoning up the courage to look underneath. He bent and flipped it over. It was lighter than before, having lost most of its stuffing, and there was nothing underneath but splintered wood and his old biscuit tin, entirely flattened. The overcoat lay in the grass where it had been tossed aside.

Miles flopped down on the disemboweled mattress and put his head in his hands. "This is what happens," he muttered to Tangerine, "when we meddle in things that aren't our business. Now the girl is missing, and we have nowhere to live." There was no answer from Tangerine.

A pinecone fell from the tree above and bounced

off the back of his neck. Another one hit the top of his head. Miles looked up at the tree. "That's right, drop your cones on me," he shouted. "Do I look like I don't have enough troubles already?"

"I'm sorry," said the tree in a familiar voice. "I just wanted to make sure it was safe."

"Little?" said Miles.

A pale face appeared in the darkness between the branches. "Have they gone away?" asked Little.

"They've gone away," said Miles. A wave of relief rose from his frozen feet and swept through him like laughter. "You can come down now."

Little scrambled down the twisted trunk. Her skin was scratched by the bark. Miles shook out the overcoat and wrapped it around her. It trailed on the ground like a royal train.

"Are you okay?" he asked her.

"Yes," she said. "I know you told me to stay out of sight, but I heard someone coming, and I knew it wasn't you. You don't smell *that* bad. So I hid up the tree."

"You're lucky you got up there before they saw you," said Miles. He looked at the small girl, who reached no more than halfway to the tree's lowest branches, and wondered how she had managed to get up there at all.

"Let's go," said Miles. "I'll carry you on my back."

Little did not seem as light as before, but Miles suspected that his old overcoat counted for much of the weight. He followed a familiar path between the rocks and gorse bushes, over the brow of the hill and down into the small wood on the other side. Dry leaves whispered under his feet, and overhead the wind rustled through the treetops, making the branches creak. Out of sight of his smashed home he could imagine that it was still there, warm and dry, waiting for him to return. To push the picture of the demented beast out of his mind he thought about the tiger who had visited him the night before.

"Little, is there a tiger at the Circus Oscuro?"

"I've never seen one," said Little. "Why?"

"I dreamed about one last night. At least I think it was a dream, but it seemed almost more real than real life. I was sitting in my barrel and a tiger came and sat near me. He looked like an ordinary tiger, but he spoke to me. He told me that he could smell the circus in me, but I've never been to a circus until tonight."

"If a tiger said it, it must be true."

"But it was only a dream," said Miles.

"Tigers don't lie," said Little. "Not even in dreams."

They came to a high stone wall, ivy bearded and crumbling with neglect. Miles made his way along the wall to a place where it had collapsed, leaving a gap like a missing tooth, and clambered across the tumbled stones.

Once inside the wall, he let Little down gently. They stood waist-deep in a swaying sea of weeds, among old trees of various shapes, some twisted and wild, others tall and dark like pillars holding up the night sky. The hulk of a derelict mansion stood with its back to them, empty windows staring blackly across the overgrown garden.

In the center of the garden stood an enormous beech tree. It was a strange tree, with two trunks growing from the mighty roots, joined together by a web of branches that clasped each other like the arms of wrestling giants. Perched among these branches was the dark jumbled shape of a tree house. It was made from an assortment of old furniture, floorboards, and tea chests, as though it had been washed up into the tree by a freak tidal wave. Little saw a cat stalk along one of the branches, and as her eyes became accustomed to the dark mass of the tree, she saw there were others—three, five, twenty and more cats, staring down at them, or washing their paws and pretending not to notice them.

Miles grabbed the lowest rung of the rope ladder that dangled from a hole in the tree house floor, and called up the tree. "Lady Partridge! It's me. I've brought a friend."

"So they tell me," called a voice from above. "Bring her up, my boy."

He lifted Little to the ladder and she hopped up it on one foot. Miles followed behind.

The inside of the tree house was unlike anything you've ever seen, unless you live in a curiosity shop with branches growing up through the floor. A large Persian rug covered the uneven floorboards, and a fire glowed in an ornate iron fireplace that was set into the crooked walls. The walls themselves consisted largely of a jumble of bookcases, kitchen dressers, and chests of drawers, stuffed to overflowing with books, fat candle stubs, prickly cacti, and jars filled with herbs, polished stones, old coins, dried fruit, broken jewelry, boiled sweets, nuts and bolts, dried petals, hairpins, seashells, and a thousand other strange things whose use could only be guessed at. There were so many books that they flowed from the lower shelves and piled themselves around the edges of the floor, among the umbrella stands, snake baskets, ships in bottles, milking stools, chopped logs, hookah pipes, china elephants, brass divers' helmets, ornate vases, butter churns, whalebones, sewing machines and parrot cages, not to mention a large stuffed crocodile that stared with a glassy eye from a dark corner by the potbellied stove.

A broad hammock was strung between the two trunks, where they passed through the tree house on their way to the sky. A large woman sat in the hammock, peering at Little over her crooked spectacles. In her lap sat a heavy book. She wore a black silk Chinese dressing gown decorated with red dragons, and her gray hair was piled up on her head with the help of several tortoiseshell combs that seemed on the verge of falling out.

"Well well," she said. "And who do we have here?"

"I'm Little," said Little.

"And I'm a great deal Larger than I ought to be," said Lady Partridge, and she burst into a great guffaw of laughter. Little glanced at Miles, who grimaced back.

"Well sit down, my dears," said Lady Partridge, dabbing at her eyes with a lace handkerchief. "If you can find a space."

Finding a space on the floor was not as easy as it sounds. The room was almost completely carpeted with cats. Tabbies, tortoiseshells, Siamese and Persians, cats as black as coal at night and as white as sugar in a china bowl. They swarmed over the tumbling piles of books, perched on every shelf and draped themselves across Lady Partridge's hammock. A small orange cat sat squarely in the middle of her book, smoothing his ears with licked paws. The whole tree house purred.

Little picked her way around the edges of the room, keeping her weight on her good foot. She peered into every nook and cranny, lifting things from shelves to look at them more closely. She listened to the ocean's call from the seashell, and held up a jar of amber nuggets to let the light pour through. On the shelf behind the jar was an old photograph with curling edges, in which a young man with a freshly scrubbed face stood by a large and fabulous contraption of wheels and pistons and jagged teeth. "Who is this?" asked Little, picking it up as she replaced the jar. She held out the photograph to Lady Partridge.

"That," said Lady Partridge, peering down through the spectacles balanced on the end of her nose, "is my late husband, Lord Partridge. He was a handsome chap, as you can see, with a head full of bright ideas. At least that's what I believed."

"Is that one of his ideas behind him?" asked Little.

"I'm afraid so. That was his all-in-one tree converter. If you fed it enough coal and ink it could chop down a forty-foot tree, chew it up and convert it into fourteen school desks, eight hundred triple-column accounting ledgers, and enough matches to keep fifty stevedores chain-smoking for a year and a half. By the time he had perfected the machine it could get through half an acre of trees in just over an hour. He called it Geraldine, although I was never quite sure why."

"It says 'Geraldine XIV' on the side," said Miles, looking at the photograph over Little's shoulder.

"Yes, they were all called Geraldine. There was a fleet of twenty-four of them at one stage, and no timber merchant could hold up his head unless he had at least two. It all came to an end when they realized they had made a dozen school desks for every man, woman and child in the land, and that the ledgers they had produced would not be used up before the middle of the next millennium. But by that time Dartforth—that was my husband's name—was very wealthy indeed. He had set up several other businesses and seemed to have completely forgotten about Geraldine."

"Did you live in the big house then?" asked Little.

"We did, my dear, and we had a butler and two

cooks and a team of gardeners. We had swans on the pond and peacocks on the lawn, and for many years I never bothered my head about Dartforth's businesses and what they might be making. Not until he was killed by an exploding pudding in one of his factories did I think to look at them more closely, I'm afraid."

"An exploding pudding?" said Miles, looking at the photograph with renewed interest. There was nothing in the young Lord Partridge's bearing or his cheerful face to suggest that he might be on course for such a sticky end.

"An exploding pudding," said Lady Partridge. "It was a prototype they were developing in secret for the army. It was cunningly disguised as an enemy ration tin, and was designed to be sneaked behind enemy lines by undercover cooks. They tried to keep the accident quiet of course, and offered me a pension that would have kept me in luxury for the rest of my days, but all I wanted was to find out the truth about how Dartforth had died. I hired an investigator, and little by little he discovered what kinds of businesses my husband had been involved in."

She sighed. "He was not a bad man, Dartforth. I believe he really thought that everything he did was for the best, but he was always in such a hurry to get on with the next brilliant idea that he had no time to see the consequences of the last one. He invented a cereal that was supposed to make children grow big and strong, but some rats broke into the storeroom and feasted on it for a week. Soon there were rats the size of sheep rampaging around the countryside and a team of python handlers had to be brought up from the south to hunt them all down. Then there was the Saltifier, for making lakes more like the sea so people didn't have to travel far to the beach, and the Jumbo-sized Cocktail Sausages that made people's fingers and toes swell up. Everything he turned his hand to seemed to produce poisonous gases, or terrible nocturnal noises, or two-headed chickens. After Dartforth died, there was only one thing to be done. I spent most of the money he had made over the years putting right the damage that he had done. I had some factories converted to making things that people really did need. Others, I'm afraid, simply had to be dynamited, in the hope that someday the grass will be able to grow over them."

"You must have been very sad," said Little.

"I was rather angry really," said Lady Partridge, "but it had to be done."

"I mean when he died," said Little.

The question took Lady Partridge by surprise. She was quiet for a moment, gazing at something beyond the tree house and many years ago. Then she took off her glasses and dropped them into a pocket in her dressing gown. "Well, we don't talk about that," she said briskly, tipping the orange cat from her book and placing it on top of a teetering pile that conveniently reached her left elbow.

"Who doesn't?" asked Little.

"Well . . . people in general, I suppose."

"Then how do people make each other feel better?"

Lady Partridge seemed completely stumped. Little put the photograph back in its place and walked over to where she sat on the edge of her hammock. She climbed the precarious stack of books, put her arms around Lady Partridge's neck and gave her a big kiss on the cheek. Lady Partridge hugged her back, then lifted her down gently.

"Well, here I am wittering on, and I'm sure you're both hungry," she said, dabbing her eyes quickly with a silk sleeve. "Sit down . . . um . . . somewhere, and I'll make you some soup."

Miles shifted a plump cat or two, to make space for Little and himself. His damp jacket steamed in the warmth of the fire. Little hopped gingerly over to where he sat.

"You're limping, my dear," said Lady Partridge.

"She twisted her ankle," said Miles.

"Well why didn't you tell me?" said Lady Partridge. "We must get you bandaged up at once." She stepped down from the hammock into a pair of worn purple slippers and produced a rolled bandage from a wooden box on the shelf behind her. She knelt down on the Persian carpet with a great deal of huffing and sighing, and began to bandage Little's ankle with a practiced hand.

"Why did you leave your house to live in a tree?" asked Little, wincing a little.

"Oh, I built this tree house over the years, with the help of my gardeners, from old furniture we no longer used in the house. Dartforth was forever ordering newer and grander furniture for the manor, but I hated to part with the old stuff. In the days before those dreadful Pinchbuckets took over the orphanage I used to have all the children around for picnics on Saturday afternoons. It was nice and cool in the tree house, and they could play up here when the sun became too high. The Pinchbuckets stopped all that many years ago. I don't think they ever let the poor things out nowadays, except for their annual trip to the cement quarry. After Dartforth died I began to spend more and more time up here myself. It was a good place to sit and think. All the staff had long gone, and I had sold almost everything in the house. It became too big and lonely, and I simply couldn't bear to be there anymore, so I moved my last few things out here where it was small and cozy. The grocer's boy comes once a week and the coal man delivers too, so I hardly need to venture out at all. Anyhow, it's rather appropriate that I should live in a tree with two trunks. That makes me a Partridge in a pair tree!"

Lady Partridge bellowed with laughter at her own joke, causing a fat tabby to wake with a start and fall off the shelf where he had been perched.

"And now, my dears," said Lady Partridge when she had calmed down, "I had better stop rambling on and see about that soup I promised you. A good tale never fares well on an empty stomach, and I can see that you both have a story to tell."

CHAPTER SEVEN

FALLING THROUGH THUNDER

Lady Partridge, book-bound, dragon-gowned, and mistress of a hundred cats, rummaged among the tins and jars on the dresser by the stove. As she did so she muttered to herself, or perhaps to her cats. She filled the belly of the stove with a shovelful of glowing coals from the fireplace, and placed a pot of soup on top.

While the soup bubbled in the pot, Miles told her a story that you and I have heard already. He told her of the strange circus and the mysterious tiger, of how he had seen Little fall, and later rescued her from her locked trailer under the nose of the Great Cortado. Over bowls of steaming soup he spoke of the nameless beast that had pursued him through the night, and how it had reduced to splinters the barrel that had kept him warm and dry for three winters under the pine tree on the side of the hill. Lady Partridge listened, and her cats listened too.

"Well well," said Lady Partridge at length, when his story had taken them up the ladder and into her tree house. "You must both stay here for the night, and in the morning we'll see what's to be done." She peered thoughtfully at Little. "Would you mind, my dear, if we took a look at those wings of yours?"

"She doesn't have them on now," said Miles. "They're back at the circus."

But Little had slipped off the heavy overcoat. The thin straps of her glittery costume left her shoulders almost bare, and as she turned her back to Lady Partridge Miles saw to his astonishment a pattern of gracefully curving lines traced faintly across her shoulder blades. As he looked closer he could see in the pattern the outline of a pair of neatly folded wings. Little gave her shoulders a shake, and the wings opened out. They were a little longer, from the bend to the tips of the primaries, than her upper arm from shoulder to elbow. They looked even more magnificent in the cluttered tree house than when he had seen them in the circus. The firelight gave a pearly glow to their fine, closely fitting feathers.

It took Miles a moment to find his voice. "They're *real?*" he croaked. "Where . . . where did they come from?"

"I think the real question," said Lady Partridge, "is where did Little come from?" She smiled at Little, who had folded her wings so neatly against her back that they seemed almost to melt back into her skin. "We should very much like to hear your story, my dear," she said. "I'm sure it would make the time fly!" She was overcome by a fit of laughter. Little and Miles smiled politely as she dabbed her eye with the corner of her dressing gown.

"I'm not really supposed to tell," said Little hesitantly.

"You can trust us, dear," said Lady Partridge. "We won't breathe a word to anyone."

Little chewed her lip thoughtfully for a moment. "Well . . . ," she began slowly, "I suppose the trouble started when I followed Silverpoint down through a cloud tunnel."

"Silverpoint?" echoed Lady Partridge.

"Silverpoint is a Storm Angel," said Little. "He's older than me, perhaps a thousand winters old. I used to watch him and the other longfeathers rolling thunderballs across the cloud fields and dodging one another's lightning. It was fun to watch, and a bit scary too. They were as quick as thought when they played, and the sound of their thunder made my head shake. Sometimes my hair would all stand up on end and you could hear it crackle, when they got too close."

"Did you say a *thousand* years old?" interrupted Lady Partridge.

"That's what he told me."

"Good gracious! Then how old are you, my child, if that's not a rude question?"

"I'm not sure," said Little. "Silverpoint once said I had lived more than four hundred years, but the seasons come and go, and I've never had much time for counting."

"Well," said Lady Partridge, pushing her spectacles up on her nose. "I certainly hope I'm as sprightly as you when I'm four hundred years old," and she chuckled to herself while Little continued her story.

"Silverpoint is the quickest of them all, and his lightning is strong and blue and always finds its mark. He would get angry if he saw me watching, because I wasn't supposed to be there. He told me that someday I would get fried, and my song would never be heard, but I still used to watch whenever I could find a hiding place.

"One day I saw Silverpoint and Rumblejack heading for the cloud fields, so I followed them at a distance. They gathered up some thunderballs, and I hid myself to watch, but they didn't play in the usual way. Rumblejack began rolling the thunderballs in a circle. Round and round he rolled them, faster and faster, and a sort of whirlpool began to form in the clouds underneath. The noise was like a thousand giants roaring. The center of the cloud sank lower and lower, like a tunnel heading downward. All at once Rumblejack shouted something to Silverpoint, and flew off back the way he had come. I saw Silverpoint look around to see if anyone was watching, so I sank down lower. He didn't see me. Then all of a sudden, he took a long run and dived into the hole. Just like that.

"Without thinking for a moment I got up and ran after him. It was a silly thing to do, but I just wanted to see where he had gone, to see that he was all right. But as I got near to the tunnel the wind began to pull me. I tried to stop then, but the pull was too strong, and the tunnel swallowed me like a huge mouth."

The coals shifted in the fireplace, sending a shower of sparks up the dark chimney. The ginger cat had returned to Lady Partridge's ample lap, and sat licking its paws among the red dragons on her dressing gown.

"What was it like in the tunnel?" asked Miles.

"It was white, and cold," said Little. "I was sliding very fast, twisting and turning, until I didn't know up from down. I tried to slow myself, but there was nothing I could hold on to. The tunnel became darker, purply gray, and darker again until it was almost black, and I was going faster still. I couldn't see Silverpoint anymore. My shouts were lost in the sound of the thunder, and the wind was racing through the clouds and spinning me around as it passed. Then suddenly there was no cloud, and I was falling from the sky in a rain of hailstones. When lightning flashed I thought I saw Silverpoint far below me, but the hailstones were so thick I couldn't be sure."

"Why didn't you use your wings, like in the circus?" asked Miles.

"I did!" said Little. "I opened my wings before I even left the tunnel, but the storm was too strong. I'm only a softwing, and in a hailstorm like that even a longfeather needs all his strength and skill.

The wind took me and threw me this way and that, and though I did slow my fall I couldn't control where I was going, not even if I could have seen what was below me.

"Just when I thought I would never stop falling, I saw the shapes of trees rushing up to meet me, and other shapes—a huge striped tent and a circle of trailers. I flapped with all my strength to slow myself down, then I fell into a big pile of hay in the back of a wagon. Right into the center I dived, and the hay covered me up completely. I didn't know whether anyone had seen me, so I lay as still as I could for a while, waiting to get my breath back. That hay was really itchy!" She wriggled her shoulders at the memory.

"The stalks of hay poked up my nose and in my ears, and the little seeds tickled me all over. I wriggled over to the side of the wagon and looked through the wooden slats to see if there was anyone around." Little giggled. "To tell the truth, I didn't know what kind of monsters I might see. I'd never been to the Hard World before, but I had heard all sorts of stories."

"Really? What kind of stories, my dear?" asked Lady Partridge. Her precariously piled hair had been gradually undoing itself, and looped in gray coils over her ears and down her neck, but she didn't seem to notice. The ginger cat played with a long strand, biting the end and swatting it with his paws.

"Oh, all sorts. I heard that people have no wings, which was true, and that they might have two heads, or hairy faces. Bluehart, the Sleep Angel, told me that some people eat without stopping until their insides explode, and others walk like skeletons and eat seeds from cracks in the earth. The first man I saw, looking out from the hay, had a white face and a round red nose like a ball. His hair was purple and it stood up on end. He was beating a pig with a long stick.

"I couldn't understand what was going on. The pig was on four legs and had no hands to hold a stick of his own. He was covered with big green spots, but they were washing off in the rain. He was tied to the wheel of a wagon, and could do nothing but stand there and squeal. I could hardly even make out what he was saying."

"Do you mean you can understand animals?" exclaimed Lady Partridge.

"Of course," said Little. " I am a Song Angel, and every language is an echo of the One Song, even the sigh of the wind and the groan of the mountains. Everything speaks. You just have to know how to listen.

"Anyway, the poor pig was crying as the man beat him. I thought I heard him saying 'not again,' then he said some things about the man that were so rude I would have laughed, if it wasn't so horrible. Nobody came to his help, so I had to do it myself. I climbed out of the hay (and anyway, I couldn't have stayed in there a second longer), and I told purple-head to stop at once."

"That was very brave of you, my dear," said Lady Partridge. "What did the man do?"

"He turned around and stared at me. He had one real eye. The other was made of glass and could see nothing. He turned back and gave the pig an extra-hard whack, then he walked over to me and raised his stick high in the air.

"Just at that moment there was a loud crack, and the man's purple hair burst into flames. He dropped the stick then, and he let out a yell. He began to run around in circles, flapping his hands at his head and shrieking. The pig was shouting, "My turn gone, your turn now! My turn gone, your turn now!" For a moment I thought the pig had somehow done it to him, then I saw Silverpoint standing there with his hands on his hips and thunder in his face, and I understood. The man with the flaming head tripped over an iron peg and fell straight into a big bucket of paint. That put the fire out all right, but when he stood up his whole head was white and dripping, and he stepped straight into something the elephants had left behind. It was really very funny." Little giggled at the memory.

"Silverpoint was angrier than I had ever seen him. I didn't know if he was more angry with me or with purple-head. He grabbed my arm, and there were sparks still coming from his fingertips that made my skin hurt. He said, 'Come!' But before we could leave, a man stepped out of the shadow of the tent."

"He was a small man, no taller than Silverpoint himself. You have met him, Miles, I think. He is called the Great Cortado. He spoke to us from behind his great mustache, and his words were kind. 'That was a very impressive trick, and funny too' was what he said to Silverpoint. The purple-haired man had wiped the paint from his eyes, and he bent to pick up his stick, but then he met the Great Cortado's eye and he dropped it again, and slunk off with his head down.

"Silverpoint thanked the Great Cortado politely and told him that we really must be leaving, but Cortado insisted that we go into his trailer to have some supper and to dry off. Silverpoint tried to refuse, but Cortado wouldn't take no for an answer. While he went to have supper made for us, we sat in his wagon and Silverpoint told me off for following him. He said that it was very foolish, but now that I was here, there were things that I must remember. He said that humans could not be trusted. I mean *he* said . . ." She hesitated.

"Don't worry, my dear," said Lady Partridge. "In some cases I'm afraid he's right, but we're not all bad! What else did he say to you?"

"He said that people must never find out who we really were. He told me never to let anyone see my wings, and above all never ever to sing my real name."

"Isn't Little your real name?" asked Miles.

Little laughed, and her laugh itself was like music. "Of course not," she said. "Little is just the name that Silverpoint gave to me, when the Great Cortado asked who we were. It's far too short a name for a Song Angel!"

"You must excuse our ignorance, my dear, but what exactly is a Song Angel?" asked Lady Partridge.

"Song Angels are the voices of the One Song," said Little.

"And what is the One Song?" asked Lady Partridge.

"It's hard to put into words," said Little. "I've never had to explain it before." She stared into the fire for a minute, a small frown on her face.

"The One Song is the music that runs at the heart of everything. It keeps the world spinning and the stars shining. Everything that exists, every insect and rock and river and flower, has a name in the One Song. Love and Sorrow, Laughter and Anger and Courage all have their places too, and they must be kept in harmony. When one of these strands is taken out from the rest, that is when bad things happen, like a rope beginning to unravel. Each Song Angel must learn a part of that song. We keep it alive and guard it, and in the end we must each add our own name to it so that the Song keeps growing and the world keeps moving along its path."

"But why can't you use your real name, instead of Little?" asked Miles, who had not understood much of what she had just said.

"If I sang my name here, its power would be spent. I would be bound to Earth, and would never be able to return home." She laughed. "Besides, my real name would not come to life on the clumsy tongues of people."

"Is Silverpoint a made-up name as well?"

"Well . . . yes and no. A Storm Angel's name is a

different thing, and does not have the same power. Silverpoint is something like his real name, but shorter and simpler. It's a name he uses when he visits Earth."

"And why did Silverpoint come down through the clouds, my dear?" asked Lady Partridge. She was trying to rebuild the unruly pile of gray hair on her head, and she held a tortoiseshell comb and several hairpins between her lips. Her question sounded more like, "Und fwoy did Filverfoint come down shoo du cloudsh, wy dear?"

"I didn't get the chance to ask him that, because the Great Cortado returned with our supper before we had finished our talk. He asked us many questions, but Silverpoint answered them cleverly and told him very little. Cortado's voice was soothing and his eyes were kind, and after a while even Silverpoint seemed more at ease. At the end of our meal we had a hot, sweet drink that glowed like fire inside us, but this was the worst mistake of all. I saw Silverpoint's head start to nod as he swallowed his last mouthful, and before I could even put down my own cup, I fell into a sleep without dreams.

"When I woke up I didn't know if it was night or day. I was in a small trailer, and a huge woman, as tall as a tree and with pictures on her skin, was wiping my face with a wet towel. She told me her name was Baumella, and that Silverpoint had sold me to the circus and gone away. I didn't believe her, of course, but I said nothing. They gave me a sparkly costume to wear, and began to teach me to walk on a rope and to balance on things. When I wasn't practicing or performing they kept me locked up all the time. Baumella treated me well enough, but she never let me out of her sight.

"I tried to find out where Silverpoint was. He wasn't anywhere in the circus. I asked the animals whenever I got the chance. One of the monkeys told me he heard the parrots say that Silverpoint had been taken to the Palace of Laughter, but none of them knew where that was. That was all I was able to find out."

Little fell silent for a while. In the firelight Miles could see tears shining in her eyes.

"I haven't seen Silverpoint since that night," she said quietly. "I don't know what's become of him, but it's all my fault. If I hadn't followed him he never would have had to save me, and we would never have been captured. I have to find him, somehow."

Miles looked at the small girl sitting among the cats and the bric-a-brac. She had pulled the overcoat back around her, although it was warm in the tree house, and was wiping her eyes with the back of her hand. Her skin still gave off that faint pearly glow, only visible in dim light. She looked lost and alone.

He thought about his smashed barrel and his disemboweled mattress. There was really only one choice to make. Whatever the dangers of her search for Silverpoint, he would go with her. He could not let her face such a journey alone, even if she did have wings and was four hundred years old. Besides, he thought, it would surely be more exciting to set off into the unknown in search of a Storm Angel, than to look for a new barrel to crawl into.

He knew what Tangerine would think. He put his hand into his inside pocket to check on the bear. Beside the familiar straggly fur his fingers felt something smooth and strangely cold. It was a card of some sort, and only when he had taken it from his pocket did he remember the silvery ticket he had picked up from the muddy grass beneath Little's wagon at the Circus Oscuro.

CHAPTER EIGHT

THE SILVER TICKET

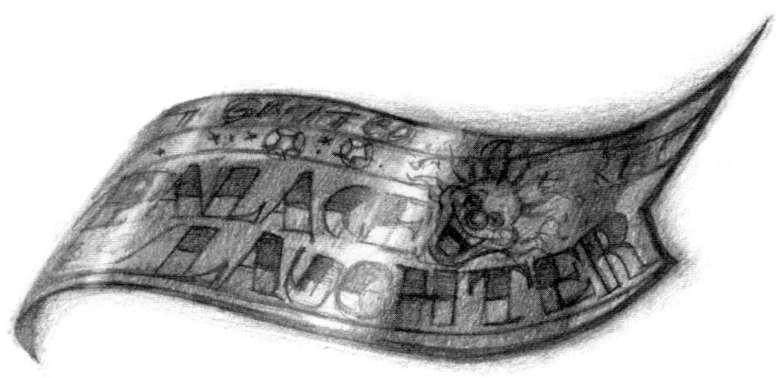

Miles Wednesday, soup-filled and fire-warmed, held the ticket up to catch the light from the candle flames that flapped lazily on the shelves. It looked something like this, although you will have to imagine how it sparkled in the light.

"The Palace of Laughter," said Miles. "Isn't that where you said Silverpoint was taken?"

"That's what the monkeys told me, and they don't miss much," said Little. Miles handed her the ticket. She frowned at the writing, and turned it over in her hands. "I can't read," she said. "Does it tell you where to find it?"

"No. It just says that the train leaves at dawn tomorrow."

"Then you shall have to try and catch the train if you are to find your friend," said Lady Partridge. "We'll find a way to disguise you, so you won't be so easy to spot. Perhaps Miles will go with you."

Miles did not answer. He was trying to remember where he had heard of the Palace of Laughter before. Crouching by wooden steps, breathing the smell of cigar smoke. That was it! The Great Cortado had mentioned it in his conversation with Genghis. Miles pictured a rambling palace, the doors standing open and the sound of laughter flooding out on the warm firelight. The thought of it made him smile. Somewhere out in the distant night, this place really did exist. He began to look forward to the adventure that was unfolding before them.

"You can't come with me," said Little. "This is trouble that I made for myself, and you've already done enough for me. The Great Cortado is a dangerous man, and he'll be very angry with you for helping me to escape."

"Then I'd better keep out of his way," said Miles. "But you can't go on your own, and anyhow the Great Cortado owes me a new home. If I can't ask him for one, I'll find another way to make him repay me."

"Quite right," said Lady Partridge, "but you shall both have to be very careful. I don't like the sound of this Circus Oscuro at all. Giantesses. Bone-crunching beasts. It's not my idea of a circus."

She sighed, stroking the ginger kitten on her lap. "I used to bring the orphans to Barty Fumble's Big Top. Now that was a wonderful show. It used to pass through here every summer, and we never missed it. It was small and friendly, and you could see that everyone really enjoyed themselves, right from the prop hands to the ringmaster himself. Barty Fumble was a real gentleman. You could tell by the way he held himself. It was said that he looked after all his performers, whether on two legs or four, as though they were his own children. I remember his pride and joy was a tiger named Variloop . . . Voopilar . . . some foreign name that I never could pronounce. There were many wonderful acts but that magnificent tiger was always the highlight of the show."

"What happened to Barty Fumble's Big Top?" asked Miles.

"I'm not really sure, my dear. It merged somehow with a larger circus, but that was years ago now. Rumor had it that Barty Fumble disappeared shortly after that, and his tiger along with him. I've never heard anything more of them since, and no other circus has passed through here for years, not until this Circus Oscuro arrived.

"Anyhow, that was all a long time ago," said Lady Partridge, "and what you both need now is a good night's sleep, or you won't be going anywhere at the crack of dawn, not if I have anything to do with it." She slipped into her purple slippers, which waited as usual below her hammock, and began to rummage in a wide drawer for bedclothes, muttering to herself as she did so. "Pillows, pillows, not in this one . . . nor that one. Now where did they go? . . . Shoo, you big furball. . . . Ah, here's Great-aunt Boadicea's embroidered cushion, that will do. . . . Now let me see . . . blankets . . . Don't get many visitors these days, you see. . . . Where did I put the dratted blankets?"

By the time she had found all that she needed, Little and Miles were asleep. She gently slipped pillows under their heads and covered them with warm blankets, then with a deep sigh she damped down the fire and shuffled through a purring sea of cats to her hammock.

Now imagine for a moment that you are an owl,

drifting silently over the garden of that deserted mansion in the middle of an October night. Your sharp hunter's eyes would see the strange jumble of Lady Partridge's tree house, nesting in the tree below you. A thin wisp of smoke is rising from the crooked pipe that serves as a chimney, before being pulled apart by the night breeze that rocks the tree house gently in the arms of the twin beech tree.

If you should perch on one of the higher branches, you would see through the single dusty window in the tree-house roof the outlines of three sleeping figures, and the twitching shapes of a hundred dozing cats. Inside every one of those sleeping heads is a world of dreams.

The dreams of the cats are much as you would expect them to be. Insects buzz through the dry grass of a summer's day, always just out of reach, and sometimes a whole fish will jump out of nowhere and land in a shower of sparkling droplets, right at the surprised dreamer's feet.

Curled up under a tartan blanket, Miles dreams of the basement laundry in Pinchbucket House. He is working with the other children, hauling damp sheets from a giant washing machine. On top of the machine sits the Bengal tiger, calmly cleaning his whiskers as though the laundry were his natural habitat, and not the jungles of Asia. Miles turns to drag his full basket over to the dryer, and sees to his horror that Fowler Pinchbucket is feeding his orphan brothers and sisters, two at a time, into the mouth of a huge machine in the corner. His mean face wears a grin of satisfaction. Miles turns to the tiger, who is paying not the slightest attention. He points at Fowler Pinchbucket and opens his mouth to shout, but no sound comes out. Two by two the children disappear, while the tiger licks his paws and the machines rumble on.

From your perch in the branches you would see Miles turn over in his sleep, rubbing the arm he has been sleeping on, while Lady Partridge snores gently in her swaying hammock. She is dreaming of a hot summer afternoon, her hammock strung between the twin beech trunks, in the shade below the tree house. Her cats are swarming over her, rubbing their cheeks against her chin and mewing loudly. She feels groggy from the heat, and she brushes them off irritably. When she opens her eyes they have disappeared, every last one of them. She has an uneasy feeling that they were trying to tell her something important, but it is too late to ask. She groans in her sleep, and the dream slips away.

But what of Little? The vast dreams that fill her

sleep are beyond anything you or I have ever imagined. She is soaring high above the Earth, riding the speeding winds among bright billowing clouds that tower above her as thunder rumbles deep in their bellies. All around her the One Song, of which we have never heard more than a lost echo, fills the skies of her dreams like a braided river of light. She sings as she swoops and climbs, feeling the thrill of speed in her stomach, and the wind sings with her. She becomes aware of two angels, riding on either side of her. They still the wind and silence the Song, and the clouds dissolve into a gray fog. "Silverpoint," says one. "Where is he?"

"Where is Silverpoint?" echoes the other, and he reaches out and lays a cold hand on her forehead. Little whimpers quietly in her sleep.

And now, if owls are as wise as they say, you will know that it's time to leave in search of that crunchy mouse you fancied for supper, for the tree in which you are resting is home to a hundred cats. They have begun to slink out along the branches and drop to the ground, and Little is waking from her sky-blown dream.

CHAPTER NINE
THE COUNCIL OF CATS

Miles Wednesday, sleep-muddled and blanket-warmed, woke to find Little shaking him by the shoulder. The tree house seemed quieter and draftier than before. The only sound was the creaking of branches and the soft snores of Lady Partridge, and he realized that the cats had all left.

"Where have they gone?" whispered Miles.

"To their Grand High Council, in the gazebo. They hold it every third full moon. We should go and see what they're saying."

Miles stretched and rubbed the sleep from his eyes. He pulled Tangerine from his inside pocket, to check that he was all right. Little watched him as she pulled on the old overcoat. "What do you call him?" she asked.

"Tangerine," said Miles. "He used to be bright orange once, but he's not too keen on baths."

"Have you had him for a long time?" said Little.

Miles nodded. "I've always had him," he said. "He's the only thing I have that my . . . that I had when I came to the orphanage."

"Your parents gave him to you?" said Little softly.

"I suppose so," said Miles. It was something he did not like to talk about, and he shifted uncomfortably on the creaky floorboards. Mrs. Pinchbucket had told him that his parents had left the orphanage laughing and driven away in a shiny car, leaving him on the doorstep. She told this to all the children, and Miles did not believe it. It was hard to imagine what kind of monsters could leave their children with nasty Mrs. Pinchbucket and her brutish husband, and he preferred to believe that his parents were dead. They had been swallowed by time, and his only link to them was Tangerine.

"Can I see him?" Little reached out her hand. Miles hesitated. He had never parted with Tangerine, not even for a moment. It felt strange to be handing him to someone else. Little took the small bear gently and propped him on her knees.

She looked into his clouded glass eyes for a long time, as the tree house creaked gently in the breeze, then she leaned close and whispered something into Tangerine's ear. She whispered very quietly, and as she did so Miles felt a strange sensation, like the warm breath of some invisible giant, passing through the tree house walls and ruffling his hair before disappearing into the night.

Little smiled to herself, and put Tangerine down on the floor. Instead of flopping straight over, Tangerine kept his feet, and as Miles watched in disbelief he began to totter across the Persian carpet toward him. It was a wobbly path that he traced, and he fell over several times, picking himself up each time until he reached Miles's knee. He began to climb, and Miles reached down instinctively to help him. His threadbare fur and saggy stuffing felt the same as they always had, but he wriggled in Miles's hand, and when Miles tried to help him into his pocket, Tangerine clung to him and squeezed, just as Miles had hugged him ever since he could remember. Suddenly he felt warmer in his thin jacket. He looked at Little, who was watching him with a smile. "How did you do that?" he whispered.

"I found his name in the One Song," she said,

"and I sang it back to him. Don't ever tell Silverpoint. He'd be very angry."

"Can you do that with just anything?"

Little shook her head. "Everything has a name in the One Song, but I am only learning, and there are many things whose names I don't know. I found Tangerine's real name there because you brought him to life in your imagination, and you made his name strong and bright, even though you didn't know it."

Tangerine wriggled into his accustomed place in Miles's pocket. With his head swimming, Miles buttoned his jacket carefully and followed Little down the rope ladder into the swaying weeds below. She set off around the empty mansion, still limping on her bandaged ankle. On the far side of the house the path curved away between the trees and around an old pond, choked now with weeds and long since abandoned by the swans. A small ornamental house with an open front perched on the edge of the pond, where Lady Partridge and her visitors had once sat on summer afternoons, fanning themselves and watching the swans sail among the water lilies. This was the gazebo, and in its dilapidated ruins the last few stragglers were just arriving to attend the Council of Cats. Lady Partridge's hundred cats had been joined by several stocky mousers from the surrounding farms, a number of strays, and a delegation of town cats from the tall houses of Larde.

Little put her finger to her lips and beckoned to Miles. He followed her to a willow tree beside the pond, whose feathery branches hung to the ground, making a sort of leafy cavern. They ducked under the tree and sat themselves on a carpet of dry leaves. Between the branches that trailed in the water's edge, they could see across the pond and into the gazebo, which was so packed with cats that those on the lip of the pond were in danger of falling into the water. A beam of moonlight shone through a hole in the roof and picked out a large tomcat. He was completely white except for a black tail and ears, as though he had been dipped in ink at both ends. He sat on top of an oblong of sandstone, carved with a tangle of leaves and a horned face, that stood on its end in the middle of the gazebo.

The black-eared cat opened his mouth and let out a low yowl, which silenced the others for a moment. Little sat forward as though to hear better. For some minutes the cats meowed and growled back and forth as cats will, especially when they are outside your window and you are trying to get to sleep. Miles listened as carefully as he could, but he could make no sense from the sounds the cats were making. "What are they saying?" he asked Little. She put her finger to her lips again, and leaned over to whisper in his ear. "We must be quiet. We would not be welcome if they knew we were here."

"I can't understand a thing," said Miles.

"You are listening too hard. You must stop trying to listen before you can hear. The voices are there, and they're not that different from your own."

Miles tried to grasp what she was saying, but it made little more sense to him than the mewing of the cats. He sat and listened for a while longer, but soon became sleepy and bored. He felt in his pocket for Tangerine, who grabbed his finger and lifted himself out. Miles put him down, and Tangerine crawled about happily, rummaging among the crackling leaves and tossing the furry willow seeds at Miles when he found them. In the distance a voice was saying, "The circus cats have a right to hunt our fields, provided their stay is short."

Somehow Miles knew, without even looking, that this voice belonged to the black-eared cat perched on his sandstone throne. He forgot Tangerine for a moment and stared in amazement at the moonlit figure in the center of the gazebo. The cat's voice sounded just the same as it had before, and he couldn't understand why the meaning had not been clear to him all along.

"What right is that?" called a bony black cat who was wedged into a corner at the back. "There's three and more big cats hunting our fields since yesterday. Fat fellows they are too, living well enough on circus leftovers. Why they need to be muscling in on our pickings is beyond me."

A large cat, stretched out on the gazebo roof, chuckled quietly at this. "No one tells us where we can hunt and where we can lie. We are citizens of the road and guests of every town. Besides, as you say yourself, there are plenty of scraps to be had at the circus, if you have the teeth to ask for them."

Several of the cats that crowded the roof and the surrounding trees sat up to look at the speaker. One hissed at him and stalked to the other end of the roof, his tail held high. "I wouldn't share food with a circus cat, nor would I turn my back on one for a second. I've heard it said . . ." He hesitated.

"Go on," said the circus cat, in a slow voice with a hint of amusement. "What's the chatter among the gutters and alleys?"

"It's no laughing matter," said the other, whose

name was Tiptoe. "I heard that . . . that a king of cats was killed in that circus, some years ago."

The circus cat was on his feet in a flash, and had swiped at Tiptoe before he had a chance to move, almost knocking him from the roof. "You heard wrong. There are no tigers in this circus," he hissed, "and there never were."

"I thought," said a fluffy cat from a low branch in a nearby tree, "that the lion was the king of cats."

The entire council erupted into yowls of laughter at this. There were cries of "Shame!" and the unfortunate cat began to clean his whiskers busily, pretending that it was someone else who had spoken.

"You've spent too much time among humans," said Blackears. "Every cat knows that the tiger wears the mark of royalty. Lions are braggarts with big hair, but there is no royal blood in their veins, no more than in mine or yours. However"—he looked up through the broken roof to where the circus cat stood—"this is a serious allegation, and it is the council's decision that you will come down here and present your case before the bench. You will not find yourselves welcomed among the local cats while such suspicions hang over your kind."

The circus cat dropped through the roof onto

the carved column, right beside Blackears. He was a heavy gray cat with a large head, and he put his face close to the other cat and sniffed at him, before dropping casually to the ground. The other cats made a space for him hurriedly.

"Well?" said the circus cat.

"Is it true," said Blackears, "that a tiger met an unnatural death in your circus?"

"It's not my circus. And there has been no tiger there in my time."

"And how long might that be?"

"I'm three and more winters old," said the gray cat, who in common with all cats could count no further than three.

"Surely you would have heard of such a terrible crime."

"No doubt," said the gray cat, yawning. "Which simply bears out that it never happened. There never was a tiger with the Circus Oscuro."

"There's a tiger on the poster," said the bony black cat in the corner. "They're all over town."

"That's right," said Tiptoe. "How do you explain that?"

The gray cat got to his feet and began to thread his way through the crowd toward the door of the gazebo. "It's obvious you know nothing about the ways of the circus," he said over his shoulder. "Every circus, even if it consists of nothing more than a pair of poodles and a clown, has a tiger on its poster. It's tradition, and circus folk would sooner blow themselves from a cannon than depart from tradition."

The circus cat left the gazebo and made his way around the edge of the pond, his tail high in the air. Blackears called the council to order and began a discussion on the strange rumors of a sheep-eating monster that some of the stray cats had reported. Miles picked up Tangerine, who appeared to have fallen asleep, and put him back in his pocket.

"Come on," he said to Little. "We had better get back. The sun will be up in a couple of hours." They made their way back through the overgrown garden and climbed the ladder to the tree house. Little fell asleep almost immediately, but Miles sat quietly by the fire, his head abuzz with strange happenings. Outside the tree house a chorus of birds sang the sun into place, just below the rim of the world.

CHAPTER TEN
THE SURLY HEN

Miles Wednesday, clean-shirted and cat-surrounded, spooned hot porridge into his mouth in the half-light before dawn, while Lady Partridge rubbed soot from the hearth into Little's hair. The result was a dirty, dark gray that would pass for black if you didn't look too closely. Against the dark hair her skin was white as a pearl.

Little was dressed in a boy's jacket, shirt and trousers that Lady Partridge had produced from an old leather trunk in the corner. They were a few sizes too big, but with the trousers turned up and the shirtsleeves rolled they fit her well enough. "These," said Lady Partridge, "belonged to Will, the gardener's boy. I used to pass them on to the orphanage when he outgrew them, until I discovered that horrible Pinchbucket woman was selling them to a stallholder at the market and keeping the few pennies for herself." She had rummaged again in the trunk and found an ice-cream-free shirt for Miles, and a cap that would at least partly hide his face. The shirt felt clean and a little stiff, as he spooned the last of the porridge from his bowl. He felt in his jacket pocket, but Tangerine was sleeping.

Lady Partridge stepped back to admire her handiwork. "You look like you've just fallen off the back of a coal truck, my dear, but I don't think anyone would recognize you too easily." She wiped her hands on an old cloth that hung from the tree trunk beside her. She looked from one to the other. "Now then," she said, "the longest journey begins with a single step. It's time you were going, the two of you, or you'll miss your train." She blew her nose loudly. "And remember," she said from behind her handkerchief, "wherever your road takes you, stick together and look out for each other. Really, if I weren't so generous of figure I would like nothing better than to shin down that ladder and come with you."

They dropped from the ladder into an early-morning mist that blanketed the deserted garden. The dark shape of the old mansion seemed to float among the trees, and the air felt cold and damp after the warmth of the tree house. Little still limped slightly. They clambered out through the gap in the wall, but took a different route through the woods, skirting around the bottom of the hill until they reached the lane that led to the train station.

They walked quickly along the lane between the tall hedges. Just as they reached the station the sun broke over the mountains, lighting the tops of the ornate chimney pots on the station-house roof. An old train stood at the platform. Its coaches were a dark mossy green and rather tattered. The platform was deserted except for the stationmaster, a tall gray-haired man who walked with a stoop, as though he carried an invisible sack on his shoulders. He was making his way along the platform, shutting the train doors as he went—slam . . . slam . . . slam. He did not seem in any hurry.

Miles opened the station gate. It squeaked loudly, but the stationmaster continued along the platform without a backward glance. "Excuse me," said Miles. The stationmaster slammed another door. "Hello?" said Miles. The stationmaster shuffled onward, his frayed gray trousers dusting the platform.

"Maybe he's deaf," said Little. The stationmaster stopped. He slammed one more door, then turned around slowly to face them.

"Not deaf, busy," he said. "I've got a lot of doors to close here, in case you hadn't noticed."

"We just want to know if this is the train for the Palace of Laughter," said Miles.

The old man sucked his teeth. He had very few teeth left, and when he sucked them, his wrinkled lips wrapped around them like gray curtains. "The Palace of Laughter," he repeated.

"That's right," said Miles. The stationmaster scratched his head. Miles produced the silver ticket from his pocket and held it out. The stationmaster barely glanced at it. "Says tomorrow," he said.

Miles looked again at the ticket. "Train leaves at dawn tomorrow," it said along the bottom. "But this *is* tomorrow," he said. "I got the ticket yesterday."

"Today is today, son," said the stationmaster patiently, "and tomorrow is tomorrow. Least it was when I went to school. Train leaves at dawn tomorrow."

"But tomorrow this ticket will still say 'tomorrow,'" said Miles. "Tomorrow is always tomorrow!"

"Aye," said the old man. "You're catching on, lad.

And dawn tomorrow is when your train leaves."

"How can we be sure?" persisted Miles.

The stationmaster sighed, his lips flapping slightly in the draft. "Because it says so on the ticket. But don't take my word for it, ask them odd folk at the circus. Them's the ones who give out the tickets. Now if you don't mind, I have a busy day ahead of me." He turned and slammed another door. It was a long train, and there seemed to be no one aboard.

"What do we do now?" asked Little as they walked back along the platform.

"I don't know," said Miles. "We can't wait around another day, and it might be a good thing if we could get to the Palace of Laughter before the train does anyhow."

"It might, but we still don't know where it is."

"I think," said Miles, "our best chance might be for me to sneak into the circus again, and see if I can find out anything more. You'll have to keep out of sight when we get closer. They might recognize you, soot or no soot."

They followed the rutted road as it curved around the base of the hill toward the long field. Birds chattered and sang in the trees by the roadside, but the sun had not yet begun to warm the air.

As they came within sight of the field, Miles stopped dead in the long shadow of a poplar tree. The red and black tent was nowhere to be seen, and the trucks and wagons of the strange circus had packed up in the night, as silently and unexpectedly as they had arrived. Not a hoop or a bucket or a rusty peg remained. A large oval patch of trampled ground was all the evidence that was left of the Circus Oscuro—that and the tangle of wheel ruts that curved from the field and out along the road toward the mountains.

"They've gone," said Miles. He turned to look at Little, but she was staring at the tree where the elephants had been tethered the morning before. Her face, if it were possible, looked even whiter than usual. Miles followed her gaze. For a moment he could see nothing, then he became aware of a figure standing in the shadow of the tree. Although he could not make out any features, nor even if it was a man or a woman, he was sure the figure was staring straight at them.

"I'll go and ask him," said Miles, "or her. Maybe they know where the circus has gone."

Little grabbed his arm, and though she was light as a feather her grip was painfully tight.

"No," she said urgently, "let's go." She pulled him

by the elbow, turning in the direction of the disappearing wheel ruts.

"Wait," said Miles. The figure under the tree seemed to be moving toward them. He felt a strong urge to see the person's face, which still seemed indistinct. It was not that the distance between them was great, but his eyes felt heavy and he found it strangely difficult to focus.

"Stay awake!" hissed Little, pinching his arm so tightly now that he tried to pull himself free of her grip. "Please, Miles." She seemed on the point of tears, and he looked at her in surprise. "Come with me, now," she pleaded.

He began to walk slowly along the road. He suddenly felt as though he had not slept for a year. "Walk faster," urged Little. He turned to look over his shoulder, and again she pinched him hard. "Don't look back," she said. "Just keep walking."

Miles forced his leaden legs to keep pace with Little, and they walked quickly and silently toward the distant mountains. A cart passed them on its way into town with the muffled clanking of full milk churns, and Miles could no longer resist the temptation to look back the way they had come, but the figure was no longer anywhere to be seen.

• • ● • •

In the shortening shadows of the late morning, Miles and Little walked along the center of the road, farther from the town of Larde than Miles had ever been before. They had followed the muddy tracks of the circus wagons until they faded into the road, and continued walking, with no plan left to them but to find the circus wherever it stopped next. Besides, as Miles had pointed out, the road followed the train tracks, more or less, which must lead eventually to the Palace of Laughter.

As they walked, Miles thought about the figure they had seen in the circus field. Little, who seemed incapable of remaining upset or anxious for long, was laughing at the chattering of the birds in the hedgerows, and he felt almost reluctant to bring the subject up, but his curiosity would not leave him alone. The tiredness he had felt had melted away, leaving only the ache of his feet in their cracked boots.

"Who was that, back there in the field?" he asked.

Little fell silent for a minute before answering. "Someone I thought I recognized," she said.

"Someone from the circus?"

Little shrugged. "Maybe," she said. "It was better not to risk it." She gave him a sidelong glance, then turned her eyes quickly back to the road.

"Look," she said, pointing ahead of them. "There's a river crossing the road."

Miles shaded his eyes and looked where she was pointing. He knew she was not telling him all she knew, but it was obvious she wanted to change the subject, and he did not see any point in pressing her further. He shook his head. "That's just a mirage," he said.

"A mirage?"

"Lady Partridge explained them to me. It looks like water, but it's just the hot air bending the light."

Little laughed. "It looks like water because it is water," she said. She sounded so convinced that Miles almost expected to find himself shortly wading through a stream, but when they reached the slight rise where the mirage had appeared, the road was dry.

"See?" said Miles. "Dry as a dragon's tongue. The water was just an illusion."

"The water was here, and it still is," insisted Little. "It just doesn't want to be seen."

"If you say so, Little," he said, but she had picked up a praying mantis and was staring into its green bug eyes as it perched grandly on her outstretched finger, the subject of disappearing water already forgotten.

Around midday they arrived at a small hamlet, little more than a cluster of farms and a small village square with a row of shops and a tiny church. A sign by the side of the road said? WELCOME TO HAY. POP. 481. TWINNED WITH CARTHAGE. At the far end of the square stood a rambling inn with benches and tables outside. The inn was called the Surly Hen, and it appeared to have been built over several generations by owners with very different notions of what an inn should look like. The main part had two steeply pitched roofs rising to sharp points, with leaded windows set into white plastered walls that were divided into neat shapes by a web of black beams. Growing out of that was a low, small-windowed extension, roofed with an untidy thatch that looked like it needed a haircut. There were several other additions ranging in style from mock Gothic to simply indescribable.

The long tables outside the inn were crowded with local farmers and travelers at lunch, shoveling chunks of bread and sausage into their stubbly faces and washing them down with pitchers of dark wine. Miles looked at them curiously. An air of resigned misery seemed to surround them like a fog, and hardly a word was spoken as they ate. Two small girls chased each other among the tables, laughing, but no one paid them any attention. At the nearest table sat a stocky man in a shapeless hat, and a plump woman with several chins. They had a large feed spread out on the rough boards before them, and they were working their way through it with a kind of sad vigor. A half-demolished pie sat in front of each of them, and with a large forkful of steak and pastry on its way into her mouth it looked like Mrs. Farmer was ahead in that particular race. Between them on the table sat a basket piled with crusty bread, and a bowl of green olives that Mr. Farmer was tossing in handfuls between his thin lips after every mouthful of pie. Two plates of sausage were all but done for.

Miles felt a yawning cavern in his stomach at the sight of all this food. His morning bowl of hot porridge seemed a lifetime ago. Mrs. Farmer caught sight of him standing in the road, transfixed at the sight of her enormous lunch. She stared sadly at him for a moment, then returned her attention to her food. As Miles contemplated the best way to get himself and Little fed, without so much as a brass penny between them, the landlady of the inn bustled out among the tables. By contrast to her customers she wore a broad grin, and sang snatches of some tune that must have sounded considerably better in its original form, or it would have been strangled at birth.

She planted her tray on the end of Mr. and Mrs. Farmer's table. "Now, ducks," she said happily. "One jug of wine and a bottle of Tau-Tau's." She took from her pocket a small bottle with a bright green label, which she uncorked and emptied into an earthenware wine jug. She picked the jug up, swirled its contents around for a moment, then slopped a generous measure into two glass tumblers, which she plonked on the table. The farmer and his wife picked the glasses up greedily and emptied the contents in unison. The farmer refilled them at once.

They carried on eating with no less gusto, but it seemed that Mrs. Farmer's cheeks were growing redder by the moment. She glanced in Miles's direction again, and stopped in mid-chew, a ribbon of cabbage hanging from the corner of her mouth. She nudged her husband sharply in the ribs. He had just put his tumbler to his lips, and took more wine up his nose than into his mouth. While he coughed and spluttered into a grubby handkerchief, Mrs. Farmer beckoned to Miles. "Come here, come here," she called, a smile breaking out on her plump face. "Don't be shy, lad."

The farmer glared at Miles as he shoved his

handkerchief back up his sleeve. "No beggin' allowed here," he grunted, tearing off a chunk of bread and wedging it into his cheek to allow other food free passage through his mouth.

"Oh put a sock in it, George," said Mrs. Farmer, whose mood seemed to be brightening by the second. "Can't you see the boy's 'ungry? Looks like he's never had a proper feed in his life. Where'd you come from, lad? Call your little sister over—there's plenty 'ere for both of you."

Mr. Farmer stared over Miles's shoulder in puzzlement. "What little sister, woman? There's only another young lad there."

"Don't be daft, George! Them's just boy's clothes. Anyone can see it's a little girl what's wearing 'em, ain't that right, lad?" Miles nodded. "She's shy," he said.

"Bless 'er," said the plump woman, chuckling, it seemed, at nothing in particular. She emptied some of the bread basket into her pie dish, filling the empty space with the remaining slices of sausage and a lump of rank cheese.

Mr. Farmer grunted, but the miserable expression seemed to be melting from his face too, like winter snow. "I don't spend the day breakin' my back to feed every 'ungry urchin that 'appens by," he muttered, though none too loudly.

"You don't spend the day breaking yer back at all, you lazy old coot, unless it's liftin' a beer tankard you're talking about." She handed the bread basket to Miles, throwing in the last few olives for good measure. "'Ere, lad, this'll stop your ribs knockin' together. Take it over to your sister and mind you share it, eh?"

"Thank you," said Miles. He hesitated by the table.

"Well?" said Mr. Farmer. "What is it, sonny? Want me socks and britches as well?" He laughed loudly at his own wit.

"I was just wondering if you knew where I could find a place called the Palace of Laughter."

The reaction to Miles's question was not what he had expected. Mrs. Farmer's face went strangely blank, yet at the same time her mouth stretched in a sort of strained grin that was quite unlike the sunny smile she had worn a moment before. A strangled whinny came from the back of her throat. Mr. Farmer stared fixedly at Miles, as though he were trying to remember where he had seen him before. "Never 'eard of it," he said eventually. He picked up the wine jug and emptied it down his throat, then he and his wife got up from their bench without another glance at Miles, for all the world as though he had become invisible. They walked a slightly meandering path to their battered old car, giggling like a couple of schoolchildren, and drove away in a cloud of dust.

Miles stood for a moment staring after them. He noticed that some of the people at the nearest tables were looking at him with suspicion, so he took the basket of leftovers and hurried over to where Little was waiting for him. She sat on the rim of a stone fountain that stood in the center of the small square, dangling her fingers in the cool water. "Why did those people leave so suddenly?" she asked.

"I don't know. I asked them if they knew the way to the Palace of Laughter, and they reacted very strangely. They said they'd never heard of it, but I don't think they were telling the truth. I suppose I could ask someone else."

Little put a piece of cheese in her mouth. She pulled a face and bit off a chunk of bread to dilute the sour taste, and shook her head. "I don't think anyone here is going to tell us. As long as we can still see the train tracks we must be going in the right direction."

They ate in silence for a while. The midday sun

was hot for October, and after they had quenched the thirst of their long walk with handfuls of clear water, they sat down on the warm paving stones, leaning against the fountain's smooth rim. With his belly full and the sun on his face, Miles felt sleepy. He looked around him for a moment, half expecting to see the strange figure the circus had left in its wake, but there was no one to be seen but the chuckling landlady, her melancholy customers and the two small girls, who had been joined by a blond boy and were squatting in the dust making patterns with pebbles. "We'll rest here for a few minutes before we go on," said Miles, but Little was already asleep.

Miles felt in his pocket for Tangerine, who gave his fingers a squeeze. He seemed tired too, although he had done none of the walking. A fly buzzed somewhere above their heads, and wood pigeons hooted softly in the trees beside the inn. Squinting through his eyelashes, Miles noticed a circus poster tacked to a pole across the square. Beneath the words "CIRCUS OSCURO," the tiger, magnificent and fierce, reared in the center of a flaming hoop, while a fearless boy in a red suit with gold epaulets brandished a whip in the background. He wondered whether he would ever again meet the tiger he had spoken to in the moonlight. It seemed such a long time ago.

Miles felt his head nodding, and the tickle of Little's soot-blackened hair as she leaned against his shoulder. "She weighs nothing at all," Miles thought as he drifted into sleep. "She must have hollow bones, like a bird."

CHAPTER ELEVEN
TANGERINE

Miles Wednesday, stone-warmed and Tangerine-less, blinked in the afternoon sun and wondered for a moment where he was. He lifted Little gently upright and . . . just a moment . . . Tangerine-less? His hand dived into his pocket, but somehow he already knew what he would find there. A silver ticket to the Palace of Laughter, and no bear. Where had he gone? He shook Little's shoulder.

"Little—wake up! Have you got Tangerine?"

"No," she yawned. "Isn't he in your pocket?"

Miles shook his head. He stood up and looked into the fountain behind them, but there was nothing in the water besides a few yellow leaves. He had a panicky feeling, as though the ground were falling away beneath his feet. The square itself was almost empty. At the inn tables the crowd had thinned out, but there were still clusters of people, hunched over beer tankards and talking of horses and hoes and the storms that came down on them from the mountain. Small bottles with green labels stood empty on some of the tables, and if Miles had not been searching so anxiously for Tangerine he might have noticed something odd. Unlike the other knots of silent, gray-faced diners, the people sitting at those tables laughed and chatted as you would expect people enjoying a long lunch and good company to do.

Miles shaded his eyes with his hand and searched the shadows beneath the tables for a sign of Tangerine. He spotted him after a moment. A wave of relief swept over him. The bear was ambling between the table legs toward the door of the inn. Miles took from his pocket the cap that Lady Partridge had given him, and pulled it low over his eyes. He made his way among the tables to the point where he had last seen Tangerine. No one paid him any attention. He bent and looked quickly beneath the table next to him. Tangerine was not under that one, but he could see him in the shadow of the table behind that. The bear had come face to face with a large tabby cat, who stood frozen with his tail fluffed, and stared at him with unblinking green eyes.

Miles ducked under the table and crawled between the muddy boots toward Tangerine. The cat hunched lower and shifted his paws, preparing to spring. Miles wriggled over a crossbar between two table legs, desperately trying to reach Tangerine, who had decided that hide-and-seek must be the cat's game, and was trying to hide himself behind a pair of ankles.

The ankles that Tangerine had chosen to hide behind were dressed in lemon yellow socks, plainly visible beneath too-short trousers. As he stuck his threadbare orange head between the ankles and stared at the slightly bemused cat, two things happened at once. A hand reached down from above the table, and the cat sprang. The tabby cat and the owner of the lemon-yellow ankles reached the small bear at the same moment, and the cat's claws sunk themselves into the man's hand instead.

Genghis (for who else would wear lemon-yellow socks?) staggered to his feet with a yell. The bench fell with a crash. He let fly several strange curses that you would only hear in a circus, and not very often at that, but he did not let go of Tangerine. He aimed a kick at the cat, who bolted for the nearest tree and ran straight up the trunk until he disappeared among the rattling brown leaves. Miles clambered out from under the table, the panicky feeling growing stronger in the pit of his stomach. Genghis was sucking the torn knuckles of his right hand, and holding Tangerine tightly in his left. Miles cleared his throat loudly, the cap still pulled low over his eyes. Genghis turned to him with a face like thunder.

"That's my bear," said Miles. He could see Tangerine pushing feebly at Genghis's thick stubby fingers. He frowned at him desperately to try and get him to lie still, but Tangerine took no notice.

Genghis took a good look at Tangerine for the first time. His sly eyes widened as he saw the bear struggling in his grasp. "Not anymore it ain't," he said. "Now take a hike before I polish my boot with your backside."

"Give him to me!" shouted Miles, grabbing Genghis's wrist. People stared from the surrounding tables, but Miles didn't care. All the love that a luckier boy might have given to his parents, Miles had given to Tangerine, and he was not about to let him go.

Genghis reached over with his bleeding right hand and grabbed Miles by the collar in a grip that was starting to feel too familiar by half. He tried to squirm from Genghis's hold, and the cap was knocked from his head. Genghis gave a start. "Well skin me alive!" he said. "It's you again, you little weasel. You seem to be everywhere, except when you're nowhere to be found, that is." He shoved Tangerine into his overcoat pocket and leaned closer to Miles, his words floating on stale cigar breath. "My boss would like a word with you, little weasel. And I don't think he'll be offering you no job, neither."

The landlady of the Surly Hen had emerged again from the inn's dark interior to see what the commotion was about. "Leave that young 'un alone, you big lummox," she said. "'E's just a boy."

"Get lost," growled Genghis, swinging around to face the landlady. As he did so, Miles twisted in his jacket, sinking his teeth into Genghis's hand at the base of his thumb and stamping on his foot with all the strength he could muster. Genghis yelled and let go of Miles's collar. He stuck his clawed and bitten hand back into his mouth and aimed a clumsy swipe at Miles with his other. Miles ducked, but not fast enough. The big man's fist hit him squarely in the ear, sending him sprawling on the dusty paving stones. Through the ringing in his ears he could just hear the landlady squawking at Genghis, her face red with anger and her finger stabbing the air in his direction. The diners were glaring at Genghis now too, and from the shadows of the inn door a large bearded man was emerging, hitching his gravy-stained cook's trousers up to an imaginary waist and squinting in the light. He had a large meat cleaver in his hand, and did not look happy to be disturbed in his work. "What is it?" he growled.

"This big lummox is pickin' on that boy, Ted," said the landlady. The sight of Ted, who was an even bigger lummox and with a meat cleaver to boot, was enough for Genghis. He turned on his heel and strode around the side of the inn to the patch of trodden and rutted earth where the carts and tractors of the inn's patrons were tethered.

The landlady opened her mouth to speak to Miles, but before she could utter a word he had scrambled to his feet and was running after Genghis, desperately hoping that Tangerine would manage to wriggle unnoticed from the big man's pocket, as he had from his own. Genghis was climbing aboard a battered blue van as Miles turned the corner of the Surly Hen. He saw the words "THE PALACE OF LAUGHTER" painted in silver letters on the side, as the engine coughed into life and the van made a sharp turn out of the lot. With no thought but to stay close to Tangerine, Miles ran after the van, but before he could reach it the battered vehicle bounced into the road and roared away up the hill, leaving a cloud of dust and the trace of a smell that might have been rotten bananas in its wake.

Miles stood for a minute, bruised and panting, staring after Genghis's van as it disappeared over the brow of the hill. He felt a strange tug, as though something deep inside him had been hooked by an invisible fishing line and was being pulled away along the dusty road. He closed his eyes and tried to fix a picture of Tangerine in his mind. "Sit tight," he said silently to the bear. "I'll come and get you." He opened his eyes again and suddenly remembered Little.

She was no longer to be seen at the fountain, or anywhere else in the square. He hoped she had had the sense to hide herself at the first sight of Genghis, and he looked around the trampled field for any sign of her. A forest of dark conifers began at the edge of the field and ran along the right-hand side of the road that the van had taken. Shading his eyes, Miles spotted Little among the nearest trees. She was standing half hidden behind the trunk of a tall fir, but she was not looking in his direction. She was staring at something a little farther into the shadows. He followed her gaze and saw to his surprise that someone seemed to have hung a circus poster well inside the wood, where it was barely visible in the mossy gloom. He could just make out the dull orange glow of the tiger's stripes, but he could not see the boy with the whip, or the flaming hoop.

In the shadows of the trees the tiger appeared to be moving. Miles walked over to where Little stood, to get a closer look. Without turning, she put her finger to her lips. He could see the tiger more clearly now, and there was no longer any doubt that he was moving. He was walking slowly toward them, his enormous paws making barely a sound on the carpet of pine needles. There was no poster after all, just a large and magnificent Bengal tiger, and this time Miles knew for sure that he was not dreaming.

CHAPTER TWELVE

SUNFLOWER AND STORMCLOUD

Miles Wednesday, bruised, bemused and bearless, held his breath as the tiger approached them in the stillness of the afternoon. The twittering birds had fallen silent, and the sound of cows lowing on the hillside had ceased. He could see the tiger more clearly now, and he recognized the pattern of markings on his face, and the deep gaze of the great beast's amber eyes. At ten paces the tiger stopped. Little glanced at Miles, as though waiting for him to speak, but what do you say to a Bengal tiger who is staring at you from springing distance, and with no bars between you?

The tiger spoke first. "What's the matter, tub

boy?" he rumbled. "Cat got your tongue?"

"No," said Miles. "Genghis got my Tangerine."

The tiger seemed to prick up his ears at this, but all he said was, "I've never had much time for riddles."

"It's not a riddle," said Miles. "I have a stuffed bear called Tangerine, and a fat man called Genghis has stolen him and driven away in his van." He pointed in the direction that Genghis had taken. "I have to get him back."

"A stuffed bear?" said the tiger. "You're wasting my time, tub boy. I could be finding myself a tasty meal right now."

"I didn't ask you to come here in the first place," said Miles, rather shortly. He had many questions he wanted to ask the tiger, but at the moment the bear-napping of Tangerine was uppermost on his mind. With every passing minute Genghis was getting farther away, with Tangerine trapped in the pocket of his smelly overcoat, but how could he explain the importance of this to the tiger?

The tiger paced slowly toward him until his eyes were just inches away. His tiger smell was musty and strong. The black markings over his eyes gave his face a slightly quizzical expression, but the eyes themselves were steady and clear. His nostrils flared slightly as he took in Miles's smell.

"Maybe so," he said. "And maybe not." He turned to look at Little.

"Who's your friend?" he said, still speaking to Miles.

"This is Little," said Miles.

"Little," said the tiger. "That's apt, I suppose. There's barely enough of her to go on a cracker."

"The kitchens are just over there." said Little, ignoring the tiger's comment and pointing through the trees to the back of the inn. "I'm sure you could find something to eat, if we could distract the cook for a minute. You'll need all your strength and speed to catch up with Genghis."

The tiger stepped back a pace and looked Little up and down.

"So you can speak," he said. "I prefer my meat on the hoof, little girl. And besides, what makes you think I would go haring over the countryside chasing a fat man with a stuffed bear?"

"I was hoping you could carry us on your back," said Little. "We're not heavy, and you are strong."

"Do I look like a donkey to you, little girl?"

"Not at all," said Little. "You look much faster, and even if a donkey could catch up with Genghis I don't think he would scare him much."

The tiger gave a deep rumbling laugh that seemed to come all the way from his hungry belly. "I suppose a little run might be enjoyable," he said, "and it so happens I was headed in that direction anyway. As for you, you may sit on my back if that's what you wish; I will not even notice you are there. But you should understand that I am not a beast of burden, and staying on will be your own concern. It doesn't matter to me if you fall off and are lost."

The tiger turned to face the distant mountains. Miles was just a shade taller than him, although he would have had to stand on his toes to see over him. He lifted Little from the ground and helped her onto the tiger's back, where she settled just behind his powerful shoulders. Then he grabbed a handful of the tiger's short pelt and hauled himself up behind her. Before he could seat himself, the tiger started off through the thin trees at the edge of the wood, and Miles had to hold on tight until he could swing his leg over and sit up properly. He had no doubt the tiger meant what he said about leaving him behind if he fell off.

If you have ever sat on the back of a fully grown Bengal tiger, you will have noticed that a tiger's body has a leaner shape than that of a horse. Whereas some horses, and especially the kind of ponies you get to ride on your holidays, can be distinctly barrel shaped around the middle, a tiger is basically a long slender slab of pure muscle, which makes gripping a tiger with the knees a little easier, especially if you are a first-time tiger rider.

Miles had no experience of riding either animal, and for the first few minutes he concentrated hard on keeping his balance with nothing for his hands to hold on to. When he became confident enough to look back over his shoulder, the hamlet of Hay and the Surly Hen had disappeared from view, and there was no sign of the horde of policemen and out-of-work zookeepers that he had half expected to see pursuing them along the road.

The tiger's stride lengthened and he began to run. Miles gripped tighter with his knees, but at each bound he felt himself lift in the air, the wind whistling past his ears. He was sure that he would part company from the tiger at any moment and find himself somersaulting through the air. Little, by contrast, sat easily at the tiger's shoulders, looking about her with delight as the sunlight flashed through the passing trees. Miles held her around the waist, as though some of her confidence might flow into him.

The tiger kept to the edge of the woods, a little

way in from the road so as to keep out of sight. They had reached the top of the hill over which Genghis's van had disappeared and descended into the valley below. Between the trees they could see a small village in the valley floor, with a tall gray spire rising from a jumble of red roofs. Neatly tended fields climbed gently up the slopes of the surrounding hills. Far off to their left there was a glint of sunlight on the railway, which curved gently away and ran out of sight into the hazy distance.

They came to a break in the trees, where a stone bridge crossed the stream that wound along the edge of the wood, and here they stopped. Miles's legs felt stiff as he slid off the tiger's back, but the tiger showed no sign of tiredness. A bend in the stream kept them out of sight of the town, and there was nobody about. They drank from the clear water that ran over the smooth brown rocks of the riverbed, then Miles and Little flopped down in the lush grass of the stream bank while the tiger waded out into the water and stood there as still as a statue. For two or three minutes he did not move a muscle, then suddenly he gave a short lunge and ducked his head into the water, coming up a moment later with a large trout flapping between his teeth, while sparkling drops of water shivered on his whiskers like dew on a spider's web. Little laughed, and the sun came out from behind a cloud. Everything seemed so new to her, and Miles wondered how she must feel to be so far from the world she knew.

"What's it like, where you come from?" he asked her.

"It's bright," said Little, "and cold, and very beautiful."

"Do you miss it?"

"Of course." She picked a flower from the grass and twirled it in her fingers. "It's very strange down here. Especially people."

"How do you mean?"

"They do funny things." She propped herself up on her elbow and looked at him intently with her sky-blue eyes. "Like you. You are helping me to find the Palace of Laughter, even though you lost your home and the Great Cortado wants you dead because of me. And you know that when I find Silverpoint I'll be going home."

Miles felt an unexpected lump in his throat. He did not want to think about the moment when Little would leave. "I have to find Tangerine," he said.

"That's not the only reason," said Little. "You tried

to save me when I fell. Then you rescued me from the circus, and from The Null. All that happened before you lost Tangerine. It doesn't make sense."

Miles looked at her. There was only curiosity in her eyes. "That's what friends do," he said. "Silverpoint's your friend, and you're going to find him, aren't you?"

Little looked puzzled. "Silverpoint is a longfeather and a Storm Angel," she said. "I am just a Song Angel."

"But you're trying to rescue him," persisted Miles.

Her gaze dropped to the flower that she twirled between her fingers. "I can't return home without Silverpoint," she said. "I led him into a trap, and now I am bound to find him."

The tiger stepped back onto the riverbank, having filled his belly with fresh fish, and shook himself, showering Miles and Little with cold water. He turned to look at them. "I beg your pardon," he said. "I thought you were just a couple of rabbits there in the grass."

Little tucked the flower carefully into her pocket and put her finger to her lips. "Something's coming," she said.

The tiger's rounded ears swiveled in the direction

of the road. He turned without a word and padded along the bank until he was out of sight under the stone bridge, where he lay down in the shade. Miles and Little followed him quickly, as the sound of hooves and cart wheels from the road above grew louder. Over the noise of the approaching cart they could hear the sound of laughter. The wheels of the cart rumbled overhead, and Miles saw a small object spinning through the air to land with a plunk in the water of the stream.

When they were sure the cart had gone, the tiger stood and stretched himself. "You'd better climb aboard if you're coming," he said. "We have some catching up to do."

"Wait a moment," said Miles. He was curious to see what it was that had been thrown from the cart. He pulled off his boots and rolled his trousers to the knee. The stream was cold and the stones slippery with weed. He waded to the spot where he had seen the small object hit the water, and found it almost immediately, lodged between two rounded stones. It was a small square bottle with a green label, like the ones the landlady of the Surly Hen had been dispensing. He fished it out and read aloud: "Dr. Tau-Tau's Restorative Tonic. Restores the natural humor and lifts sagging spirits. Just two spoonfuls of this miracle remedy will bring the laughter back into your life. Do not operate heavy machinery or perform surgery for six hours after dosage."

"The tiger is leaving," said the tiger. "Are you finished prospecting for rubbish?" Little was already perched behind his shoulders. Miles nodded, and slipped the bottle thoughtfully into his pocket. He pulled his socks and boots back on over his wet feet, and climbed onto the tiger's back.

The forest through which they had been traveling ended at the stream. On the far bank was a field of sunflowers. They stretched into the distance like a tall green army, their yellow-fringed heads heavy with seeds and drooping slightly. Beyond the fields the mountains rose steeply, their lower slopes terraced with vineyards. The sunflower fields, still lit with the late-afternoon sun, showed a dazzling yellow against the purplish black rain clouds that hung low over the mountain.

"The railway turns away to the north here, but the road looks like it continues straight over the mountain," said Miles.

"Of what concern is the railway, tub boy? I understood your were pursuing a fat man in a van."

"We are" said Miles. "We're also looking for a place called the Palace of Laughter. The train goes there. But it looks like the van might be going there too."

"Then the obvious thing would be to take the shorter route, which would appear to be over the mountain," said the tiger.

Miles and Little nibbled on sunflower seeds that they managed to snatch as they passed through the tall flowers with their thick hairy stems. In the distance they saw a lone farmer, staring in puzzlement at the sight of two children's heads traveling at some speed, just above the level of the sunflowers. They waved at him, and he blessed himself and turned quickly away. The sunflowers seemed to go on forever, but eventually the ground began to rise, and they emerged into the lower terraces of the vineyards. To their left they could see the road beginning to loop from side to side as it climbed the steep slopes toward the gathering storm. The tiger made better speed now, following the paths of packed earth at the edges of the vineyards. When he reached the next terrace he paused for a moment, and Miles could feel he was gathering himself to spring. Little took hold of his pelt, and Miles held her around the waist, and the tiger jumped, soaring through the air to land with his huge paws sinking slightly into the loose earth.

Miles, who had slid back almost onto the tiger's tail, pulled himself forward again as the tiger took off toward the next level.

The tiger leaped from terrace to terrace, and Miles learned to grip tightly with his knees and lean forward at the moment of the jump. Little laughed with delight as they sped through the bushy vines. Miles had never heard anything quite like this laugh. It seemed to be made of sunlight and sweet air, all the things he had never felt in Pinchbucket House, or in the leaden laughter of the tired people of Larde. There was something else there too, a feeling that he imagined might be the thrill of flying. He looked over his shoulder and was surprised to see how high they were. The town was already a distant jumble threaded on a silver stream, where the dark green of the forest met the gold of the sunflower fields.

Ahead of them the vineyards were coming to an end, and the rocky mountain, dotted with scrubby vegetation and isolated pines, rose into the dark stormclouds. As they left the last neat rows of young vines, fat drops of rain began to fall, and in a few moments they were riding through a heavy downpour that soaked them to the skin. The rain battered the earth with a hissing roar and stung their faces, but the tiger's pace did not slacken. He ran on, bounding from rock to rock and forging through wild shrubs as though the storm were a figment of their imagination.

They could not see far through the curtains of rain, but presently the ground leveled off and they began to descend. Before long Miles realized they were climbing again, and he guessed that the moutain rose in a series of peaks, each one higher than the last.

The sky began to lift at last, and the rain eased off. A cold breeze made them shiver in their wet clothing. The tiger stopped, and they found themselves on the highest ridge of the mountain, looking down the other side. A little way down the far slope an almost circular lake lay in a hollow like a giant cauldron, and beyond that a hilly plain stretched away into the darkness. Miles felt strangely like a small giant, perched on the mountain ridge with the sun setting behind him, and before him a thousand possible futures waiting for him in the mountain's shadow.

CHAPTER THIRTEEN
VARIPPULI

Miles Wednesday, rain-soaked and tiger-carried, stood on a windy ridge at the top of Mount Bare-knuckle and surveyed the twilit hills beyond. To his left stood a Bengal tiger, and to his right a girl, smaller than he was but several centuries older, who had fallen from the sky. He felt light-headed and free, as though he could step out onto the wind and sail down from the mountain like an untethered kite.

He tried to make out the course of the road they had been following, but as it wound down from the ridge it soon disappeared into the shadow of the mountain. They made their way down toward the circular lake, which shone faintly with the last remaining light. Miles walked to loosen his legs, while Little sat sidesaddle (but without a saddle, of course) on the tiger's back. A dense pine wood bordered part of the lake, and in the wood they found a small clearing that opened on one side onto the still waters. In the center of the clearing stood three enormous stones, with another flat slab laid across the top. The standing stones were about three paces apart for a tall man, and the ground between them was dry, sheltered by the stone roof.

"We will spend the night here," said the tiger. "I suggest you build a fire, while I go and catch myself some supper. After all that running I could eat a small village."

Under the pine trees there was plenty of dry wood. They piled it just outside the standing stones, and Miles, who always kept an old brass lighter in his pocket, soon had a good fire blazing. They sat on the dry ground between the stones, and their clothes steamed in the heat. The waters of the lake were now as dark as night. The sky was cloudy still, and only a few patches of stars could be seen here and there. Miles stared into the embers of the fire, glowing orange and black like the tiger's flanks. The ground beneath him seemed to sway slightly, echoing the rhythm of the tiger's muscular back that had carried him through the afternoon. He wondered where Tangerine was now. He pictured him somewhere on a tavern table, being poked and prodded and laughed over by drunkards and fools, and he hoped at least that he was still hidden in Genghis's stale, smoky pocket.

The tiger emerged from the darkness and settled himself in the grass beside the fire. His stomach no longer rumbled, and now and then he licked his lips and sighed deeply.

The questions Miles had been storing up for the tiger came crowding back into his mind. He hardly knew where to start. "Do you have a name?" he asked.

"Yes," said the tiger.

Miles smiled to himself. He felt unaccountably pleased that the tiger had given him the same reply that he had given the Great Cortado. "My real name is Miles," he said to the tiger.

"I prefer 'tub boy'" said the tiger.

"But why?"

"It's hard to eat someone with whom you are on first-name terms," said the tiger, "and you never know when the larder will be bare. If I told you my name you might get the notion that we are friends."

Miles looked at Little. She seemed to be miles away, smiling to herself in the soft glow of the fire. He thought of the night before, surrounded by cats as Lady Partridge told stories of her husband, his untimely death by exploding pudding, and the circus that used to visit Larde each year.

"Did you ever hear of Barty Fumble's Big Top?" he asked the tiger.

The tiger made no answer.

"Barty Fumble owned a tiger who was the star of his circus, but I don't know what he was called," persisted Miles. "I just thought you might have heard of them."

"The tiger's name was Varippuli," said the tiger, "and Barty Fumble did not own him. No tiger can be owned by a man. You will find it was the other way around."

"So you did know them?" said Miles.

"I know something of the story," said the tiger.

"Will you tell it to us?"

The tiger sighed. "I suppose I won't get any sleep until you have heard it," he said.

In the glow of a pine fire by the edge of the dark lake, the tiger told Miles and Little what he knew of the story of Barty Fumble and Varippuli. His rich, deep voice brought the tiger and his man alive in the night, and the story he told went something like this:

"Barty Fumble was a dark-haired, barrel-chested man with a huge beard and a laugh that could rattle windows. His eyes laughed all the time beneath his thick black eyebrows, and when his mouth joined in, it was impossible not to laugh with him. The circus had been in his family for five generations, and he treated everyone in it as one of his own children. From his most famous clown to his smallest parrot, from the elephants to the tent boys, they were all family to Barty Fumble, and for this he earned their undying respect and love.

"Barty's circus followed a well-tried route through the country, and its arrival was eagerly awaited in every small town along the way. Indeed, some towns were almost emptied of people when Barty Fumble's Big Top was camped nearby, as all but the most miserable souls crowded into his patched tent to marvel at his majestic animals and lose their worries in the antics of his clowns, who were generally considered to be without equal. But the greatest attraction without a doubt was the famous tiger, Varippuli."

The tiger got up and moved around to the other side of the fire to escape the smoke. He settled himself with a sigh. "Varippuli," he said, rolling the name like distant thunder. "Now there was a magnificent beast. The tiger is the king of cats, as I'm sure you know, and Varippuli was a king among tigers. He could wrestle a bull elephant to the ground, and when he roared, small birds fell stunned from the sky. He was the handsomest and noblest of animals, and though he would suffer the ownership of no man, nonetheless his loyalty to Barty was as strong and enduring as the mountain beneath us.

"One year a cold wind from the east blew all through March, and with it came the Circus Oscuro. It was a big circus, with over a hundred wagons. There were animals from every dark corner of the world, and death-defying acts that could amaze and terrify in equal measure. It was said that this circus had swallowed up other, smaller circuses, and that was how it had grown so large. Whether or not that was true, it was certainly swallowing up Barty Fumble's paying customers. When Barty Fumble's Big Top arrived in Arktown, they found that the Circus Oscuro had rolled out the night before, and their posters were still hanging on every lamppost. No more than a handful of people came to see Barty's Big Top. It was the same in

Shallowford and in Nape, and when they arrived at the village of Botox they were met by the sergeant of police, who told them they could move right along, and had better arrive earlier next spring, as one circus a year was quite enough."

"Why didn't they take a different route?" asked Little.

"They did, little girl. Barty was no fool, at least so I heard, and had been in the circus all his life. He struck off to the west, but found himself still chasing the new circus's tail. He doubled back and tried the coastal towns, but the Circus Oscuro had already been there too. He tried taking a short cut over the mountains to Frappe, but even before he got there he could see the dark snake of the Circus Oscuro winding out of the town in the first light of dawn.

"Now Barty Fumble was a resourceful and optimistic man, but even he was beginning to get very worried. They had not had a successful show in over two months, and the kitty was empty. The animals were short of food and of temper, and the acts were losing their spark from playing to empty houses. What's more, Barty's wife was expecting their first child, which made it the worst possible time to be facing ruin.

"The time came for Barty to make a difficult choice. He got up from his bed well before dawn one morning, and rode ahead on his favorite horse without a word to anyone. He returned late that night with whiskey on his breath and a deal in his pocket. The following morning he gathered his performers together and announced that Barty Fumble's Big Top would merge with the Circus Oscuro for the summer season, and that when winter came they would once again go their separate ways. Some of the performers were not entirely happy at the news, but they knew that the situation was becoming desperate. They trusted Barty's judgment, and many of them realized how hard it must have been for him to swallow his pride and go cap in hand to a larger circus."

The tiger yawned and fell silent. Miles fed the fire from the pile of branches he had collected. The dry wood crackled and spat, and sparks flew dizzily up into the darkness. Crickets creaked in the grass just beyond the circle of firelight, telling their own stories back and forth in the night.

"I heard that Barty and his tiger . . . I mean Varippuli . . . disappeared after his circus joined with the Circus Oscuro," said Miles.

"More questions, tub boy? You should stop bothering me and get some sleep before the sun comes up."

"But I'm curious. You seem to know the story well, and I'm very interested in tigers."

The tiger gave a long sigh. "Then perhaps you're not as foolish as you might be," he said. "And you are certainly as persistent as a mosquito. All right, I will tell you what I remember, but if you're hoping for a happy ending you will be disappointed.

"The combined circus had a very successful summer. They were playing to bigger audiences than ever, and many of Barty's performers forgot their doubts about the wisdom of his deal. In time Barty himself became friends with the Circus Oscuro's ringmaster, who called himself the Great Cortado, but Varippuli never took to him."

"Why not?"

"I don't know, tub boy, I am simply relating what I heard. Now are you finished with the interruptions?"

"Yes, for the moment."

"Very well, then I will continue. Barty's son was born on a rainy autumn night in a small town named Iota, but what should have been a happy event turned to tragedy. His young wife died in childbirth, and neither the midwife nor the town quack could save her. The child was a fine, healthy boy, but Barty was driven out of his mind with grief.

He stayed with the circus for a while, but he never uttered another word. In the end he left in the night, taking his infant son with him. I never met anyone who has seen or heard from Barty, from that day to this."

The wind had changed direction once again, and the tiger got up and circled the fire. He padded silently to where Miles and Little sat between the standing stones, and settled himself behind them on the dry ground. His head was less than an arm's length from Miles's right ear, and although Miles had felt a little sorry for the rabbits who had laid down their lives for the tiger's supper, he couldn't help wishing that a few more might come and join them in case he got peckish in the night.

"Did Barty take Varippuli with him?" he asked.

"Of course not, boy," rumbled the tiger in his ear. "Only a fool would wander the countryside with a fully grown tiger. Besides, Varippuli met his end on the same night that Barty disappeared."

"How did that happen?" asked Miles.

The tiger said nothing for some time, then he sighed deeply and continued. "After his wife's death, Barty Fumble retreated into his grief, and there was no one in the circus who could persuade Varippuli to perform again. The Great Cortado, who did not understand the mutual respect that the tiger and the man had shared, became impatient with him. He starved Varippuli for days at a time, and then tried to make him perform for food. Naturally the tiger would never give in to such an ignoble trick. He ate nothing, and he bided his time. When one night the Great Cortado entered the tiger's cage with a whip and a bellyful of whiskey for courage, Varippuli attacked, and opened the little man's chest from neck to navel."

Miles shuddered at the memory of the scar that the Great Cortado had shown him the night he had helped Little escape from the circus. "How did he survive that?" he asked.

"Ah," said the tiger, "nature gave the tiger a most fearsome set of weapons with which to defend his honor, but though men are weak and soft at the edges, they were given the weapon of cunning. While Varippuli gathered himself to finish Cortado off, the little man managed to crawl into his trailer and get hold of his blunderbuss. As the tiger entered the trailer, he cut the magnificent beast down with a blast from the gun at point-blank range. It took two surgeons and a visiting tailor from Marrakech to stitch the Great Cortado together, so I heard, and over a year passed before he could stand on his two feet and wave a whip about again. When he was well enough to listen, he was told that Barty had left the circus, and none could say where he had gone."

The tiger fell silent for a while. Miles turned the story of Barty and Varippuli over in his mind, as the stars wheeled slowly overhead. Little had fallen asleep against the tiger's warm flank. The jacket had slipped from her shoulder, and her pearly skin shone faintly in the firelight. Miles leaned over and pulled her jacket back around her.

"That's a remarkable little friend you have found yourself," said the tiger. "She has more wisdom than you would expect to find in such a small parcel, and you will be glad of it before your journey is done, or I'm a tree frog."

"I'm not sure if she's my friend, exactly," said Miles, thinking back to their conversation by the stream. "She'll be leaving soon, anyway."

"A friendship should be judged by its depth, not by its length," said the tiger. "And not many adventures are better followed alone, unless of course you are a tiger."

"Do you always travel alone?" asked Miles. "Didn't you arrive with the Circus Oscuro?"

The tiger snorted. "I would sooner eat a putrid

donkey than perform tricks for that outfit."

"But you were once with a circus yourself, weren't you?"

The tiger gave a low growl. "That was a long time ago, tub boy, and another story entirely. Now if you have any more questions you will have to swallow them again, because I don't care much for talking, and tonight I've done enough to last me through the winter and into next summer."

The tiger settled his head between his paws, and the crickets wound down gradually in the darkness. Miles sat beneath the roof of stone with his arms wrapped around his knees, gazing into the embers of the fire. Tales of acrobats, rolling roads and tiger-striped revenge played themselves out in glowing shapes before his tired, smoke-stung eyes, until at last he drifted into sleep.

CHAPTER FOURTEEN
BALTINGLASS OF ARABY

Miles Wednesday, dawn-chilled and hungry, woke with a pale sun peering at him from just above the horizon. Little was kneeling by the lake, splashing cold water onto her face. The tiger was gone.

His first thought was to build up the fire, but then he remembered that they had nothing to cook on it. His stomach was as empty as the pocket where Tangerine lived. He put his hand in the inside pocket anyway, as if by some miracle he might find Tangerine back in his accustomed place. There was nothing there but the silver ticket. He sat up and shaded his eyes. The pale snake of the road looped down the wooded flank of the mountain, visible here and there between the trees. It was the trail down which Genghis had passed the day before with teeth marks in his hand and Tangerine in his pocket—a trail growing colder with each passing hour.

"Where did the tiger go?" he asked Little as she returned from the water's edge.

"I don't know. He was gone when I woke up."

"Then we'd better get going. We must be at least half a day behind Genghis as it is."

When Miles had quenched his thirst they left the lake and started down in the direction of the road. The slope of the mountain was covered with patchy forest giving way to frequent clearings. They scrambled down a steep slope of mossy boulders and tree roots onto the road. On the far bank the tiger sat, looking down on them with an air of mild amusement.

"You're going to walk all the way? You'd better get a move on."

"We will," said Miles. As he strode down the road he called back over his shoulder, "I can see you're too busy licking your paws to offer us a ride."

There was a soft thump as the tiger's weight landed on the packed earth of the road, and a moment later he was walking beside them.

"As it happens, tub boy, I am also headed this way. And before you ask, it's none of your business. I might consider letting you ride today, especially if your little friend with the better manners were to ask me."

Little laughed. "Please, King of Cats, lend us your speed and strength, and may the world turn ever toward you," she said.

The tiger stopped. "You see?" he said to Miles. "A little poetry goes a long way. Now climb on before I change my mind."

Once on the tiger's back, Miles felt as though he had been riding tigers all his life. Little sat in front again, and the tiger set off at a steady pace down the center of the road. They ran in silence for a while. The morning sun began to warm the air, and soon it was abuzz with insects. From time to time they caught a glimpse of the mountain's foothills between the knotty trunks of the tall pines.

"Shouldn't we get off the road?" asked Miles.

"No need," said the tiger. "After all, what stringy peasant would dare stand up to the king of cats?"

"One with a blunderbuss," said Miles.

He could feel the tiger's muscles stiffen beneath him. "Some day you'll be bitten by your own mouth, tub boy," he said, but all the same he left the road a little farther on and entered the cover of the trees.

They made good speed through the patchy forest. The tiger bounded over twisted roots and dodged between trees with obvious enjoyment. Sometimes he almost seemed to be flying. The clearings became larger and more frequent, and as they reached the lower slopes the woods dwindled into isolated copses rising from the long grass. Here the tiger went more cautiously, threading a path through the longest grasses and pausing before leaving the cover of each copse.

Below them they could see a range of low, gently rounded hills stretching to the horizon. The road wound between the hills like a dusty river. Not far ahead of them it swung to the right and climbed a small hill that was crowned by a village of white-washed, red-roofed houses.

"We need to get something to eat," said Miles.

"If you're thinking of going to that village," said the tiger, "you'll be going on your own."

"That's what I plan to do. There's an olive grove on the slope, just below that tower. You and Little can wait for me there."

"As you wish," said the tiger.

Miles and Little dismounted from the tiger as

they approached the village. An occasional donkey cart appeared on the road, rocking through the potholes and moving with no apparent hurry, and once a tractor chugged by with a train of beige dust. They kept their distance from the road, and when anyone passed by, the tiger simply froze like a statue, so that even from a few paces he was invisible in the tall grass.

They reached the olive grove, which lay at the foot of the village in broad terraces. Rows of olive trees stood on twisted trunks in welcome pools of shade. Not a breath of wind stirred the leaves. Built into the wall of the second terrace was a sort of man-made cave where the olive pickers could rest and eat in the shade. The tiger stood at the mouth of the cave, his whiskers twitching as he investigated it with his nose. Once he was satisfied he disappeared inside.

"I'll come with you," said Little. Miles shook his head.

"It's better if I go alone," he said. "You wait here with the tiger. I won't be long."

The road wound steeply up into the village. It was lined with a parade of crooked houses, with small windows and little courtyards with electric-blue walls and shady trees. He came to a long high wall on his right-hand side. Behind that wall, although he couldn't see it, was a small apple orchard. What Miles could see was the long branch of an apple tree hanging right out over the wall, weighed down by a handful of ripe green apples. If you've ever traveled for miles on a dusty road in the hot sun with a Bengal tiger and a four-hundred-year-old girl, you will be able to imagine just how cool and tasty those apples looked. He stopped in his tracks and stared up at the branch, trying to figure out a way to reach them. He felt in his pockets for something to throw. The apples looked ready to fall at the slightest touch.

"It'll never work," said a voice behind him, making him jump. "They don't fall off so easy."

A plump boy about his own age sat on a low wall across the street. He had close-cropped hair and eyes that looked too small for his face. He smiled, and tossed a large apple butt over his shoulder.

"How did you get that one?" asked Miles.

"Easy," said the boy. "I can tell you how to get a sackload of them without breaking a sweat. He's got so many he doesn't know what to do with them."

"Who has?"

"Old Baltinglass of Araby," said the boy. "That house with the apple orchard belongs to him. He used to be a famous explorer, or so he says, but he's been blind as a bat ever since I can recall. He's lived in that house for years, with no one but a dozen chickens and a garden full of apple trees."

The boy jumped down from the wall and crossed the road. He lowered his voice. "All you've got to do is knock on the door and say you're Rufus and you've come about the apples. That's my name, Rufus Weedle. My mam sent me to pick up a bag of apples from old Baltinglass, but if you pretend to be me he won't know any different."

"Why don't you get them yourself?" asked Miles suspiciously.

"Well," said the boy, putting his plump arm around Miles's shoulder as though they'd been friends for years, "there's a small snag. Baltinglass's chickens have the run of the orchard, and they lay their eggs wherever they like. Baltinglass likes his eggs, but he can't go and collect them himself, on account of he's as blind as a bat, like I said. If he went looking for them he'd only step on them, and end up with a load of scrambled eggs, wouldn't he?"

"I suppose so."

"Exactly. So usually my mam picks them up for him on her way to the bakery, and he gives her a bag of apples in return, only today she says her knee is giving her hell and her kidneys feel like they've switched places, so she sent me instead, even though she knows I can't go near chickens."

"Why not?"

Rufus took a step backward and stared at Miles as though he had two heads. "Why *not*? Cause they're 'orrible, that's why not. The way they walk, like little broken machines with feathers, pecking at your ankles. And crawling with vermin too. They give me the creeps! But if you tell him you're Rufus Weedle you can pick up the eggs and be out of there in no time. My mam says there's only a dozen to find, and it never takes more than five minutes. Then we'll split the apples between us, because if I go home to my mam on a bad-kidney day with no apples, I might as well be going home to a crocodile without a dead pig under my arm."

Miles shrugged. "All right," he said. "But I don't see why I can't just tell him that your mam sent me instead."

"Because he's expecting me, not you, dummy!" said the boy in a loud whisper. "And he's not just as blind as a bat, he's as batty as one too. He thinks foreign agents are combing the land for him, looking for some priceless treasures he brought back from the Orient. He once chased the new postman halfway down the street with a sword because no one remembered to tell him that the old one had died. As long as he thinks you're me, he won't slice you in half, will he?"

Miles looked doubtfully at the weathered door of the old house. It was studded with square iron nails. A worn horseshoe hung in the center, and a knotted rope hung to the right of the door. He thought about Little, waiting in the olive grove, and pulled the rope. A jangling din came from inside the house, as though there were a few pots and pans instead of a doorbell on the other end of the bell rope.

A muffled shout came from within the house, and after a minute a tap-tap-tapping could be heard on the other side of the door. A bolt rattled, and the door opened abruptly.

"Whaddya want?" barked Baltinglass of Araby. His wrinkled head stuck horizontally out of his shirt on a neck like a cluster of ropes. He wore a knitted hat despite the heat. On either side of a large beaky nose his milky eyes stared, in slightly different directions, into the fog of his blindness.

"I'm Rufus Weedle," said Miles, hoping he had remembered the name right. "I've come about the apples."

"Ah, Weedle junior!" said Baltinglass. "I used to know your grandfather, though I don't think my life was richer for it." He stepped back once, twice. His house was dim inside. The small high windows were filthy and let in hardly any light. Miles could just make out a cluster of pots and pans hanging on the end of the bell rope.

"Well, step inside and be quick about it," said Baltinglass sharply, "before all the air gets out."

Miles took a deep breath and stepped across the stone lintel. The old man slipped around behind him and slammed the door, locking it with a key that he produced from a chain around his scraggy neck. As the door shut, Miles caught a glimpse of the real Rufus Weedle making a mock salute, a funny little smile on his face.

"Now!" barked Baltinglass of Araby, in the dimness of his musty hallway. "The mightiest task begins with a hitch of the trousers, young Rufus. You get stuck in right away and work like a bull ant's nephew, and you should be finished and free in three days flat!"

CHAPTER FIFTEEN
APPLE JELLY

Miles Wednesday, apple-hungry and self-kidnapped, stared in dismay at the wrinkled features and toothless grin of Baltinglass of Araby.

"Did you say three *days*?" he asked, hoping he had misheard.

"That's what I said, boy. Three days. Sun comes up, sun goes down again!" He swished his cane up and over his head as he said this, hitting the candleless chandelier and showering himself with dust. "Up again! Down again! Up one more time, and if you're still working like a team of mules you'll be all done by sundown on the third day, barring sandstorm and snakebite. But if you're going to stand there gawping like a fish, it'll be four days at the least, so put your best boot forward, young Weedle."

He turned and stumped away into the darkness. Miles followed, his head spinning. He could dimly see an impressive collection of swords, crossbows, and grimacing masks arranged on the walls of the drawing room. A human skull with ornate silver decorations sat on a small round table. Yellowed newspaper cuttings hung in crooked frames near the French windows. One showed a picture of a much younger Baltinglass standing by a rectangular hole in a rocky bank. The headline read GULLIVER P. BALTINGLASS DEFIES THE CURSE OF THE EMPEROR'S TOMB. They stepped out into the blinding light of the orchard.

"How can it take three days to find a dozen eggs?" asked Miles.

Baltinglass stopped in his tracks and swung around to face him, his sightless eyes staring at the source of Miles's voice. "Are you trying to be funny, Weedle?" he bellowed.

"No sir!"

"Where would I be getting eggs from, since you stole my prize-laying chickens and wrung their necks?"

"But Ru . . . but I can't go near chickens!" said Miles in surprise.

"Listen to me, young Weedle," said Baltinglass, stabbing his cane in Miles's direction. "We may not have crossed swords before, but it's my eyes that are blind, not my wits, and if you take me for a fool you might just end up on a wooden plaque on my wall. I've heard all about your lies and your trickery. You were caught red-handed selling my chickens for boilers. How you got your thieving little hands on them I don't know, but it's time to settle your debt and you ain't going to worm out of it."

He marched into a corner of the orchard and pulled out a rickety wooden stepladder. "There's nine trees here, and at least two hundred apples on each. That's eighteen hundred apples, as you'd know if you ever bothered to show up at school. You've got to pick every last one by nightfall. Tomorrow you'll peel and core 'em. Day after that you'll be boiling them up for Baltinglass's Famous Homemade Apple and Thyme Jelly. If I had my way you'd be laying eggs for me too, but Justice O'Hooey felt that'd be a bit too much to ask of a young lad, so count yourself lucky."

He shook the old stepladder open as though he were wrestling a crocodile, his cane clamped between his teeth like a hunting knife. "Grab a basket and up you go, lad. I've got blades to polish, and it's time for my gin and tonic. Keeps the malaria away, you know." He leaned toward Miles like a blind turtle and shouted in his face, "If the malaria jumps on my back you'd better run and hide, boy. Tends to make me lose my calm demeanor altogether."

He turned on his heel and disappeared into the gloom of his house. Miles picked up a large wicker basket and climbed the wobbly ladder. It was not the first time he had visited an orchard in his life, and he was something of an expert in twisting apples quickly from their stems. As he filled the basket, his mind worked overtime. What was he to do? He couldn't possibly stay here for three days. Little and the tiger were expecting him back at any moment, and with each passing hour his chances of finding Tangerine were growing slimmer.

He took a good look at the wall that surrounded the garden. It was high and smooth, and topped with nasty-looking spikes that curved inward and looked almost impossible to get over. He could try telling Baltinglass that he was not Rufus Weedle at all, but as the old man was busy polishing his swords, it might not be the best time to interrupt him with this startling news. It was hard to tell if Baltinglass really was mad, or whether this had all been part of Rufus's ruse. His face flushed hot at the thought of the mock salute the chubby chicken thief had given him as Baltinglass slammed his front door. "I'll flatten his nose for him, if ever I see his fat face again," he muttered to himself.

The basket was getting too heavy to hold. He climbed down the ladder and tipped the apples into a large barrel in the corner. Already his right arm and shoulder ached from picking the apples above his head, and it looked as though he had cleared less than a quarter of the first tree. The garden was filled with the drone of bees, but on listening closer he could hear that it was mixed with another sound. It was the sound of snoring, coming from inside the house. He put the basket down quietly and tiptoed to the open doors that led into the drawing room. Baltinglass of Araby sat in a high-backed cane chair, a straight-bladed Chinese sword across his lap and his head nodding onto his chest. His wide mouth hung open like a torn pocket, and long stretched-out snores escaped from it.

Miles stepped over to the barrel and filled his trouser pockets with as many apples as he could stuff into them. He crept back into the drawing room and over to where Baltinglass slumped in his chair. One of his milky eyes was half open, and Miles had to remind himself that it could see nothing. He held his breath and reached for the silver chain that hung around the old man's neck, the one that held the key to the front door. He drew the key as softly as he could from Baltinglass's shirt. His snores didn't falter, and Miles allowed himself to take a breath. He paused for a moment before attempting to slip the chain over Baltinglass's woolly-hatted head. As he lifted the key the old man sprung like a bear trap, and Miles found his wrist caught in a surprisingly hard grip and the sharp tip of the Chinese sword pressed up under his chin.

"Hah!" bellowed Baltinglass, both eyes wide open now and inches from his own. "Thought you could catch me napping, eh, Weedle? I can grab a sand viper as he strikes, boy, and twist his head so he bites his own backside!"

"I didn't think snakes had backsides," said Miles with difficulty. The pressure of the sword in his throat was making him feel sick.

"Ignorance is a wide sea," said Baltinglass, flecks of spittle on his wrinkled lips, "and you're a very small fish." He withdrew the sword and made a grab for Miles's pocket. Two apples fell out and rolled across the dusty floorboards. "Just as I thought," he bellowed. He struggled to his feet without loosening his grip on Miles's wrist. "Not content with pinching all my chickens—first chance you get you're trying to escape with an armload of my apples too. You're a slippery little savage, young Weedle, but you're not slippery enough to escape Baltinglass of Araby. Now give me one good reason why I shouldn't run you through here and now."

Several good reasons flashed through Miles's mind: Justice O'Hooey was one, the mess that would have to be cleared up was another, and there were always the eighteen hundred apples waiting to be jellied. Instead he said simply, "I'm not Rufus Weedle."

"Not Rufus Weedle, eh? Who are you then—the Sheikh of Djibouti? You told me who you were yourself, in case you've forgotten."

"I lied," said Miles, "My real name is Miles Wednesday."

"And I'm the king of the baboons. You'll have to do better than that, my lad." He let go of Miles's wrist, and opened a glass-fronted cabinet in a shadowy corner. He took out a large glass jar and held it out to Miles. "Know what this is, Weedle?" he barked. "This is the finest apple jelly money can buy. You'll find jars of Baltinglass's apple jelly on the tables of all the world's royalty, the ones with any class at least. But it doesn't make itself. It's taken me years to perfect the recipe. One of the miracle ingredients is hard work, and this year you're going to do the hard work for me, whether you like it or not."

Miles took the jar and read the label aloud: "Baltinglass's Famous Homemade Apple and Thyme Jelly. Excellent for fevers and disorders of the intestine, and a fine accompina . . . accompaniment to lamb dishes."

Baltinglass raised his bushy eyebrows in surprise. "Well blow me down! You've been lighting your fires underwater, young Weedle. The judge told me you were as thick as yesterday's porridge and hadn't caught more than a fortnight's schooling in your life. Where'd you learn to read like that?"

"I told you, I'm not Rufus Weedle, I'm Miles Wednesday. A friend of mine called Lady Partridge taught me to read from her encyclopedias."

At this Baltinglass's eyebrows disappeared altogether into his woolly hat, and he dropped his cane with a clatter.

"Lady Partridge? You mean Lady Gertrude

Partridge of Larde?" he barked. "How the devil do you know her?"

"I live near her. I once brought her a litter of abandoned kittens, and we became friends," said Miles. "She found out that I couldn't read, so she decided to teach me."

"Well skin me alive and cure me in salt!" said Baltinglass. "You mean to say you've *really* come all the way from Larde? You must be something of an explorer yourself, Master Wednesday. In that case I expect you'll know my nephew too, Radovan Flap."

For a moment Miles could not imagine who he was referring to, then he realized that it must be Constable Flap. His ear could feel the skinny constable's hard pinch at the mere mention of the name.

"Yes, I know Constable Flap." He thought about the nights he had spent locked in the cell at the back of the police station. "In fact I've accepted his hospitality several times."

"Well well, young Miles. It seems we've got off on the wrong foot altogether. You had better tell me what you're doing here, and why the blazes you would ever want to be Rufus Weedle of Cnoc."

They sat on a rough wooden bench in the sunny orchard, and Miles told Baltinglass of Araby his story, but he was as brief as he could be, and left out many details. He made no mention of the tiger, nor did he say much about Little except that they were searching for a friend of hers, and that Little herself was waiting for him to return with some food so they could continue their journey. When he got to the part where Rufus had tricked him into changing places, Baltinglass snorted in disgust.

"Rufus Weedle, eh? Rufus Weasel, more like!" he said. "I'll say one thing for the little savage, for all his lack of schooling he has an agile mind. He's managed to stitch the two of us up like a pair of ballet slippers. But you're a bold lad, why didn't you just knock on my door and ask for a few apples yourself?"

"Because Rufus told me you might slice me in half with one of your swords."

Baltinglass stroked his stubbly chin. "He's got a point there," he said.

"Do you think I could have a few apples to bring with me?" asked Miles. He had mangaged to eat one as he picked them, but his stomach was still rumbling. Baltinglass leaped to his feet. "By the trousers of the Sphinx!" he bellowed. "Your friend is waiting, and the sands are running on your mission, while we're sitting here nattering in the sun like two old men. Come to think of it, I am an old man, but you've got a fate to catch. By all means take as many apples as you can carry, my boy. You'll find a bag in that cupboard there, and while you're loading it I'll have a rummage in the supply depot and see what else I can provide you with. An ill-equipped explorer is like a camel with no hump. . . ."

Miles took a bag and began to fill it with apples. He took as many as he could fit in.

". . . and only three legs," shouted Baltinglass from the darkness of the house, amidst the clattering of tins and the squeaking of corks in bottles.

He emerged after a while with an assortment of foods—dried sausage, bread, cheese and olives, a jar of his apple jelly and a bottle of elderflower wine. "Open up another one of those bags, my boy, and I'll drop these in. They should keep you going for a while."

"Thank you," said Miles.

"Not at all, not at all. I have a very fine Berber sword I could lend you too, with a hilt of black horn, or a Gurkha knife if that's more your size. Just in case you come across that Weedle lad. He'd get up to no more mischief if he were diced like a carrot."

"I don't think that would be a very good idea," said Miles.

"You don't, eh?" said Baltinglass, sounding slightly disappointed.

"You need him to pick and peel all those apples, for one thing."

"Ah, you've got a point there. I used to do it all myself, you know, but I'm getting a little stiff around the joints for that sort of thing nowadays."

"How did you manage to do it on your own?"

"Well the ladder's not hard to find, my boy. I fall over the blasted thing every day. The trees are always where I left them last, and the apples smell so sweet I can almost see them in front of my face. They have a green smell, Master Wednesday. The greenest smell there is."

He led the way to the front door and unlocked it. Miles stepped out into the empty street, the sack of provisions and the bag of apples slung over his shoulder. He turned and shook Baltinglass's hand. "I'm sorry I lied to you," he said.

The old man wiped a tear from the corner of his eye. "Tactical necessity, my boy. Think nothing of it. I only wish I was able to come with you. My heart is like a swallow in this old rib cage, Master Wednesday. Now you get on with your adventure before it leaves without you, and may good luck dog your heels."

"Thank you," said Miles again. As he hurried down the dusty street toward the olive grove, he heard Baltinglass bellow after him: "And give my regards to Gertrude when you see her. Tell her she could have seen the farthest corners of the world with me, if she hadn't married that benighted fool Partridge."

CHAPTER SIXTEEN
BIG LAUGHING HEAD

Rufus Weedle, sly-eyed and slick-witted, sat in the lee of a haystack boring a hole into one arm of a forked stick. The stick was thick and smooth, cut from a branch of ash with the bark stripped off. With a length of strong elastic it would make a lethal catapult, and woe betide any small bird that showed its beak once he had it finished. He heard someone walking through the hay stubble, and wormed his way quickly back into the haystack, but not quickly enough.

"There you are!" said Miles. "I've been looking for you." He could tell that Rufus was more than a little surprised to see him.

"Looking for me?" said Rufus. His small eyes squinted nervously up at Miles.

"Of course. How else can I give you your share of the apples?" He swung the bulging sack off his shoulder and held it up for Rufus to see.

"But . . . how did you get them?"

It was Miles's turn to act surprised. "Exactly as you said. I collected his eggs for him and he gave me the apples. Gave me lots of other stuff too, but I forgot to ask for another bag to put your share in. Look—my friend is waiting over there in the olive grove. Come over with me, and we'll sort everything into the two bags so you can have one to take home with you."

Rufus stood up and shook the hayseeds from his collar. He looked baffled to find that his tall story had somehow twisted itself into reality, but curiosity had got hold of his devious little mind, and he followed Miles down among the olive trees. They reached the shelter in the stone wall. Miles poked his head into the shadows and said, "It's me. I've brought you some lunch." He stood aside and motioned Rufus in before him.

We will never know who the boy expected to meet in the darkened cave, but it's a safe bet that he was not expecting to find himself face to face with a Bengal tiger. This tiger was staring at him with interest, and he appeared to have already caught a small girl. Rufus let out a sort of whimper, and tried to reverse out of the shadows, but Miles was standing right behind him. He winked at the tiger over Rufus's shoulder, although he was not at all sure that winks worked on tigers.

"Well that's very gracious of you, tub boy," purred the tiger. "It's nice to see you bring back someone with a bit of meat on him for once. I don't suppose you've got any sauce, have you? I do like a bit of relish with a plump boy."

Rufus let out a long moan of fear. His knees had gone wobbly and he had to support himself on the wall with one hand. The apples he had stolen from the tree must have been bad. Not only did the tiger sound like he was talking, but the little girl appeared to be grinning at him.

"I've got some Baltinglass's Famous Homemade Apple and Thyme Jelly," said Miles. "Apparently it's a big favorite with royalty."

"That sounds like just the thing," said the tiger, but at this point the terrified Rufus found his voice.

"A-a-actually, n-now that you mention it, I ha-have to help an old m-man to make some apple j-jelly," he stammered.

"So you do," said Miles. "He mentioned something

about that. Eighteen hundred apples' worth, I think he said."

"What a pity," said the tiger. "It's not often we have someone for lunch. Are you quite sure you have to go?"

"P-p-positive," said Rufus. He turned and shoved past Miles, his face drained of color, and took off at a fast if shaky pace toward the house of Baltinglass of Araby. He didn't once look back.

"I trust he deserved that, whoever he is," said the tiger.

"More than you can imagine," said Miles. "Would you really have eaten him?"

The tiger met his eyes with his cool gaze. "You should not play games with a hungry tiger," he said, "if you care what happens to the players. And now I think we had better get back on the road before the whole village comes out with their best pitchforks."

"You don't have to worry about that," said Miles. "If he does tell anyone, they won't believe a single word."

Miles and Little ate their fill of the food that Baltinglass of Araby had given them. They offered some sausage to the tiger, who looked at it as though it were a rotten egg and politely declined. After washing down their meal with a little elderflower wine, Little wandered out of the shelter, while Miles set about repacking what remained into one sack.

When he stepped out into the sunlight he could see Little sitting in the shade of an olive tree a little way off. She appeared to be talking to a tiny old man with a big nose, his hands clasped behind his back. As he got closer, Miles could see it was not a miniature person at all, but an ancient and bedraggled crow. The bird was almost completely bald, and most of his feathers were gray, as though summers beyond counting had all but bleached the night out of them.

If you have ever heard crow talk, you will know that it sounds like an old witch with a sore throat who has just caught her fingers in a door, and this old crow's voice was hoarser and wheezier than most. Little was speaking to him in his own language, of course, but the sound of her "Crow" couldn't have been more different. She somehow made it almost musical, and unlike the old crow's speech, Miles could get at least a vague sense of what she was saying. He crept forward slowly, afraid that the old bird might take fright and fly away, but the crow ignored him.

"He says that he knows of a place that he thinks might be the Palace of Laughter," said Little to Miles. "He calls it 'Big Laughing Head,' and he says it's in the big city, about two days away as the crow flies."

"Two days?" said Miles in dismay. "That's farther than I thought."

"Are you sure it's that far?" Little asked the crow. He wheezed something, nodding at a tree a few feet away.

"He says it depends on which crow is doing the flying. He's over twenty years old, and he can barely make it to that tree over there without having a little sleep to recover. He says a young crow would make it in an afternoon."

She turned back to the crow. "Which way is it?" she asked. The bird croaked a long reply.

"He says keep the sun behind and to the left in the afternoon, pass two wooded hills on our right, look for a rock that looks like a three-headed turtle, bear a little to the left and keep going downward until the ground begins to rise. If we reach the old cork tree we've gone too far to the east, and should go back about five hundred paces and bear farther left, heading straight for the hill that looks like it has been cut in half. When we get to the birch woods we should cut through them in a southeasterly direction, crossing two small streams and turning to the right after the second one. When we come out of the woods we will be near the top of a small ridge, and from the top of that ridge you can see the city below. In the middle of it is a wheel that's bigger than the biggest tree, and beside that is Big Laughing Head."

The crow said something else.

"Or we can just follow the road. It goes straight there," said Little.

The bedraggled crow took a couple of hops to one side, and cocked his head as though to see around Little. Miles followed his gaze and saw that the tiger had emerged from the cave and was stretching himself in the sunlight. The crow stared at him for a moment through bleary eyes, then he croaked something to Little. She laughed. The old bird flapped his great wings, made a little run and took off slowly down the olive grove. He made it all the way to the far end of the grove before alighting in a tree, where he shuffled along the branch until he was hidden by the foliage.

"What did he say?" asked Miles.

Little stood up and whispered in his ear, "He said that he had never seen such a large cat, and that we must be giving him far too much food."

CHAPTER SEVENTEEN
HALFHEADS

Miles Wednesday, saddle-sore and sun-browned, felt the breeze in his tangled hair as the tiger ran on through field and forest. He had become so used to traveling on tigerback that he wondered how he had ever been satisfied with walking. The smooth rhythm of the mighty animal's pace, which was somewhere between running and a sort of long leaping, was hypnotic. Sometimes it seemed as though they were not moving at all, but were suspended over a river of grass and wildflowers that flowed fast beneath their feet. "This must be the next best thing to flying," thought Miles.

"Is this as good as flying?" he asked Little.

She laughed, and looked over her shoulder at him. "This is fun!" she said. "But flying is living."

The hills stretched before them like irregular green waves. They passed a large rounded rock perched near the top of a hill. Smaller outcrops of stone were clustered around its base, and Miles could make out the shape of a tortoise with three heads. "We must be on the right track," he said to Little, but she was lost in thoughts of swooping between the bright clouds, and gave no answer.

As the afternoon wore on, the sky paled and a cold breeze began to blow. The tiger followed the road into a birch wood. They ran through fern and forest, leaping each of the two streams with a single bound. Up ahead Miles could see the trees begin to thin out toward a rocky ridge that was silhouetted against the sky. He knew from the old crow's directions that the city was near, but nothing could have prepared him for the sight that would meet them from the top of the ridge.

Below them the city of Smelt spread across the floor of the valley like a lake of red roofs and tall steeples and gray chimneys and bridges, and stone buildings with more windows than you could count. It seemed to go on forever. A broad river wound through the heart of the city, glinting yellow in the late afternoon sun, and here and there columns of smoke stood like purple pillars, all tilting at the same angle and rising silently into the pale autumn sky.

Miles whistled. "It must be fifty times the size of Larde," he said.

"It certainly smells fifty times as bad," said the tiger, wrinkling his nose. "Not that it's any surprise. Nature never intended any of its creatures to live in boxes with a neighbor at the end of each whisker."

"Look," said Little. "Is that the big wheel that the crow told us about?"

Miles shaded his eyes and looked where she was pointing. Away in the distance he thought he could see a shape like a spoked wheel rising out of the haze and the gray buildings. He could not imagine what it might be for.

"I'm not sure," he said. "We'll have to go down through the city to reach it."

"Then I suggest you start without delay," said the tiger. "The farther you can get before nightfall the better."

Miles felt his stomach fall. "Aren't you coming with us?" he asked.

The tiger shook his massive head. "This is as far as I go, tub boy. From here on, you must rely on your own mettle, and on your little friend's considerable charm."

"But . . . ," said Miles, and stopped. He had known in the back of his mind that the time would come when the tiger would leave them, but the thought of going on without him filled him with dread. He had already lost the comforting feel of Tangerine in his pocket, and now he felt as though some of his own strength and confidence would leave with the tiger and disappear back into the forest.

" . . . couldn't you come with us, if we waited for night to fall?"

"Night or day, it makes no difference," said the tiger. "Cities are not made for tigers, nor tigers for cities, and there's no doubt I would draw unwelcome attention on the streets. Besides, I have other places to be."

"Where will you go?" asked Little, but the tiger gave no answer. He stood a moment longer, looking out over the city below. His nostrils widened and he drew in a deep breath, as though preserving the odor of the city, or perhaps of Miles and Little themselves, for his journey. He turned to look at them. "Now keep your eyes clear and your claws sharp, both of you," he said. "The city is a jungle, by all accounts, though I have more experience of the leafy kind myself. I suspect your journey so far will turn out to have been the easy part."

He turned and padded back toward the forest until he slipped out of sight among the trees, like a dream retreating from the morning sun. Miles felt like a small boy again, exposed on a rocky ridge and about to enter a city that was larger than anything he had imagined, in search of a place he knew nothing about. He looked at Little, who had already begun to slither down the rocky slope into the valley. He knew that when they found Silverpoint she would be leaving him too, but right now she was all he had left, and he pushed thoughts of the future from his mind and called after her, "Wait for me!"

She stopped and waited for him to catch up. "I think we can join the road now," he said. "Genghis must be half a day ahead of us, and like the tiger said, I don't think anyone else will be looking for us here."

They picked their way across the rocky slope until they reached a loop of the road. The road wound down into the valley, and as they walked quickly along it they soon reached the outskirts of the city. There were low square buildings with blind windows on either side that looked like factories, and between them wooden houses with peeling paintwork and sunken steps. On the sides of the buildings were large posters advertising strange things: Type-o-matic Writing Machines, Golden Meadows Rest Home for Elderly Poodles, Cuffe's Shirts of Distinction. They passed several large posters advertising Dr. Tau-Tau's Restorative Tonic. The posters showed ruddy-faced, happy families holding up bottles like the one Miles had fished out of the stream, and laughing as though they hadn't a care in the world. BRING THE LAUGHTER BACK INTO YOUR LIFE read the slogan, in huge red letters.

There were rails like train tracks that were sunk into the cobbles, running straight down the center of the road, and a narrow tram with a clanging bell that swung out of a side street and almost ran them over. Here and there were people, walking quickly with heads down, dragging wide-eyed children who stared at Miles and Little as though they had blue skin and horns. Most wore the same expression, tired and slightly sad, that Miles had noticed on the faces of the diners at the Surly Hen.

A little farther on, a small striped tent had been erected over a manhole in the street. Outside the tent a single roadworker warmed his hands at a makeshift stove made from a punctured metal can.

Miles felt the warmth from the fire as they drew level with the tent. A wave of weariness crept over him, and he felt a strong urge to curl up inside the warm tent and slip into a dreamless sleep, where all his fears and his tiredness would slip away from him for good. He looked at the man who stood by the tent, but he could not make out his features. It was as if he were looking at someone standing in a patch of twilight, though the rest of the street was lit by the pale afternoon sun.

Miles became aware that Little was saying something to him repeatedly. "Stay awake. Stay awake. Keep walking," she said. She gripped his hand tightly and was almost dragging him along the road. He wanted to turn and ask the man if they could rest in his tent, but Little's voice reached him again through the humming fog in his ears: "Look at me. Stay awake, Miles." He felt as though he were wading through molasses. Little began to sing snatches of some strange tune, a running song. There was a tremor in her voice, but some of the heaviness lifted from his feet and he began to run with her. Their boots clattered on the cobbles, and people stared at them as they ran by.

"Don't look back," said Little. They came to a side street and turned down it without either one saying a word. The road was a short cul-de-sac, ending in a high wall with a pair of rusty iron doors in the middle. The words "Scrap Metal" were painted in clumsy white letters across the doors. They were closed with a heavy padlock and chain, but a smaller door was set into one of them. Miles tried this door and it opened with a push. They stepped inside, and he bolted it behind them.

The junkyard looked like a miniature city of rusting iron, built by a colony of cross-eyed lunatics. It was another world. Every kind of broken-down car and carriage, printing press, machine and motor was piled up in row upon untidy row, with narrow passages running between them, littered with bolts and tires and bottles and pipes. They turned quickly down the first passage, staring up at the piles of silent junk that towered over their heads. At the end they turned left into another passage, and then right into another, trying to keep an idea of their direction. Somewhere above them a large iron wheel broke loose and bounced heavily down the stack before plunging into a muddy puddle, making them jump.

Miles turned to look behind him. The junkyard was deserted. "Who *was* that person . . . ," he began, but Little interrupted him, a determined look on her face.

"What are all these things doing here?" she asked.

"They're scrap," said Miles patiently. "Things that people don't want anymore."

"Can't they make them into something else?"

Miles shrugged. "I suppose they could, but it's easier to throw them away and make new stuff."

"But won't the whole world fill up with these things in the end?"

Miles didn't answer. He had stopped dead at the end of the row and was staring at something that drove the strange figure from his mind. An enormous and oddly familiar-looking machine squatted in a corner of the junkyard. A forest of pipes sprouted from a copper tank that was mounted on the front (or was it the back?), and there were two massive mechanical arms, one ending with a giant pincer and the other in a rusting circular sawblade. Empty sockets gaped where more arms had once been. Pistons, cogs and other spare parts lay scattered around where they had been torn off and discarded. The machine looked strange and silent, like a sober monument to a man of great curiosity—a man who had been killed by his own exploding pudding.

"It's Lord Partridge's big idea!" said Little.

Miles hoisted himself onto the broken caterpillar track and rubbed some of the rust from the nameplate on the machine. "It's Geraldine XIV," he said. "The very one that's in the photo with him." He poked his head into one of the empty arm sockets. "Hello!" he called. He expected nothing back but an echo of his own voice, but instead he saw a blur of movement in the darkness, and something blunt poked him hard in the chest. A wild idea flashed through his mind, that this was Lord Partridge himself, back from the grave and hiding in the ruins of his own creation. He gave a gasp of surprise, lost his footing and fell backward off the track. Before he could get to his feet, a head appeared through the opening. It was not Lord Partridge's head, of course, but that a boy of about Miles's age.

The boy looked down at Miles. "Hello," he said.

Miles stared back. The right half of the boy's head was shaved, leaving a tangle of black hair on the left side with a number of small gray objects knotted into it. He jumped out of the machine and dropped to the ground beside Miles. His clothes were stiff with dirt, and he carried what looked like a large leg bone in one hand. A bandage was wrapped tightly around one end of the bone, to give him a better grip.

"What was that for?" asked Miles, scrambling to his feet.

"What, this?" asked the boy, giving Miles another hard poke with the end of the bone. Miles made a grab for it, but the boy jumped back. "Halfhead challenge is what it is," he said. "What's yours is mine. Empty your pockets or name yer weapon."

"I don't want a fight," said Miles. "We're just passing through."

"We?" said the boy. He turned and looked Little up and down. "Very handy! I'll have her too. Need a new creeper, and there aren't many windows she wouldn't fit through. Chimneys, neither." He turned back to Miles. "You haven't emptied your pockets yet."

"There's nothing in my pockets that you'd want," said Miles, "and I wouldn't give Little to you even if she was mine to give."

The other boy laughed. "You're not from around here, are yeh?" he said. "You look like a peasant to me. Live in a barn, do you, pez? Well you're in Halfhead territory now, and there's no such thing as passing through, so I'll say this one more time. Empty yer pockets or name yer weapon." He jabbed the bone at Miles again, but this time Miles was the one to skip backward.

There was a laugh from behind him. "You're gettin' slow, String. Can't even clobber a pez now!"

Miles turned, keeping half an eye on the boy with the bone. Another boy with a half-shaved head sat on top of the junk pile behind him, and another to his right, and more were appearing from among the scrap with every second. Little moved closer to Miles and away from the newcomers.

"Ten against one's not fair," said Miles.

"You really don't know anything, do you, pez?" said the one called String. "Fights with outsiders is always one-on-one. If you lose, I keep all your stuff and you run as fast as you can until you're off our turf. That's if you can run at all by the time I've finished with you."

"And if I win?" said Miles.

"You don't need to worry about that," said String, "'cause you're not going to win."

"Get on with it, String," shouted the other boy. He also carried a bone, and a scar ran from the corner of his mouth across his left cheek. "You're nattering like an old woman, and I'm getting hungry. I bet the pez has some grub on him."

String turned to answer him, but he never got a chance. The moment his attention shifted, Miles reached out and jerked the bone from his grip. Before String could recover himself, Miles hit him with the bandaged end, knocking him sideways. He jumped on the boy and sat on his back before he could get to his feet.

"Bone!" shouted Miles. "Or should I have named it first?"

String twisted like an eel and tried to sink his crooked teeth into Miles's leg, but Miles pinned him with the bone across the back of his neck. The boy struggled and spat. Miles was just wondering what was considered a win, when a loud clang sounded from above him.

"Twelve seconds," called the boy from the top of the junk pile. He swung his own bone again and hit the end of a metal drum beside him. "Halfhead out, Halfhead in."

"Halfhead out, Halfhead in," repeated the other boys in unison.

String stopped struggling for a moment. Miles got off him cautiously, keeping a wary eye on his opponent and a firm grip on the bone. String got to his feet and spat. "Gimme my bone," he said.

"Not till I'm well out of your reach," said Miles.

"Not then either," said the boy with the scar, clambering down the junk pile. "Bone's yours now, pez, and he knows it."

"I don't want his stinking bone," said Miles. "I just don't want to be hit with it again. He can have it back as soon as we're gone."

"No he can't, pez," said the other boy, "'cause he's not a Halfhead no more. He's out. You're in. Them's the rules, and Halfhead rules don't bend nor break."

"Look," said Miles, "I don't want his place. I just want to get to the Palace of Laughter."

The scar-faced boy looked at him as though he were planning to visit the moon. "Hear that?" he shouted. "Pez thinks he's going to the Palace of Laughter."

The Halfheads roared with laughter, all except String. "Let him go then, Jook," he said sullenly. "Fight wasn't fair anyhow. It don't say in the rules that an outsider can use a Halfhead's bone in a fight."

"It don't say that he can't, neither," said Jook. "Face it, String. The pez fought smarter than you. He's in. You're out."

"Fine," said String. For a moment his tough face crumpled, and he looked on the verge of tears, then it hardened, and he fixed Miles with a look of pure malice. "I'll see you again, pez," he said, and without another word he turned and disappeared down one of the junkyard alleys.

CHAPTER EIGHTEEN
BONEYARD

Miles Wednesday, chest-poked, half-shaved and hungry, sat on a stone slab in a ruined church as a small boy named Henry tied bones into the remaining half of his hair. His scalp was stinging from the razor, and his stomach rumbled. Little sat quietly beside him.

"Toe bones," said Henry. "Least, they're supposed to be, but it's hard to find real toe bones anymore so these are mostly just from back of the butchers." His quick little fingers knotted as he spoke. "Jook, he got real toe bones back in the old days, when there was still bones left in the broken graves. That was before I became Halfhead. There was another

Jook then, but he got took by the cops and then they growed him up. Now he's a cop himself. I seen him in his brass buttons and coat, and he's just as mean as the rest now. Meaner even."

As Henry chattered on, Miles tried to think his way out of the situation they found themselves in. They seemed to have escaped the shadowy figure for the time being at least, but it did not look likely that the Halfheads could be persuaded to let them continue on their way. Henry had told him that now that he was Halfhead, any attempt to leave would be considered desertion, which carried a punishment of a week locked in the sheds behind the junkyard. "Not many has tried it," he said, "and no one's ever got away with it neither."

A fire crackled in the center of the ruined and roofless church, keeping back the twilight. Around the fire sat a dozen Halfhead boys on large stones. Jook, the boy with the scar across his cheek, was eating some of the food that the creepers had stolen from the pantries and kitchens of the big houses on Elm Hill that day, and the others had to wait until he had finished before they would get their share. The creepers were generally the smaller boys, who could fit through narrow windows or scurry unnoticed under tables. Henry was one of them, and when he wasn't being a creeper he was a nonstop talker.

"Boneyard, junkyard, and bullring, them's the three corners of Halfhead territory. No one passes through here but answers to us. Any Halfhead that catches an outsider has to challenge him. Mostly Halfhead wins, and he gets everything outsider has on him, and runs him to the borders. But if outsider wins, like you did, Halfhead loses his place to outsider. Them's the rules."

Miles said nothing. It seemed the only sure way to escape the gang was to lose a fight with an outsider, but he could hardly wait around until a suitable candidate happened by. Even if the opportunity came quickly and he lost the fight, he was not sure if they would let Little go. "We have to escape tomorrow," he told himself, but he did not want to risk spending a week locked in anyone's shed. They would have to keep their eyes clear and their claws sharp, as the tiger had put it, and wait for the right moment.

"What will happen to String?" asked Miles.

Henry yanked at Miles's hair. "Don't say that name again—it's not allowed," he whispered. "Once Halfhead's gone, he's gone, and his name goes with him."

"But wasn't he your friend?" asked Miles, twisting

around to look at Henry's face in the flickering firelight. Henry looked at him defiantly. "Once Halfhead's gone, he's gone," he repeated. "And yer bones are all done, pez."

He jumped down from the stone slab and took his place by the fire. Little leaned in close to Miles and whispered in his ear with a voice that was tiny and clear. "I'm not hungry," she whispered. "Keep them talking. I'm going to take a look around." Miles nodded. "Be careful," he said under his breath, and he got up to join the other boys.

Jook had finished eating, and the food was being passed around. "Sit, pez," said Jook, sucking meat juice from his fingers. Miles could feel his stomach rumble. He looked at the other boys who sat around the fire. They passed the food back and forth—half-eaten chops, apples and onions, stale bread and sausages—and they talked and laughed as they ate, an odd brotherhood of the unwanted and the lost. "In other circumstances," thought Miles, "I could feel at home here." He emptied his own pockets and passed around the half bottle of elderflower wine and what remained of the food that Baltinglass had given him.

Jook took a swig of the wine. He looked at the bottle (although it had no label) and nodded wisely.

"Now," he said to Miles, "tell me where you was *really* headed."

"I told you," said Miles to Jook. "We need to get to the Palace of Laughter urgently." The other boys laughed again, but Jook rapped on a stone with his bone, and they fell silent.

"You'd never get near the Palace of Laughter, pez. Why do you want to go there anyways?" asked Jook.

"We lost a friend of ours, and we think he's been taken there." He did not mention Tangerine. A stuffed bear that could walk would require too much explanation.

"If your friend is in the Palace of Laughter," said Jook, "he won't be the same no more. And like I said, you'll never make it there."

"Well we're not afraid, even if you are," said Little. She had returned from her investigations, and when Miles looked at her she gave her head a tiny shake. "Come on, Miles" she said.

Jook laughed again. "The kid can go if she wants," he said, addressing Miles as though it were he who had spoken, "but you're Halfhead now, and you ain't going nowhere. Besides, the Palace of Laughter is in Stinkers' territory. They'd tear you to pieces."

"Stinkers?" asked Miles. "Who are they?"

Jook turned to Henry and gave him a rap on the

head with his bone. "Didn't you learn him nothing, Henry?"

Henry stood up, his cheek stuffed with meat, and began to recite the missing parts of Miles's Halfhead lesson, spitting crumbs of food into the fire as he spoke.

"Halfheads, Gnats, and Stinkers. Them's the three gangs. Halfheads got the yards, Stinkers the bad-egg factories and the fun park, and Gnats got the alleys. Crossing to another territory is a raid; raid means war, war means prisoners, prisoners means Pigball."

"What if I just fought one of the Stinkers, like I did with . . . like I did today?"

Henry swallowed his last mouthful and stood up again. "One-on-one is for outsiders. You're Halfhead now, pez, and if you step into Stinkers' territory, it's a raid. That means they all got a right to fight, no matter if there's one of us or twenty-four. And that means a war, cause no Halfhead gets left to fight solo."

Henry sat down, his speech finished. He yawned and stretched, then settled himself by the embers of the fire. "Sleep before creep," he said. Most of the other boys were curling up in their favorite sleeping spots. Jook produced a small box of blackened wood from his pocket. There were several half-smoked cigars of various thicknesses inside. He selected a fat Havana that had hardly been smoked, and lit it. They sat and watched the slow blue smoke, listening to the crackling of the flames and the hiss of sap bubbling from the firewood.

"That kid your sister?" said Jook after a while, nodding his head at Little as though she were deaf.

"No," said Miles. "She's . . . my friend."

"Friends come and go," said Jook. "You got to get rid of her tomorrow."

"What do you mean, get rid of her?" asked Miles, trying not to sound too alarmed. He glanced at Little, who looked more indignant than worried.

"What do you mean, get rid of me?" she echoed.

"What I say," said Jook to Miles. "There's never been a girl Halfhead, and that's not going to change on my watch. Long as she's here she's using up food, and if it comes to a raid or a war she'll slow us down. Tomorrow you got to run her off the territory. I'll send some of the boys with you, make sure it's done right."

Miles frowned. He did not like Jook's attitude toward Little. He tried to think of how it might be turned to their advantage.

"I thought she was to be used as a creeper," he said.

"Did you?" said the older boy, blowing out a column of smoke and looking sideways at Miles. "And what gave you that idea?"

Miles knew it had been String's suggestion, but he was not about to fall for that one. "She's small and quick," he said, "and she moves without a sound. You know she'd bring more food than she eats."

"I don't know nothing of the sort, pez," said Jook.

"Maybe you could try her out," he said quickly. "You might be surprised." He winked at Little, and she gave him the ghost of a smile. Jook smoked his cigar silently, until Miles began to think his suggestion would simply be ignored. Eventually he took a last pull on the cigar and flicked the butt into the fire, then he reached out with his bone and gave Henry, and another small boy curled up beside him, a sharp poke each.

"Henry. Ignatz. Wake up. Got a job for you," he said. Henry opened his eyes at once, as though he had slept a full night on a feather mattress. The other boy sat up and yawned.

"Time to do your rounds, boys. You're taking the pez's girl with you, see if she's got the makings of a creeper." He turned to Miles. "Not a Halfhead, mind. A creeper."

"You mean right now?" said Miles. His suggestion had been a delaying tactic, and he had not meant Little to be sent out to sneak into sleeping houses before they even had a chance to formulate a plan.

"Why not?" said Jook. "You waiting for her to grow wings and a tail?"

Miles thought that question would be best left unanswered. "Are you sure this is a good night for creeping?" he asked instead. "There's no moon."

Henry laughed. "That's what makes it a perfect night for creeping," he said. "Cloudy sky, and no wind for blowing things about when the windows is opened. Just the night for breakin' in a new creeper."

"Maybe I should go with you," said Miles. Little smiled at him, but in the flickering firelight he could read nothing more in her expression.

"You're too big for creeping, pez," said Jook. "And I don't fancy having to come and prize you out of a tight window."

Little stepped forward to whisper in Miles's ear. He expected to hear something she had spotted on her brief investigation, but instead she whispered, "Am I really your friend?"

"Of course," said Miles, taken aback. Little nodded. "Then I'll be fine," she said, and she turned and disappeared after Henry and Ignatz into the darkness.

The fire died down, and he moved closer by degrees as the pool of warmth shrank toward the ashes. He pictured Little creeping through the night with the two boys, and all the dangers that might be waiting to ambush her. He chewed his nails, and missed having Tangerine to confide in. Talking to the bear made things clearer in his head. "What now?" he muttered to himself, trying to imagine that Tangerine was listening from his inside pocket, but the only answer was the snoring of small boys, and the faint hissing of the dying fire.

Miles slept fitfully on the hard ground, waking at every sound. The night seemed to drag on forever, but it was still well before dawn when he heard someone dropping from the window onto the broken tiles of the church floor. It was Ignatz, and he was alone and limping, and smelled of something indescribably rotten.

Miles sat up at once, straining for a sound of Little or Henry. "Where are the others?" he asked Ignatz. "And what happened to you?"

"Got jumped by Stinkers, up near the borders," panted Ignatz. "We was outnumbered, and the other two got taken. They would've got me too, only I can run like a snotty nose."

Miles felt his heart plummet. "We have to go after them," he said.

"No point," said Jook. He and Lob, his lieutenant, had awoken at the sound of Ignatz's return. "They'll be well inside Stinker territory by now."

"You can't just give up on them!" said Miles.

"Course not, pez. Henry's our best creeper. We'll have to win him back at Pigball."

"What exactly *is* Pigball?" asked Miles.

"Pigball's played in the bullring," said Ignatz, who was beginning to get his breath back. "It's real simple. Each team has a big oil drum, up on the top terrace. You got to get the ball into the other team's drum to score. That's all there is to it."

"Then we have to play for both of them," said Miles. "Henry and Little."

"The girl's not Halfhead. Pigball's never played for outsiders, and there's nothing in the rules says they have to give her back," said Jook.

"Rules were made to be broken," said Miles.

"Not our rules, pez," said Jook. "Pigball game starts at midday after prisoners are took, and you're on the team, so you better get some sleep."

"But I've never played before!"

"Don't matter," said Lob. "You won Halfhead's bone, you get his place on the team."

Miles Wednesday, sleepless and ash-dusted, crept through the back lanes in the morning haze with a gang of half-shaved boys. He gripped a leg bone in his right hand, and his breath fogged the air. Thoughts of Little and the upcoming game knotted his stomach. The rest of the Halfheads, by contrast, seemed unconcerned, and most of them had slept through the morning while Miles fidgeted and practiced swinging his bone.

Now Ignatz, limping along beside him, was describing how the three creepers had been jumped by a small party of Stinkers as they crawled through a hole in a hedge, close to the border between the territories. He had been felled by a Stinker club, which he described as a sort of stocking with a ball of hard slime in the end of it, and knocked almost senseless. "It's the stench," said Ignatz. "It's worse than the whack itself. That smell would knock you out on its own." He had crawled free of the ensuing scramble, but they were outnumbered, and Henry and Little had been tied up in a matter of seconds. Ignatz (by his own account at least) had managed to land a few blows with his bone, and with his speed and slipperiness he had escaped the Stinkers and run all the way back to the churchyard.

The mist had almost cleared as they reached the bullring, a dozen bone-wielding Halfheads slipping through the broken turnstiles. Miles looked about him as they entered the dilapidated arena. The Stinkers were waiting at the far side. He could just make out Little and Henry sitting on the crumbling stone terraces, guarded by a couple of the larger boys. He waved at her, but he was not sure if she could see him. Besides the Stinkers, a scattering of small long-haired boys sat around the terraces. Some nudged each other and pointed at the Halfheads as they entered. They were mostly barefoot.

Lob grunted. "Gnats is here already," he said.

Three of the Stinkers were crossing the arena toward them, swinging their clubs in their hands. The top halves of their faces were painted black, as though they wore masks over their eyes. Two of them wore kilts, and the smell of rotten eggs preceded them like an invisible tide. Miles fought the impulse to hold his nose. Jook casually lit a cigar, and stepped forward to meet the chief Stinker.

"Got us one of your creeps," said the Stinker in chief through a broken-toothed smile.

"You got two prisoners," said Jook. "We want to

play for 'em both." Miles looked at him in surprise, but Jook's eyes were fixed on his opposite number.

"We got one prisoner," said the Stinker, "and a girl that was with 'em. You taking girls in now, Jook? Your boys not tough enough?"

"She's not Halfhead," said Jook, blowing a cloud of thick smoke at the chief Stinker. "She belongs to one of my boys. You can throw her in with my creeper, and we'll say no more about it."

"Finders keepers, even creepers," said the other boy. "She's not Halfhead, like you said, and we don't have to give her back. Might make a good lookout, if her eyes are sharp. We play one game for the creeper. First to three scores. You lose, you got to play for him again next week." He turned on his heel and began to walk away.

"Wait a minute, slime head," said Miles.

The Stinker in chief whipped around and scowled at him through his painted mask. "I don't know your face, squirt," he spat. "And you're not going to know it either, once this game is done."

He turned to Jook. "I'd teach him to keep his mouth shut if I was you."

"Well you're not me," said Jook, "so you can keep your own mouth shut."

"*I'll* play for both of them," interrupted Miles.

"The girl and the creeper. Just me against your team."

There was a moment's silence. Halfheads and Stinkers alike stared at Miles in disbelief, then Ignatz slapped his hand to his forehead and groaned, and the Stinkers burst out laughing.

"You've never played Pigball, have you, squirt?" said the Stinker in chief. He stepped forward and stuck out a filthy hand. "You're on. It'll be a short match, but it'll be fun to watch. Better get a wheelbarrow, Jook."

The three Stinkers walked back across the bullring, still chuckling. Jook let out a long stream of smoke, and stubbed out his cigar butt. "I like you, pez," he said, shaking his head. "That's why I stuck my neck out for you. But that's got to be the stupidest idea I've ever heard."

"It's just a game, isn't it?" said Miles. "How bad can it be?"

"Ever been run over by a tram?" laughed Lob.

"It ain't funny," growled Jook. "You'd better give a good account of yourself in the few seconds you're going to last, pez."

"How many are on a team?" asked Miles.

"How many? The whole gang is a team. You'd have to get the ball across the bullring, up the terraces and into their drum, playing against fourteen of 'em, plus the crowd of course."

Miles felt his stomach sink. "The crowd can play as well?"

"They can't leave the terraces, and they can't score," said Jook. "But they can foul whoever they like."

Miles looked around at the scattering of long-haired boys on the terraces. "They all look very small," he said hopefully.

"That's 'cause they're Gnats, pez. None of 'em's more than six or seven. Some of them's not much more than babies. Henry was Gnats, once. When he got too big we took him as a creeper."

"They shouldn't be too much of a problem then," said Miles.

Jook laughed. "Don't count on it, pez. Gnats sting."

"I think you'd better teach me the rules so I can work out a strategy," said Miles.

"No eye gougin'," said Ignatz, scuffing the dirt with the end of his bone.

Miles waited for a moment. "What about the rest of the rules?" he said.

"That's it," said Ignatz. "No eye gougin'. That's the only rule there is."

CHAPTER NINETEEN
PIGBALL

Miles Wednesday, stomach-knotted and hopelessly outnumbered, looked around him at the crumbling arena with its scattering of tiny spectators. He could just make out the rusted oil drum, painted with black and yellow stripes, on the top terrace at the Stinkers' end of the arena. It seemed impossibly far away. The Halfheads had slapped him on the back and left him alone, finding themselves places to sit on the terraces. The Gnats fidgeted and squinted in the sunlight, and on the far side of the ring, the Stinkers gathered in a dark huddle, from which laughter broke out from time to time.

A Stinker was dispatched from across the bull-ring. “You the new face?” he said. Miles nodded. The Stinker produced a tightly bound ball of rags that looked like it was a veteran of many matches. “You understand the game?” he asked.

“I think so,” said Miles.

The boy turned and pointed to the arches that ringed the top of the terrace. “See the black an’ yellow drum under the bigger arch?” he said. Miles nodded. “That’s where you got to put the ball. Your drum is up there.” He pointed to another large arch above where the Halfheads were seated. “That’s where we got to put it. Usually a game is first to three, but the chief says you only got to score once. An outsider’s not worth three scores, and besides, you’ll never make it out of your corner.” He spat on the ball and held it out for Miles to do the same.

“The rest of you Halfheads is out of this game, by agreement,” said the Stinker. “Otherwise all bets is off, and you don’t get the outsider, nor your creeper neither.” He turned back to Miles. “It was nice knowin’ you,” he said. “Game starts in three minutes.” Halfway across the arena he placed the ball carefully on the ground, and went to rejoin his team.

The sun was high now, and the heat was beginning

to rise from the packed dirt of the arena. Miles took off his jacket, but despite the warmth he felt a cold chill down his spine. He thought of the scoop of ice cream he had unwittingly collected while under the benches at the Circus Oscuro. He paused for a moment, then a smile crept across his face. He moved into the center of the knot of Halfheads and took off his shirt as well. He rolled it into a ball, knotting the sleeves around it as tightly as he could. He put his jacket back on, and stuffed the shirt into his pocket.

Jook was watching him closely from his seat on the terrace. He took half a cigar from his pocket and put it between his lips, unlit. "I'll bet two toe bones on the pez to score," he said. "Any takers?"

"You're on," said Lob, removing the necklace of bones he wore under his shirt. "I say he never gets to the terraces."

"Get ready for the whistle, pez," said Jook. "Your only chance is to get to the ball first."

A moment later a shrill blast on a whistle echoed across the arena, and Miles took off as fast as he could. His seven escape attempts from Pinchbucket House had made a sprinter of him, and he covered the ground like a whippet. The entire Stinker team, with the exception of the two who were guarding the prisoners, was charging toward him from the opposite side, yelling and whooping and whirling their stinking slime-filled stockings over their heads as they came. Miles carried the bone he had inherited from String, but he concentrated on running and left the whooping and whirling to his opponents. It looked like they would reach the ball at the same time, and Miles tried to block out all thoughts of the coming impact from his mind. He was only yards from the ball now—nine, eight, and the leading Stinkers were almost upon him, eyes staring from their blackened faces, seven, six, tongues hanging out as they ran, the smell of bad eggs turning the air before them. He took a last lungful of clean air at three yards and dived for the ball, still holding his bone in one hand, and a second later he was buried under a pile of smelly boys, scrabbling and grabbing for the ball, and flailing wildly with their slimy clubs.

Miles could feel the ball under his chest. He wormed his fingers in among the knotted rags to tighten his grip. He couldn't breathe for the weight on top of him, and with the weight being composed entirely of Stinkers he wasn't sure he wanted to. A knee dug into his back and a bang on the side of his head made his ear sing. The weight shifted, then eased, as the pile of boys toppled over, and with a mighty wriggle he was out from under them and struggling to his feet. A hand gripped his jacket. He swiped with his bone and felt the grip loosen. He lowered his head and charged a couple of Stinkers who stood in his way, knocking one of them over, and he was free and running again.

He could just see the terraces through a film of sweat that was running into his eyes. He leaped onto the first terrace, hoping that he was heading for the right arch. The Stinkers were hot on his heels. One of their slime clubs wrapped itself around his ankle. He tripped and half fell, then recovered his feet and jumped another few terraces, landing among a crowd of Gnats. Too late he remembered that audience participation was a part of the game. He felt a stabbing pain in the back of his leg, then another, and he fell to the stone terrace with a crowd of small boys swarming over him like wasps on spilled jam.

Once again he was at the bottom of the pile, but this time they were mostly Gnats, although his nose told him that more Stinkers were joining the scrum by the second. His bone was snatched from him, and he could hear it clatter down the steps and out of reach. The real ball was wedged underneath him, and with his free arm he rummaged in his pocket for his balled-up shirt. Instead his fingers found his pocketknife. He was nose to nose with a Gnat who could not have been more than four years old, grinning through his long stringy hair. "Fun, ain't it?" said the boy.

Miles produced his knife, and the boy's eyes widened. "You want this knife?" he gasped. The boy nodded. Miles put it back in his pocket with difficulty. He shoved the ball quickly under the other boy's chest. "Take this up to the Stinkers' drum and wait for me," he said. "Then I'll swap the knife for it."

The Pigball pile shifted and heaved. Elbows were jammed in ears, and feet between teeth, and minor fights and scuffles broke out until the heap of boys collapsed outward onto the terraces. Miles seized his chance. He pulled his filthy rolled-up shirt from his pocket and broke out from the scrum, holding the bogus ball tightly under one arm and leaping down the terraces. He took off at a sprint across the ring, straight toward the Halfhead side. He could hear the Stinkers laughing as they chased him. "Hey, Halfwit," one of them called. "Keep going straight. You're going to score."

Three of the fastest Stinkers were right on his

heels. A blow from a slime club stung his ear, and he felt his sleeve grabbed. He spun around as he fell. The three Stinkers were on top of him, shoving him into the dirt. "Here, we'll do that for you," laughed one, then they were up and running toward the Halfheads' drum, one of them with Miles's rolled-up shirt clutched under his arm. Miles scrambled to his feet again. He caught a glimpse of the shocked faces of the Halfhead spectators, and flashed them a grin. He turned and ran as fast as he could toward the terraces. He did not make directly for the Stinkers' end, but reached the midpoint, where the terraces were empty, and leaped onto the first step. His lungs were burning, and his legs stung where they had been cut by the Gnats. The laughter of the Stinkers, and the watching Gnats, echoed across the bullring. "He's lost the ball," someone shouted. There was more laughter.

"No he ain't," came a shout from up beside the Stinkers' drum. The Gnat had reached his target unnoticed, but he could see that Miles was on the way with the fine knife he had promised him, and he could contain himself no longer.

"It's up here! I got it!" yelled the boy, holding the ball over his head and hopping with excitement. The Halfheads broke into a roar of delight. Miles leaped the next terrace. The heat and the exertion were making him dizzy, and his legs felt like wet string. The chief Stinker was roaring now too, and not for the same reason. "Get after him, you boneheads! Where's your defense? Flatten the Halfbrain!"

Miles looked across at the Stinkers' end. A crowd of them had started up the terraces to cut him off before he could reach their drum. He was making his way around toward them with each step he climbed, but he was still only halfway up, and the top terrace seemed a lifetime away. The Gnat had stopped jumping up and down now. He had stuffed the ball behind him on the step and was looking worried. The Stinkers were whooping and swinging their clubs as they swarmed up the terraces, the black on their faces smeared with sweat. Miles pushed himself up step after step until he felt his lungs would burst. He reached the top terrace and ran on rubbery legs, following the wide curve beneath the colonnade of arches.

It was cooler up here, where the breeze could reach him and the sun could not. Everything seemed to slow down and fall into place. He could see the Stinkers, clambering up to cut him off, and he could see the Gnat with the ball, looking wide-eyed from him to the approaching horde and back again. He could see Little down below, standing on the terrace between her guards, waving both arms in the air and shouting, and most of all he could hear the roar from the Halfheads, a wave of surprise and delight that seemed to carry him the last few yards to the Stinkers' drum without his feet touching the stone. He grabbed the ball from the Gnat's outstretched hands and paused for a moment at the mouth of the oil drum. The Stinkers were two steps below him, mouths wide as they gasped for air, defeat already in their eyes. He held the ball high, and dropped it into the drum. *Thunk!*

His legs gave way from under him, and he collapsed onto the terrace beside his small accomplice.

"So this . . . is . . . Pigball," he panted as he handed over his knife.

The small boy nodded. "Fun, ain't it?" he said.

CHAPTER TWENTY
A NEST OF ANTS

Miles Wednesday, freshly minted Pigball legend, smiled as he was carried shoulder-high by cheering Halfheads down the bullring terraces. The Stinkers waited below in a surly knot, arguing about the outcome of the game. Tempers flared and scuffles broke out. Little and Henry were still under guard on the Stinker terrace. Jook approached the chief Stinker, and the rest of his gang fell silent.

"Halfheads claim the prisoners back," said Jook.

The chief Stinker shook his head. "Stinkers demand a rematch. Spectators aren't allowed to score."

"The Gnat didn't score," said Jook. "You seen

it—our pez dropped the ball in the can."

"Maybe so," said the Stinker in chief, "but he played two balls. That's not allowed."

"The way I heard it, that's only not allowed if one of them is an eyeball," said Miles. "Anyhow, I can't help it if your Stinkers are dumb enough to run off with my best Sunday shirt."

Jook laughed. "Pez is right, and you made a deal. Now hand over the prisoners."

"Or else what," sneered the Stinker in chief. Some of his fighters began to close in behind him.

"Or else the cops will get you," said Miles.

"What are you talking about, farm boy?" said the chief Stinker.

"Big fellas, shiny buttons, just picked up your two guards," said Miles, pointing over the Stinker's shoulder. The Stinker in chief laughed. "You don't expect me . . . ," he began, but he never got to finish his sentence. Miles was gone, his tiredness forgotten, sprinting in a wide arc around the surprised Stinkers toward the Stinker terraces, where two policemen were hauling Little's guards roughly up the stone steps. Another large meat-faced man made a lunge at Little herself, but she ducked between his legs and jumped down the last three terraces, almost landing on top of Miles as he reached the bottom step.

"Miles!" she said. "You were brilliant!"

"No time for that." Miles grinned. "Here's our chance. Let's get out of here."

The police were streaming out from under the arches and cantering awkwardly down the terraces. They had managed to catch a couple of Gnats by surprise, though the small boys were mostly too quick for them. The arena was suddenly like an ant's nest that had been poked with a stick. Halfheads and Stinkers ran in every direction, pursued by police blowing whistles and shouting—now that the element of surprise had passed—about burglary and painted 'ooliganism, and grabbing whoever they could get their hands on.

Miles took Little's hand and ran toward the mouth of a narrow alley between the terraces. He stooped to grab his discarded bone on the way, and shoved it into his belt. They ran down the alley, through which angry bulls had once charged, rubbing the walls smooth with their coarse flanks and trampling the earth iron-hard beneath their hooves. At the end of the alley their way was blocked by a tall iron gate, topped with curved spikes.

"It's too high," said Little.

"Not for you," said Miles. "You've got wings."

Little shook her head. "I . . . I won't go without you." She seemed almost surprised to hear herself say this, but before Miles could answer he felt his ankle grabbed by a small hand, and he looked down in surprise to see Henry's head poking out from a small semicircular window in the alley wall, just above ground level.

"Sssssh," said Henry. "They'll hear you. Get inside!" He disappeared back into the hole, and before Miles could say anything, Little was wriggling in after him. Miles was not sure he would fit, but the pounding footsteps of a heavy man on the terrace above made him drop down and squeeze through the narrow opening, and at the cost of a couple of buttons he was soon crouched in the dank darkness with Little and Henry.

Before long they could see a parade of boots and bare feet passing by the semicircular window. There was a loud clang and the squeal of rusty hinges as the police forced the iron gate open and marched their captives outside and into the waiting vans. The three fugitives huddled in their small cell without daring to whisper.

Some time after all the police boots had passed, and the sound of the departing vans had faded away, they saw the feet of two boys running quietly down the alley toward the gate. There was a rusty screech as they forced the old gate open slightly, then moments later they heard a man's voice shout, "Two more there, Tom," and the sound of a brief struggle, then silence.

"They've left sentries," whispered Henry.

Miles looked about him, but they were in pitch darkness.

"There's no other way out," whispered Henry. "I checked. There's one door, and it's locked. We'll have to wait till the night."

Miles put his head in his hands. His felt bruised and numb and his knees ached from crouching. He would have liked to sit down, but the floor felt slimy under his feet. He patted his pocket from force of habit, as though Tangerine might have magically reappeared, but his pocket was empty. He had had enough of waiting.

"Can't we get back out through the bullring?" he asked.

"Too risky," whispered Henry. "There'll be men on the terraces too, for sure."

"What's outside the gate?" said Miles.

"Cops," said Henry.

"Apart from them," said Miles. "What if we can get past them?"

"I know a way down to the canal," said Henry after a moment. "There's an old pipe. If we can get from the gate to the pipe without being seen, we might get away."

Miles felt impatience rising up inside him. "Let's go then," he said. He poked his head cautiously out through the window. There was no one to be seen in either direction, and he hoisted himself out onto the alley floor. He turned to give Little a hand up, but she was already beside him. He got to his feet and crept along silently to where the gate stood ajar, and peered cautiously through the gap, being careful not to open the noisy gate any farther.

A single police van stood nearby, facing away down the rutted road that circled the bullring. The back doors were locked, and he could see one of the policemen in the cab, pouring himself a steaming drink from a tartan thermos flask.

Miles turned to Henry. "You first," he whispered.

Henry slipped through the gate, silent as a fox, and ran swiftly through the tall weeds in the opposite direction to where the van was parked, with Miles and Little following close behind.

A large concrete pipe ran half buried among the weeds. A little way along it there was a gaping hole where the concrete was broken, and Henry stuck his head in to take a look, before dropping down into the pipe. It had not carried water for a long time. There was a layer of dried silt underfoot, and light filtered in through frequent cracks and holes. They moved rapidly and quietly in the dim light, the pipe sloping gently downward. After a couple of minutes they saw a circle of light ahead, which grew steadily larger as they approached. Henry stopped when he reached the end, and peered out cautiously in both directions. The pipe opened onto the canal, which too was almost dry, with just a thin channel of green water meandering along the mud bottom.

"Where are we?" asked Little.

"Gnats territory," whispered Henry. "I reckon it's safe enough, them being distracted by the cops, but it wouldn't do to get caught here all the same."

"Why are we going this way?" asked Miles.

"I'm taking you to the fun park," said Henry. "That's where you want to go, isn't it—to the Palace of Laughter?"

"Yes," said Miles, "but I thought that was in Stinkers' territory."

Henry nodded. "It is, but this is the best way from here. If we stick to the canal, it'll take us all the way along to the fun park. Used to be a hole in the fence there. If it hasn't been closed up you can get through into the park, and once you're in there you're in Stinkers' territory. I owe you that much for takin' on the whole Stinker team for us, but from there you'll be on your own. Fun park's not a place I'd go to for fun, if you see what I mean."

They dropped from the pipe onto the dried canal bed, and ran along as quickly and soundlessly as they could, keeping close to the stone wall.

"Do you think they'll be all right, the rest of them?" asked Miles as they made their way quickly along the canal bed.

Henry shrugged. "There was lots of cops. More than I ever seen. I reckon someone must've tipped them off."

"What will happen to the boys they caught?"

"They'll try to put 'em in reform school and grow 'em up. Reform school couldn't hold a Halfhead though, not if he wanted to escape."

"How will you get back to the boneyard?" asked Little. She never seemed to tire, and her feet left no mark on the soft mud of the canal bed.

"I know lots of ways that others don't," said Henry. "Been a creeper for nearly two years now, an' Jook says I'm the best he can remember. This whole town's full of holes, like a big cheese, and I reckon I know most of 'em."

The canal took a shallow right turn, and the shape of the big wheel came into view ahead. It was strange and still, like a thick spiderweb nailed to the sky by its rusting cars.

"The fun park," said Henry. He looked nervous. "That big wheel is the Stinkers' HQ. If they catch you, they'll put you right up in the top car for three whole days, no food and nothing to drink but the rain puddles on the floor." He shivered. "Ignatz says people used to pay money to go up on it in the olden days, but I don't believe that."

As they trotted along the canal bed, Miles felt his boots grow heavier with the mud they were collecting. His stomach formed into a knot. He slowed to a walk, letting Henry draw ahead. The sky was beginning to cloud over, bringing a cold wind that whistled along the canal. The wheel grew bigger and bigger as they approached, until it seemed to half fill the sky. Its metal spokes were as thick as tree trunks, and the cars squeaked as they swung in the breeze, rust speckling their faded paint like a brown disease.

Through the spokes of the big wheel he could see a strangely shaped hill looming. In the haze it looked like an enormous head, facing away from them over the outskirts of the city. He remembered the old crow's name for the Palace of Laughter—"Big Laughing Head"—and he knew that this must be the place. It was not as he had pictured it back in Larde, a theater overflowing with laughter and light. Jook had said that anyone who went in would never come out the same, and now that he could see the menacing outline of the place, Miles found it easier to believe.

"That must be the place," whispered Little. "I don't like the look of it."

Miles took her hand and squeezed it. "It'll be okay," he said.

"You don't have to come with me," said Little. "Silverpoint will know where to look for Tangerine." She laughed. "Though I'll be in trouble for singing his name out."

Miles looked at her in surprise. Rain had washed most of the soot from her hair, leaving it dirty white and tangled. She smiled up at him, but her eyes seemed to be searching his face for clues.

"I do strange things, remember?" he said. Little nodded. She looked relieved.

"Ssssh!" whispered Henry, who had stopped in front of them. "This is it," he said, almost inaudibly. They were right below the corner of the fence that enclosed the fun park now.

Miles could not see any gap. "Where's the way in?" he whispered.

"There's a hole in the fence behind those bushes," said Henry. "I'll show you which one, then I'm off." He scanned the length of the fence, a small frown of concentration on his grubby face. There was no one to be seen. "Now," said Henry. They climbed up onto the canal bank, and Henry crept along the narrow space between the fence and the bushes that grew beside it, until he came to a place where the wire had been cut. He pulled the broken fence outward and wriggled through the gap. Miles and Little waited, holding their breath. Henry turned and beckoned to them from the shelter of a pile of old tires, painted in different colors. "Quick," he hissed. Little went through next, and Miles followed, squeezing himself with difficulty through the small hole.

Henry crawled around to the other side of the pile of tires. "This is as far as I go," he whispered. "Stinkers can see the whole park from up in that wheel," he said, "so you need to keep out of sight." He pointed to two long rows of old canvas-covered stalls that started near where they crouched, and ran along beneath the wheel toward the looming head. "You can get inside the back of the stalls and run the whole length of them. If you keep under the canvas you'll be out of sight most of the way, then you'll just have to run across the open space till you get to the Palace of Laughter. I don't know how you'll get in there, 'cause I never heard of anyone who's done it, not even Stinkers."

"Don't know why you'd want to either," said a voice behind them. They spun around in unison like startled fish. A boy sat by the gap in the fence, a stem of grass dangling from his lips. What little hair was left on his shaved head was tied up in a top-knot, and a black mask was painted across his eyes. He appeared to be on his own. The boy spat out the grass stem and grinned. There was something familiar about him. "Is this a scoutin' party," he asked, "or is it the whole invasion force?"

"That you, String?" said Henry nervously.

The boy's grin widened. "You look worried, Henry," he said. "I'm not going to eat you."

"I was just leavin' anyway," said Henry. He looked around him. "Where's the rest of 'em?"

"My new brothers? The slower ones is in the police cells, waitin' to be reformed. The rest of them is waitin' in ambush down by the railway yards. I told them Halfheads was plannin' a raid along the railway line, but I knew you'd more likely come this way, 'cause I knew you'd most likely be doin' the scoutin', Henry. And being an old Gnat, I reckoned you'd probably come sneakin' up the canal. Looks like I was right too."

"What are you doing here then?" asked Miles.

String's eyes narrowed behind their mask, and his grin faded. "I'm here to help you get where you're goin', pez. You'd have no chance of crossin' this territory without me."

"Why would you do that?" Miles asked suspiciously.

"Firstly, 'cause I don't like you," said String. "And if you're dim enough to want to be swallowed up by that madhouse, I'm only too pleased to help. If you do get in, you'll never come out the same."

Miles said nothing. He had heard that phrase too many times for his liking.

"And secondly," continued String, "when you and your little creeper is safely tucked up in the giant's mouth, me an' Henry here are going back to Halfhead territory, and with you gone I'll get my rightful place back."

"They'll never let you back in! Halfhead's gone, he's gone," said Henry. "'Specially since you joined up with the Stinkers. Anyway, like I said, I was just leavin'."

String leaned over and pulled back the fence. "Off you go then, Henry. The Gnats is just returning from the bullring. I can see a swarm of 'em coming up the canal, and they don't look very happy. Mustn't have been much of a game, eh?" He let the fence swing shut, and grinned. "Look, Henry, it's me, String. We've always been mates, you and me." He glanced at Miles. "The pez, he cheated me, and he's not one of us. Never will be."

Henry looked away, fidgeting with a frayed bootlace. String got to his feet, and the sly grin returned to his face. "I know Jook will see sense on this, 'specially when I tell him what I've learned about the Stinkers. They're not so careful with their secrets once you pretend to join up with 'em.

"Now we'll have to move fast if you want to get over to the Palace of Laughter before sunset. That's when the doors open, and they shut again soon as all the people are inside. If you miss 'em today, you won't get another chance till tomorrow at the earliest, and they don't have a show every day, so I'm told."

Miles stood cautiously and looked around, half expecting to find himself surrounded by Stinkers. The park seemed deserted.

"Don't trust me, eh, pez?" said String. "Very smart.

You might've made a good Halfhead, eventually. But you're not thinking it through. If I let Stinkers get you, they'll just trade you back at Pigball—after a few nights on the sky wheel—and I'd be stuck in this freaky place with these blackfaced animals for good, wouldn't I?"

He turned and trotted across the short stretch of cracked concrete to the first row of stalls with their faded canvas awnings. He turned and beckoned to them, then he ducked under the loose canvas.

"What do you think?" said Miles.

"I don't know," said Little. "He sings out of tune."

"What about you, Henry?" said Miles. "You know him better. Can we trust him?"

Henry looked uncomfortable. Things were simple once you followed Halfhead rules, but this was outside their scope. The rules said that once a Halfhead was out, he should never be mentioned again, but they didn't say what to do if you met an ex-Halfhead in foreign territory who had pretended to join another gang but wanted to gain back the Halfhead place that he believed he was cheated out of in the first place. Besides, he had known String for a long time, and he'd only known Miles and Little for one day. And Little was a girl, but then, he liked her. And Miles was a Pigball hero.

His head spun with all the details. He looked nervously over his shoulder, as though he expected to see Gnats swarming through the hole in the fence.

"I don't know about singin'," he said finally, "but I don't see what choice we got. He's goin' the same way I suggested anyway. I think we should go with him."

Miles looked across at the gap in the canvas through which String had disappeared. A stiff breeze was blowing dark purple clouds across the reddening sky, and the sun was close to the horizon. "Let's go then," he said.

Henry laid a hand on his arm. "Wait," he whispered. "Creeper goes first."

Henry took off, running at a crouch. He was almost as soundless as Little. He did not make directly for the near end of the stalls, where String had disappeared, but ran swiftly along between the two rows until he had reached the third or fourth stall. Here he dropped to his knees, lifted the canvas and peered underneath. He poked his head inside, then quickly withdrew it, but not quickly enough. Several pairs of hands reached out from under the stall and grabbed the small boy. He just had time to shout "Ambush!" before a rag was stuffed into his mouth and he was dragged in under the canvas.

"Run!" said Miles. He took Little's hand and they ran along the alley between the stalls, straight toward the Stinker ambush. There was no point in going any other way. They were too close to the Palace of Laughter to turn back now, and behind them there were only Halfheads and Gnats. Dozens of Stinkers were wriggling out from under the stalls, their eyes white in their black masks and their putrid clubs in their hands. Miles leaped high over the crawling boys. "I've outrun them before," he thought, "and I can do it again." Little hung on to his hand, and though her wings were hidden away her feet barely touched the ground.

As he ran, Miles felt a sick feeling in his stomach at the thought of leaving Henry to his fate, perched in the sky for three days and drinking rusty water. He hoped that Henry had the story wrong, or that he would somehow manage to escape, but there was no more time to think of this now. As they neared the end of the stalls, a Stinker stepped out in front of them, and in the blur of movement Miles recognized String's sly leer. String was pointing at him with one hand, beckoning the converging Stinkers with the other. "That's him," he shouted. "He's the one that brought the cops on us! I seen him—"

But that was as much as he got to say. Miles had

pulled the bone from his belt, and was holding it out in front of him as he ran full tilt toward String. "Here's your bone back," he said, as it dawned on String's face that he had no intention of stopping. The gnarled end of the bone met its original owner square in the chest, and with a gasp of shock the winded boy went down, and Miles and Little leaped over him without breaking their stride.

The big wheel loomed directly over them now. They ran past its gigantic metal feet, fixed to the ground with bolts the size of a man's head. A swarm of painted boys clambered down the wheel with the practice of spiders in a web and dropped to the ground. The Palace of Laughter towered ahead of them, even bigger than Miles had imagined. For the first time he could see it clearly, and it was by far the strangest of all the strange things he had seen since the night the Circus Oscuro arrived in Larde.

Imagine an enormous clown, as tall as a mountain, wading through solid earth up to his chin. If you can picture such a thing at all, you may have some idea what the Palace of Laughter looked like. It was a large, domed hill, carved into the shape of a giant clown's head. His great stone eyes bulged from their sockets and his blue-lipped mouth was frozen in a huge laugh. Set into the open mouth was a pair of huge wooden doors. The crown of the hill was bald and smooth, with a fringe of cedar trees sprouting like fuzzy green hair above the enormous carved ears. Around the hill lay a moat of greenish water, crossed by a drawbridge that looked like a huge wooden tongue.

They ran toward this strange hill, the boy and the angel, with no idea of how they would get in, indeed with no thought in their heads but to escape the top-knotted, club-wielding army that was hot on their heels. Just before the drawbridge stood an abandoned ticket booth. Miles headed for it instinctively, though it was hard to imagine what protection the dilapidated hut with its glassless windows could offer them.

As they reached the booth and began to scramble through the window, the sound of a great gong rang out from somewhere inside the hill. The enormous wooden doors swung inward, and a moment later a troupe of tumblers and stilt walkers emerged onto the drawbridge, blowing whistles and tooting horns. There were three tiny men in top hats, with whitened faces and each wearing a different-colored nose. They cartwheeled across the wooden tongue of the drawbridge without losing their hats, followed by two men on stilts so tall that they had to duck to avoid the stone teeth as they left the giant mouth. After them came a number of other clowns, some banging drums and others waving firecrackers on sticks above their heads, and the whole motley procession marched along the cracked concrete path, past the booth in which Miles and Little crouched, toward the wrought-iron gates of the park entrance.

Miles peered back the way they had come, through a crack in the boards. The Stinkers had melted away at the approach of the crowd. It was as though the park, which a moment ago had been swarming with angry boys, was empty but for Miles and Little, and the strange parade that passed before them on its way to the gates of the fun park.

When they reached the gates the stilt walkers unlocked them and swung them open, and a crowd of people surged in from the street outside, led by none other than Baumella the giantess herself. The clowns and stilt walkers turned and fell in on either side, playing their chaotic music and cartwheeling along beside the people, who shuffled toward the great clown's head as though they had just had a long journey and an uncomfortable night, which indeed they had.

Miles and Little crouched, panting, on the floor of the empty booth, listening to the approach of many feet and the babble of voices belonging to people who were more used to giving their own opinions than listening to other people's. They seemed to have plenty of complaints to get off their chests, and the cheerful tooting and banging of the clowns was having little effect on their mood. Miles could hear snatches of their conversations as the visitors passed close to their hiding place.

"They could have laid on a coach from the hotel, instead of making us walk."

"Hotel, you call it? I'd have swam through thin porridge in me undies to get out of that flea pit, myself."

"Maybe you would, Thacker, but I'd still have liked to be brung on a coach."

"Get on! You've been sitting on your fat behind for the best part of two days. Last thing you need is to sit down some more."

"It's all right for you. I'm a martyr to the gout, and me ankles is still ballooned up with sittin' in that stuffy train."

Whatever Thacker had to say on the topic of gout was lost in the babble of voices as the crowd flowed past. The names were unfamiliar to Miles, but the voices might just as well have belonged to the citizens of his hometown. It seemed that half the population of Iota or Shallowford or Frappe had spent two days and a night cheek by jowl, crawling through the countryside on a crowded train and shacked up in a cheap hotel on the promise of a night of laughter such as they had never seen before. It was a wonder they had not strangled one another.

"I tell you what," said a woman's voice, its owner tottering past on a pair of high heels that were not made for walking on cracked concrete, or for swimming in thin porridge for that matter. "This show had better be as good as it's cracked up to be, or I'll be wanting my money back."

"We didn't pay any money, dear. We won these tickets," said her husband.

The woman snorted. "Us and half the town. It's not a very exclusive prize, is it?"

"Well, you can't expect it to be, if it ain't cost nothing."

"*Didn't* cost nothing, William. You'll never amount to nothing if you don't learn to talk properly."

And so it went on, a parade of grumbling people, tired from a journey that was twice as long as they had expected, and all on the promise of shining a little laughter on the grayness of their lives. The drums and bugles and the sound of footsteps passed by, and Miles risked another look out the window. Baumella had reached the wooden doors, and stood to one side to usher the people in. They straggled onto the drawbridge behind her and began to crowd their way in through the doors.

Miles watched carefully the progress of the crowd. Their only chance would be to try and sneak in at the tail end, just before the doors closed again. They would have to time it just right. The lucky silver-ticket winners were ten deep on the wooden drawbridge, which was fortunately made of very stout oak planks. Many of them were fonder of beer and pastries and pies than was good for them, and had the bridge not been made of such sturdy stuff they might well have found themselves in the moat instead.

As it was, there was a good deal of elbowing and shoving, and those who had not reached their full quota of grumbling earlier were taking the opportunity to squeeze a few more complaints out while they pushed their way inside. It was a strange sight to be sure: an enormous clown's head with green cedar hair and mossy cheeks, its vast stone eyeballs staring out over the city as a long snake of people fed itself into its cavernous mouth. They reminded

Miles vaguely of a dream he had had, and not for the first time he wondered what he was doing, far from home and without his Tangerine, staring into the mouth of a nightmare with a four-hundred-year-old girl.

The music of a hurdy-gurdy spilled out from between the stone teeth, mixing with the chaotic sounds the clowns were making. Silver tickets were waved in the air, but no one seemed to be collecting them, and the crowd surged into the mysterious hill without a backward glance, until the last few stragglers were swallowed up and the mighty doors began slowly to swing shut.

CHAPTER TWENTY-ONE
A MOUTHFUL OF NAILS

Baumella the giantess, straight-boned and tree-tall, began to swing the great oak doors shut after the last few people had entered the Palace of Laughter. She had spotted the two little maggots hiding in the ticket booth, yes she had, but she said nothing to anyone. She saw that one of them was the tiny girl she had looked after at the circus, and she guessed that the other might have had a hand in her disappearance. She was surprised to see them here, skulking around the Palace, and rather impressed that they had made it this far. Had they run all the way on their tiny legs? The great doors creaked as they swung closer to each other, and through the narrowing gap she could see the two little ones break cover and run for the drawbridge. They were persistent wee creatures!

She knew they could not see her in the gloom behind the doors, and she chuckled quietly. "I won't turn you in, little maggots, but I won't make it easy for you either," she thought. As they reached the drawbridge, she closed the doors—*kerlunk!*—and smiled to herself. "Let's see what you do now, little ones." She turned to the tall pillars, as cool and unbending as herself, and hauling a large chair from the shadows between them, sat herself down with her back to the great wooden doors.

Miles and Little almost ran full tilt into the hobnail-studded doors. They appeared to have been closing slowly by themselves, and Miles had timed his run to get in at the last possible moment. But they had shut more quickly at the end, or he had misjudged the distance, and now it was too late. He stood with his hands flat on the doors and pushed them with all his strength, but he may as well have been pushing at solid rock. A few flakes of yellowing paint drifted down from the huge stone teeth that lined the top of the doorway. Above the teeth stretched the faded blue lip of the laughing mouth, and above the lip a nose, with its two enormous nostrils like bear caves, jutted out into the sky. Ragged clouds raced over the clown's head, making it look as though the hill were gradually toppling forward. Miles felt dizzy. He became aware of a deep rumbling sound that seemed to be coming from inside the hill.

"There's thunder trapped in the hill," said Little. She pressed her ear to the doors, and Miles did the same. He could hear the sound more clearly now, a grinding of gears with a regular squeak running through it. Now the ground beneath their feet seemed to be tilting upward. For a moment he thought it was just the dizziness, then he realized what was happening.

"The drawbridge," he shouted. They turned and began to scramble up the wooden tongue, which was rising rapidly, getting steeper by the second. The surface was worn smooth by years of shuffling feet, making it hard to get a grip. By the time they made it to the top, the drawbridge was almost upright. Miles could see that Little was trying to shake her jacket and shirt off her shoulders when the drawbridge stopped with a mighty jolt. He barely managed to keep his balance, but Little, with one wing partly freed, tumbled from the top of the wooden tongue, down into the murky green water of the moat.

Miles hung on for a few seconds, expecting to see Little's head appear above the water. He could see a faint whiteness moving in the moat, caught in the tangled reflection of the big wheel, but she did not surface. He took a deep breath, and jumped in after her.

If you've ever been thrown into a river or a pool by someone bigger and meaner than you, you will know how it feels to be plunged into water against your will. There is the shock of the cold, and the muffled rumble of water in your ears, and a feeling that you should have had the right to choose for yourself when you are dunked into water and when you would rather remain on dry land.

This was exactly how Miles felt as he somersaulted slowly in the moat. His ears were filled with muffled sounds, and he could not tell which way was up. He forced his eyes to open. He was in a swaying underwater forest, and he could just make out the white of Little's skin among the weeds. He righted himself and swam toward her. The oversized jacket that she had been trying to shrug off when she fell had wrapped itself around her at the elbows, and her left foot was tangled in the thick stems of the weeds. She stopped struggling when she saw Miles, and looked at him with wide eyes.

He felt that his lungs would burst with the air he was trying to keep in, but there was no time to get to the surface to take a breath. He reached for his knife, then remembered that he had given it to the small boy at the Pigball match. He grabbed the weeds that were wrapped around Little's ankle as near to the roots as he could, and pulled.

The roots of the weeds were tough and the stems slimy, and they seemed to wriggle out of his grasp as though they had a life of their own. He managed to uproot some of them, and grabbed at the remaining handful. He looked up at Little's face, half afraid that he was too late. He knew that he would have to get to the surface within the next few seconds himself, or take in a lungful of murky moat water. Snowflake patterns were fizzing at the corners of his vision, and through them he could see Little, her mouth slightly open, and her stare becoming fixed. Without stopping his frantic tugging, he glanced over his shoulder in the direction of her stare, and immediately wished he hadn't.

An ugly gray-green face was staring at him from among the weeds, a face with bulging eyes, fat lips and a miserable mouthful of sharp nails. It was an enormous pike, barely an arm's length away. Now a pike is a fish best seen at the end of a long fishing line, or not at all, and certainly not when you are trying to unwrap river weeds from the ankle of a drowning friend and your next breath is long overdue. This particular fish was enormous, mean and constantly hungry. He had spent many years fattening himself on the other citizens of the moat, and he was not used to meeting anything in the water that he could not bite in half with ease. The struggling Little had caught his eye as a particularly tasty dinner, and he was not pleased that Miles had got in his way. The shock of seeing him made Miles lose his lungful of stale air in a rush of bubbles. "I've got to get to the surface now," he thought desperately, and at that moment the stubborn weeds gave way and he grabbed a handful of Little's shirt and kicked hard against the slimy floor of the moat, up toward the light.

Miles Wednesday, weed-wrapped and waterlogged, held on to a ledge of rock at the edge of the moat. As he choked and spat, he felt Little pull free from his grasp and hoist herself onto the rock. He was afraid that the pike would take a chunk out of his leg, but he did not have the strength to pull himself up beside her. When he had cleared out all the moat water from his mouth and nose, he realized that

Little was smiling down at him as though nothing had happened. She reached out a hand and helped him climb out of the water.

"You can't breathe when you're underwater, can you?" asked Little.

"Of course not!" coughed Miles. "Can you?"

"Yes, but it's not very nice. It's a bit like being in the middle of a cloud, but much thicker."

"You mean I nearly drowned getting you free and you could breathe all along?"

"Yes, I could breathe. But if you hadn't freed me from the weeds that big fish would have bitten me in half before I could find his name, and anyway I'm not sure if I could sing it underwater."

Miles leaned back against the rock face and spat out more scummy water. Now that he had recovered he could see that they had come up on the inside bank of the moat and were leaning against the gigantic cheek of the clown-shaped hill. They were on a narrow ledge, barely wide enough to lie down on, which was exactly what he wanted to do. There was still no sign of the Stinkers.

"Do you think they're gone?" asked Little, following his gaze.

"I can't see them," said Miles. "Maybe they think we drowned." He lay back and looked up at the twilit sky. "I just need to rest for a minute, then we'll figure out a way to get back across the moat."

"I could fly over, since there's no one in sight," said Little. "But my wings wouldn't carry you. Besides, why do we need to cross the moat when we want to get inside the hill, and not back on the Stinkers' side?"

"Because we can't get to the door from here," said Miles. "The ledge doesn't go around far enough." He watched the small black shapes of a number of bats darting about in erratic circles against the sky, feeding on the insects swarming around the trees that fringed the clown's giant ear. Some of the bats seemed to be flying in and out of the ear itself. "It must be where they roost," he thought. There seemed to be more of them coming out than going in. A sudden thought struck him, and he sat up. "On the other hand," he said, "maybe we should have a word in this clown's ear."

Little looked up at the ear for a minute. "It's a long way up," she said.

"It is, but it might be a way in. If it is, it will be better than trying to get through the doors unnoticed."

He stood up and examined the sheer wall of rock in front of him. The rock was relatively smooth, but here and there were small cracks and fissures, and in places tufts of heather grew from them, as though the clown were not very good at shaving. Little took a careful look around, then she removed her jacket and shirt, and tied them by their sleeves around her waist. She still wore the sparkly circus costume underneath. "You never know when it might come in handy, my dear," Lady Partridge had said.

"I'll fly up ahead of you and find the best way to climb," said Little.

Miles looked doubtful. "I'm not sure that's a good idea. Someone might see you." His eyes scanned the sagging stalls and the boarded buildings of the old fun park, but it seemed that the Stinkers had vanished into thin air. "I can't see anyone," he said at length, "but you'd better be careful."

Little nodded. She gave her shoulders a little shake, and her wings unfolded with a flutter. They were a beautiful pearly pink in the sunset, and to his surprise Miles felt his heart leap at the sight of them. He had not seen her fly since that night in the circus, and he watched with fascination, and a little envy, as she lifted from the ledge like thistledown and rose above his head. It must have felt good to be flying once again, and she let out a musical laugh as she soared up toward the giant ear, scanning the rock for a path that Miles could take.

Miles sighed, and began to climb. "Come on, slowcloud," said Little, swooping back down toward him. "Go to the right here—there's a place for your feet, and those plants just above you will hold your weight." He grabbed the tuft of heather and hauled himself up. There were not many toeholds, and for some time he inched his way up the rock with his clawed fingers and the tips of his boots. The moat was a long way below him now, but as he neared the top of the clown's fat cheek, it began to slope inward a little more. He could see the huge earlobe almost level with him, and he edged slowly to his right until he could reach it. As he scrambled into the ear's hollow one of his bootlaces snapped and the boot made a break for freedom, bouncing off the stone cheek as it tumbled downward, and finally kicking off a sharp point of rock and splashing into the dark waters of the moat below.

Miles sat in the huge ear, which was smooth and hollow and comfortable, waiting for his breath to return. He unlaced his other boot with his bleeding fingers, and tossed it after its twin. He was about level with the hub of the big wheel. A small knot of figures was inching up one of the spokes. It looked like two of the Stinkers, carrying Henry between them as they climbed. They were too far away for him to see clearly, and with their backs turned, it was not likely they would see Little. He called to her urgently nonetheless, and she fluttered down beside him and tucked her wings away.

"That was good," she said. "I'm sorry you had to climb."

Miles shrugged casually, "It wasn't that difficult," he lied.

He stood up and looked into the dark cave of the ear. The ceiling of the cave was alive with bats, crawling over one another and squeaking like pram wheels. Miles clicked his tongue to listen to the echo. It sounded like the cave went back a long way. He took a few steps into the darkness, the smooth stone cold under his bare feet. His outstretched hands touched nothing.

"I don't suppose you can see in the dark as well?" he said over his shoulder to Little.

"Not very well. I once got lost in a stormcloud, and everyone laughed at me for days." She followed a few paces and bumped into Miles's back.

"I believe you," he laughed. He wondered how they could make a light. The wick of his brass lighter would be soaked with moat water. "We'll just have to go slowly. It can't be dark everywhere in this hill."

They moved cautiously onward through the pitch darkness, Miles in front with his hands out, and Little hanging on to the tail of his jacket—possibly the only two people in history ever to have been swallowed by an ear.

Outside this strangest of hills, night had swiftly fallen. In the old broken-down stalls with their faded canvas, String was lurking in the shadows, thinking over the things he had just seen. An entrance in the clown's ear, and stranger by far, a girl with wings, who rightfully belonged to him. He would have won her if the pez hadn't cheated in the fight. He did not really want to go back to the Halfheads of course. That had just been a ruse to lure Miles into his trap, and he knew in any case that they would never have him back. But imagine what he could do if he had a scout that could fly! He could become a legend among the Stinkers, among all the gangs. Someday he would be chief Stinker himself. He thought about these things, and he looked at the darkening waters of the moat with a shiver. He steered clear of water whenever he could, and in all his twelve years he could not remember once having a bath. "You won't catch me going in there," he said to himself. "I'll have to try my chances at the front door tomorrow. If that fool Jook is right, they won't be coming out anytime soon."

And so Miles and Little crept deeper into the darkness of the Palace of Laughter, while down below in the watery gloom the nail-toothed mayor of the moat took a bite out of the worn leather boot that had half buried itself in the mud, and chewed it for as long as he could. It was the worst thing he had ever tasted, and he thought with regret of the nice, wriggling white snack he dimly remembered seeing earlier, and spat out the mouthful of tough, smelly leather in disgust.

CHAPTER TWENTY-TWO

BACK TO FRONT AND INSIDE OUT

Miles Wednesday, barefoot and bearless, stopped for a moment and listened. His eyes were smarting from the effort of staring into nothingness, and he had stubbed his toes several times. He had been imagining a faint sound for some time, and now he was sure that it was real, but it was still too far off to hear clearly. The tunnel had begun to rise steadily, and the sound seemed to cascade down toward them like waves breaking against a distant beach.

"Do you hear that?" he asked Little.

"Yes," said Little. "It makes me shiver." She untied her shirt and jacket from her waist and struggled back into them in the narrow tunnel.

Miles strained his ears, but the sound was no more than a faint rushing. "Why does it make you shiver?"

"I don't know," said Little. "There's something strange in it, but I can't hear well enough yet."

They continued through the darkness. A draft of cold air followed them deeper into the hill, and Miles guessed that they were in some sort of air vent. At one point the tunnel became so steep that it was easier to crawl, then suddenly the ground fell away beneath them and began to descend just as steeply. They reached a point where the distant sound became noticeably clearer. It was a strange music, jangly and discordant, and it was coming from somewhere to their right.

"There's another tunnel joining this one," said Miles. He could faintly see a circle of light. "We'll follow the music."

"I don't like it," said Little. "It's . . . back to front and inside out."

Miles listened again. It was certainly unlike any music he had heard before. There were gongs and flutes and other sounds he couldn't name. Somewhere in the middle was a hurdy-gurdy. The notes seemed to fight with one another, and the rhythm would now rush onward like a strong current, then catch so suddenly that you felt like you had come to a cliff with no time to stop. It made the hair stand up on Miles's scalp, yet it was also strangely funny. He shook his head as though emptying water from his ears, and entered the tunnel. "Come on," he said. "It's only music, and music can't hurt us."

The new tunnel was smaller than the one they had come from, and they had to crawl. There were more openings branching off now. At one point they passed over hollow-sounding wood, as though there might be a trapdoor in the tunnel floor. Now each turn they took brought a little more light, and the music grew stronger until it seemed to be drawing them toward it like an invisible rope.

Suddenly the music rose to a nerve-jangling crescendo and abruptly stopped. Miles and Little stopped too. Silence washed along the tunnel, followed by a voice that was at once familiar and different. It took Miles a moment to identify it as the smooth voice of the Great Cortado. It sounded louder and deeper than it had during his brief job interview in Cortado's trailer. It was impossible to tell how close or how far away it was. He sat back against the tunnel wall and listened. Little was still too. She seemed relieved that the music had paused.

". . . your Immense Privilege to witness the most spec-tac-u-lar, the most Fan-tas-tical, the most Hil-lar-ious Ex-travaganza of Laughter ever performed," the voice was booming. " . . . Ladies, Gentlemen, Lords and Laddies, Sages and Peasants and Persons of Superfluous Learning, it is my Pleasure and Delight to present for you this ver-ry night the Funniest, the Wittiest, the most Side-splitting troupe of Fools, Funnymen, Boobs and Bobos, Tumblers and Tricky-Dicks that has ever been assembled in one place since Cortez presented his Hunchbacked Aztec Buffoons to Pope Clement the Seventh."

With a roll of drums, a clash of cymbals and the boom of a mighty gong that sounded more in the chest than the ears, the crazy cacophony started anew, twirling itself like a musical vine around the closing lines of the Great Cortado's introduction: "Tonight, Ladies and Gentlemen, be prepared to be entertained as you have never been entertained before! Tonight the greatest comics in the Wide World will take you Beyond Laughter, and your Lives will be Transformed, FOREVER!"

The music raced and plunged like a wild thing, accompanied by squeaks and shrill whistles that seemed to be hanging on to the music by their teeth. Miles laughed at the sound, despite himself.

He began to crawl toward it, but the music seemed to be coming from everywhere at once, and it was difficult to decide which route to take. The swell of laughter added itself to the sound—a great crowd of people laughing at something that was hidden from view. He had to find a vantage point from which he could see this fabulous show. He forgot his bleeding fingers and his stubbed toes, and the clammy chill of his moat-drenched clothes, his mind drawn by the hypnotic music and the waves of laughter that followed it. This, he imagined, would be more like the picture he had first had of the Palace of Laughter, and he felt an overwhelming urge to see for himself the greatest clowns on Earth. The thought of Tangerine slipped into his mind, and he brushed it aside impatiently. There was no point searching for Tangerine while the show was in full swing, he told himself, better to wait until the people had left and the place was quiet. They were nearly there now, he could tell.

"Miles!" called Little from behind. "Wait for me." He glanced over his shoulder. Little's face looked worried and anxious. "What was the matter with her?" he thought irritably. She could find something to laugh at in a cow or a fence post, but now that they were about to witness the funniest show on Earth, she looked as if she were lost on the way to a funeral.

"Just hurry up, will you?" he called. "You're always slowing me down."

His voice sounded sharper than he had meant it to, but they seemed to have been crawling in circles forever, and the show was going on without him. The strange acoustics of the tunnels made the sound confusing. Sometimes it seemed as if people were choking or wailing, then he would turn a corner and it would sound like hysterical laughter again. Little was no longer complaining. She followed him silently, and when he looked back at her he could not read her expression.

The tunnel they were in began to slope downward gently. He turned a corner, and suddenly there was bright light ahead, and the sound became almost deafening. He crawled cautiously to the tunnel mouth and found himself looking out into a huge theater of some sort, hollowed out of solid rock in the center of the hill, from a vantage point high on the wall. Above him was a domed ceiling, supported by a circle of massive pillars that were carved from bottom to top with curling vines and strange animals. Just below the tunnel mouth a stone ledge, shaped like a seashell, jutted from the wall, and he dropped down onto it and lay flat on his stomach, peering over the edge.

The roar of laughter washed over him. Some sixty feet below him he could see an enormous circus ring in the center of the floor, surrounded by banks of stone seats that were packed with people. Miles could see the crowd and the ring through a gantry of bars, pulleys and ropes, suspended from the ceiling at the level of his balcony. The gantry supported rows of spotlights, wired together with cables so frayed and tangled that they looked like the work of Fowler Pinchbucket. One spotlight hung just in front of him, and several ropes were fastened within his reach, each one bound at the end with a different-colored tape. Sandbags of various sizes dangled from the ends of some of the ropes as counterweights to the props and lights. Little dropped down softly and squeezed onto the narrow space beside him, and together they peered through the gaps in this tangle of metal and rope to get the best view of the performance.

Watching a group of people from almost directly above—through a network of bars, cables and spotlights—can make it very difficult to piece together exactly what they are doing. There appeared to be about twenty clowns on the stage at the same time. He caught a glimpse of the three small clowns with the different-colored noses. They were trying to oil an elephant's knees with a large grease can. They kept grabbing the can from one another, and slipping and sliding on the spilled grease. The crowd sat in banked circles around the ring, mouths open and tears streaming from their red-rimmed eyes. Miles had never seen people laugh so hard. The sound of it was so infectious that he began to laugh himself.

The ring was full of chaotic movement, but from their vantage point it was almost impossible to make out what was going on. All the time the music looped and raced and clattered around the auditorium like an invisible beast running laps around the walls. The men in the audience guffawed and honked, and the ladies screeched and whinnied. The more he looked at them, the less sure he was that they were really enjoying themselves. It was hard to tell from so high up, but he thought he could see fear in their eyes.

The look of anxiety had left Little's face. She was laughing at something that he could not see. There was something unfamiliar about the sound of her laughter, but he was so distracted by the music, and the little he could see of what was happening below, that he couldn't put his finger on it. Instead he found himself laughing with her. The audience roared. Some seemed to have developed a sort of lockjaw, their mouths fixed open so wide that they could no longer close them. One red-faced woman was cackling so hard that she toppled forward into the ring. Her husband leaned forward to look at her, but seemed unable to help. He slumped back in his seat, clutching his stomach and crying with laughter. The guffawing face of the priest behind him had turned the color of a ripe plum, and his eyes were fixed on the center of the ring as though they were glued in their sockets.

Miles turned his attention back to the ring. Through a triangular gap he could just see a pale-faced clown sitting cross-legged in the sawdust in front of an enormous pie and clutching an oversized knife and fork. He had a straight back and a calm expression, and sat in the center of that whirlwind of hysteria like the eye of a storm. He was dressed in an outfit that was so white it seemed to glow, and wore a very tall chef's hat, as tall again as himself. Suddenly a ragged clown on a unicycle appeared and rode straight through the center of the pie, hotly pursued by the three tiny clowns, now dressed like undertakers in long black tailcoats and top hats, who trampled what was left of it into the ground. The chef clown leaped to his feet. A small blue bolt of lightning shot from his outstretched finger toward the last of the tailcoated clowns. It hit his top hat fair and square, and the hat flew from his head and burst into flames. The crowd shrieked. Little gave a gasp and grabbed Miles's arm, and Miles knew at once that this must be Silverpoint.

CHAPTER TWENTY-THREE
TOP HAT AND SANDBAG

Miles Wednesday, bootless and buttonless, craned his neck to try and get a better look at Silverpoint. He had marched off in pursuit of the little top-hatted clowns and Miles could no longer see him. Little still held tight to his arm. She was biting her lip.

The music spiraled faster and faster, higher and higher, until it was almost a continuous shriek. In the middle of the ring, a clown dressed as a tramp jumped up from under a sheet of newspaper he had been using as a blanket. The ground beneath him began to shake. He picked up his little white dog with a comical wail and ran hotfoot for the edge of the ring. A trapdoor burst open in a cloud of green and purple smoke, right at the spot where he had been lying a moment before. All over the ring, clowns stopped their hammering and honking and squirting and cartwheeling, and turned as one to face the opening trapdoor. From the fog of colored smoke a figure rose slowly out of the ground. Miles could just make out the outline of a man sitting on a sort of throne. The hysterical bellowing of the crowd began to subside into a babble of groans and gasps. Some had fallen silent with their mouths still stuck open. Every eye in the theater was fixed on the throne.

The throne rose on a pillar of steel. It was midnight blue, and on its high back was painted the same laughing clown's face that was on the side of the Great Cortado's wagon, the same face into which the very hill itself had been carved. Looking down on it now, Miles could see it in a different light. The wide-open mouth looked ready to devour anyone or anything that came near, and there was danger in the staring eyes. Seated beneath that manic face was the Great Cortado himself. As the throne reached its full height, he stood up (which didn't make a great deal of difference, it has to be said) and began to speak in the same deep, hypnotic tones with which he had introduced the show. There was no "Ladies and Gentlemen" this time, no "Immense Privileges," no flowery introduction at all. This time the Great Cortado got straight down to business.

"Now you have felt the true power of laughter," he said. **"Elemental laughter, that has reached deep down into the center of your being and cracked you open like a tree root cracks a rock."** The audience stared. Their mouths hung open. Miles spotted Genghis sitting at the back, his arms folded and his mouth very definitely shut. His eyes roamed around the stupefied audience, and his face wore a smug look. Miles tried to see his pockets, as though he might catch a glimpse of Tangerine's grubby head peeping out, but it was too far, and too dark, and there were too many things in the way. As though awaking from a dream, he remembered what he was doing here, and he missed the feel of the bear in his pocket more than he could ever have imagined.

"Now you know the weakness of humanity," the Great Cortado continued in a quieter voice. "The debilitating millstone of laughter that hangs around the neck of the human race. Neither beast nor fish nor fowl carries this flaw. It is a cruel trap that nature has made for man alone, for it comes uninvited and saps the strength of whoever is afflicted by it. It distracts and confuses the mind and lies like a thick fog across the path of progress."

The crowd soaked up his poisoned words like blotting paper. Their jaws were slack, their eyes were glazed, and everything the Great Cortado said went in one ear and stayed there.

"Tonight," he continued, his voice growing stronger, "**you have finally been set free. With the help of our unparalleled entertainment, you have emptied your souls of every last drop of useless laughter. When you leave this place you will remember nothing of what you have seen, yet so complete is our treatment that you will be cured of laughter forever!**"

His voice was as smooth as polished stone and as rich as chocolate, and the audience listened without a murmur. Miles, perched in his balcony, could not help thinking that the Great Cortado's words made a certain sense. Now that the music and the performance had abruptly stopped, he could not quite remember what the point of laughter was, or why it had always seemed such a missing element in his Pinchbucket House childhood. Yet moments earlier he too had been laughing at the mere fractured glimpses he could catch of the performance. He felt confused and a little light-headed, and he shook his head as though to clear it. He knew that there was something twisted about the Great Cortado's words as they wrapped themselves around his thoughts like a snake.

He leaned out from the balcony to see if he could spot Silverpoint. A large sandbag of yellowing canvas blocked his view. It hung from a pulley just above Miles, on the end of a rope that stretched out from the center of the gantry. He felt the weight of the sandbag as he tried to push it to one side, and this gave him an idea. He looked at the point where it appeared the far end of the rope was tied. He looked down at the Great Cortado, and he made a quick calculation. The little man seemed to be nearing the end of his speech.

"Ladies and Gentlemen," he was saying, **"I, the Great Cortado, have finally got laughter on the ropes. With the help of the learned Dr. Tau-Tau, I have tamed it and bottled it. If ever you find yourself with the foolish inclination to indulge in this intoxicating waste of time, you may purchase it by the bottle (ten cents from all reputable dealers), and cork it when you are done. Collect your free sample on the way out. Thank you for coming."**

Miles reached up and began to pry the taut rope over the rim of the pulley wheel. Little looked at him, and her eyes widened. "Are you sure . . . ," she began, but she never finished what she was about to say. The rope came free with a sound that would have to be spelled *"Thungg,"* if it could be written down at all. The bag dropped like a stone, then swung out in a long and graceful arc across the huge auditorium. The Great Cortado was still standing on his throne with his arms outstretched like a letter "Y," and the heavy sandbag was swishing through the air, aiming straight for his head. There was no doubt about it. Little held her breath, and Miles held his. He had time to wonder, as the sandbag curved through the air in slow motion, if this was his most brilliant idea yet, or whether it was an act of foolishness that would have consequences more terrible than any he could possibly foresee.

At the very moment the Great Cortado caught sight of the approaching sandbag, the raised throne jerked into motion and began its descent back into the floor. The sandbag whistled over Cortado's head, ruffling his hair as it passed. He looked up in surprise as it swung over to the other side of the theater and up, up into the spidery gloom among the bars and wires. It reached the top of its swing and punched the glass out of a large yellow spotlight. The yellow glass rained down in a sparkling shower. Most of it landed behind the outer row of people, but one piece fell, as though it had been given precise directions, and stuck itself into the back of Genghis's right hand, already bandaged where it had been scratched by a cat and bitten by Miles himself. Genghis jumped up with a roar. The stupefied people sitting around him did not even turn their heads.

The sight of Genghis hopping around and holding his injured hand distracted Miles for a moment, but the sandbag was on its way back to him. It curved back across the auditorium, spinning now from its impact with the spotlight, and sailing well over the head of the Great Cortado, whose throne was sinking rapidly into its trapdoor.

As it passed over the ring, the three small clowns in their top hats and tails watched it closely. Suddenly the clown with the green nose hopped up onto the shoulders of his two companions, and without a word or a signal they tossed him high in the air, as though releasing a racing pigeon. Although the circus band had fallen silent, the drummer was unable to contain himself, and began a long roll on the snare drum. Green Nose somersaulted twice and landed on the sandbag as it flew past, grasping it with his legs and flinging his top hat into the air with a shrill blast on his whistle. The drumroll ended with a clash of cymbals. The audience stared, but did not laugh. They seemed to have forgotten how. Genghis watched from below, glaring and sucking his knuckles. The trapdoor in the floor swallowed the Great Cortado, throne and all.

So quickly did all this happen that Miles didn't know what to do. The sandbag that he had released had failed to connect with the Great Cortado's head, and now it was on its way back to him, complete with a small wiry man in a funeral suit and a green nose. If he scrambled to his feet he would be in plain view of Genghis and the other clowns. If he stayed where he was he would be a sitting duck.

"Get back from the edge," he whispered urgently to Little, but he himself seemed to be glued to the spot. The little man was getting closer by the second. The drummer had fallen silent.

When he remembered afterward what had happened, it always seemed to Miles that this part had been a dream. As the clown on the sandbag approached the balcony, Miles could see him in sharp detail. His head was covered in black curls that shone like raven's feathers. He had wide, green-painted lips that matched his nose, and bushy black whiskers on either side of his whitewashed face. His glinting eyes were like tiny black olives. The sandbag slowed as it drew level with the balcony, and Miles found himself inches away from the small clown, who was suspended in midair, waiting for gravity to recover its grip. Suddenly he reached out, quick as lightning, and pinched Miles's nose hard with his bony fingers. His mouth opened in a grin of little pointed teeth, and he said something that sounded like "Ommadawn!" Then before Miles could even say "Ouch" he was gone.

CHAPTER TWENTY-FOUR
SILVERPOINT

Miles Wednesday, light-headed and nose-pinched, stared in disbelief at the retreating figure of the clown riding the sandbag like a Wild West cowboy. The clown spun with the sandbag, and whistled as he spun, and all at once he let go. Just like that. He curled into a ball as he fell, and hit the middle of a waiting trampoline as though he had been doing it all his life, which indeed he had. As he bounced high in the air the unicycle wobbled past with his two brothers perched on it, one on the other's shoulders. Green Nose landed on top, and the three clowns did a lap of honor around the ring.

The audience stared, glassy-eyed. They were

wiping their mouths with their sleeves, and patting their pockets as though they had forgotten something, but couldn't remember what it was. The red-faced woman had picked herself up from the ring and was brushing sawdust from her rumpled skirt. Behind her the priest hitched up his black trousers and tucked in his black shirt, and the thin man beside him straightened his tie and ran his fingers back through his floppy hair. They all seemed somehow grayer than they had been before.

Genghis was talking to Silverpoint and a clown dressed as a tramp with a downturned mouth. He pointed up at the balcony where Miles was hidden, then turned and moved out of view. The other clowns led the people out through the doors that stood at intervals around the theater. A stilt-walking clown stalked among the shuffling people with a tin megaphone. "Don't forget to collect your free gift on the way out," he was calling in a pinched voice. The clowns were still in their bizarre outfits, but now as straightfaced as undertakers, all except for Red Nose, Yellow Nose and Green Nose. They had jumped off the unicycle and were helping to herd the audience out, but there was a skip in their step. Now and then one would steal another's hat or do a quick cartwheel, as though they couldn't help it.

The theater was almost empty now. Miles sat up and found that Little was gone. He looked up at the mouth of the tunnel. "Little?" he said. Her head poked out of the hole.

"Just hurry up, will you?" she said. He recognized his own words and smiled sheepishly as he scrambled into the tunnel mouth. Little was waiting for him inside.

"We have to find a way to speak to him," she whispered.

"To the Great Cortado?" said Miles

"No, to Silverpoint. We have to find out what he's doing here."

"I don't think that would be a good idea. He might just bring us to Cortado," said Miles.

Little looked at Miles as though she had been slapped. "You don't know him!" she said. "Silverpoint could never do anything like that."

"But you saw him. He was right in the thick of things. He can hear the Great Cortado just the same as us, and he knows what's going on."

"It doesn't matter. If he's doing it, he must have a good reason."

"Maybe he has," said Miles, "but we will have to be very careful." He could see that it had come as a shock to Little that Silverpoint was taking part in the Great Cortado's scheme, and he didn't want to upset her any further.

"Little . . . ," he said.

She looked at him, her eyebrows raised. Miles searched for the words. He had never been very good at apologies.

"I wasn't very nice to you earlier," he said. "I'm sorry."

Little smiled at him in the gloom. "Forget it," she said. "There is bad music going on here. It turned your soul for a while. I could feel it too."

"It was just music," said Miles.

"There's no such thing as 'just music,'" said Little. "Trust me. Now we have to find a way out of these tunnels. There are so many of them we could be lost in here forever."

"I think we crossed over a trapdoor on our way in," said Miles. "That must lead somewhere."

They went back the way they had come, making the steep climb at the start of the tunnel with difficulty. There was no sound now, except for their own breathing and the shuffling of their hands and knees on the stone floor. Miles found that the way back was easier to find if he didn't think about it too hard and just went with his instinct. The tunnels twisted and turned until he began to feel as though he had been swallowed by a giant snake. Some trick of acoustics made the sound of Little's breathing seem louder by the minute, and Miles had the uncomfortable sensation that she was getting heavier and larger at the same time. A panicky feeling was growing in his stomach. "Are you okay?" he called.

"I'm okay," said Little, "but I think somebody's following us."

A chuckle followed them down the dark tunnel. "She's right you know. Got it in one. Bang on the nail! The cat's on yer tails, little mouses." It was a man's voice with a nasal sound, as though its owner had one of those nasty sore throats that make it difficult to speak.

"Go faster," hissed Miles. Terrified as he was, he would have preferred to let Little get in front, but the tunnel was narrow, and he was afraid that they would simply get jammed.

"Faster, he says," came the voice from behind him. It was getting closer. "Faster's no good. Better if yiz stop now and make it easier on all of us. Well, easier on me anyhow. I reckon youse two are dog meat either way."

Miles could feel his chest tighten. He was sure that they should have reached the trapdoor by now.

"Keep with me," he called to Little.

"I'm right here," panted Little.

"Me too, little mouses!" chuckled the man's voice. "Right behind yiz."

Thunka thunka thunk went Miles's hands and knees on the wooden boards. He was moving so fast that he was over the trapdoor before he realized it. "Stop there," he hissed to Little as he squeezed himself around in the narrow tunnel. His fingers scrabbled around the edges of the trapdoor until they felt a smooth brass ring. He yanked at it. Nothing happened. He took a deep breath and pulled again, but the door was stuck fast with time and dirt. "Hurry," said Little.

Miles wished the tiger could have come with them into the dark tunnels. The memory of the smooth power of the animal's muscles working effortlessly beneath him seemed to fill his tired arms with new strength, and he heaved at the trapdoor again. This time there was an unsticking sound, the trapdoor lifted, and light flooded up into the tunnel.

"Gotcha, little mousey " shouted the nasal voice. Little squealed and reached out for Miles across the open trapdoor. Half blinded by the light from below, he could just make out the battered hat and downturned white mouth of the tramp clown behind her in the tunnel, holding on to her ankle. Miles leaned forward and grabbed Little's outstretched hand. He pulled as hard as he could. The man holding her ankles was taken by surprise. He lost his balance and fell forward through the open mouth of the trapdoor, but he did not let go of Little's ankle, and a moment later all three were out of the tunnel and tumbling through the air. Miles did not have time to see what was below them before the boy, the clown and the angel landed in a heap on the floor.

Unfortunately for the clown, it was he who landed first. Fortunately for Miles and Little, the clown was heavily padded in his tramp's outfit, and it was almost like landing on a rather lumpy sofa. The clown said, "UFFFFF," and lay winded on the floor. Miles grabbed Little's hand again and jumped to his feet, ready to get a good head start before the clown could regain his breath. He turned to see which way offered the best chance of escape, and found himself face to face with Silverpoint.

They were in a long corridor that curved away into the distance in both directions. It was lit at intervals by gas lamps. Now that his eyes were becoming accustomed to the light, Miles could see that in fact the lamps were rather dim. Silverpoint stood right in front of them. Even without the ludicrously tall chef's hat, bent sideways by the ceiling, Miles would have had no trouble guessing that this was the Storm Angel they had been searching for. He was slightly taller than Miles and, forgetting for a moment that he had lived for a millennium or more, looked just slightly older too. His face was pale, almost white, with a thin, straight nose and eyes so dark it was hard to tell if they had any color. He watched as Miles and Little picked themselves up off the floor, much as an eagle might watch rabbits far below him.

"Well done," he said, and Miles realized he was talking not to them, but to the tramp clown, who had picked himself up and stood panting behind them.

A smile lit up Little's face. "Silverpoint!" she said. Miles gripped her arm, but she did not seem to notice.

Silverpoint looked at her coolly, with no sign of recognition. "There is no Silverpoint," he said.

Little opened her mouth to speak, but Miles squeezed her arm tighter. The smile faded from her face, and she looked down at the floor. "You're hurting my arm," she said quietly.

Silverpoint turned his gaze to Miles, looking him straight in the face for longer than most people feel is comfortable. Miles stared back, determined not to be the first to look away.

"Come," said Silverpoint at last. He turned on his heel and marched down the corridor, his hat swishing against the ceiling. The tramp clown gave them both a shove from behind, but they would have followed anyway. They had, after all, come to this place to find Silverpoint (and Tangerine, of course), and besides, there seemed to be little option. As they walked, Miles looked at Little out of the corner of his eye. She was fighting back the tears.

"We'll get to the bottom of this," he whispered.

"What does that mean?" she whispered back.

"It means . . . we'll find the answer," he said.

"Oh," said Little.

The corridor ended in a pair of elevator gates, with the darkness of the elevator shaft beyond them. Silverpoint pushed the brass button, and the cables shuddered to life with a grinding sound inside the shaft. A rectangular stack of iron weights, coated with a layer of grease and dust, slid past them slowly on its way down. The cables continued to move and the grinding grew louder, and still the elevator did not come.

"Where are you taking us?" asked Miles.

"Down," said Silverpoint.

The tramp clown, who had been so talkative in the dark tunnel, seemed to have dried up in Silverpoint's presence. It was not hard to see why. Silverpoint, even though he looked like a boy of eleven or twelve, had the air of a person whom you would not question lightly. He folded his arms and looked at Miles again, a slight frown on his face. He no longer seemed to notice Little at all.

The ornate brass roof of the elevator came into view, and the grinding stopped as the cage drew level with the floor. They entered and Silverpoint closed the doors after them. Now that they were jammed together in a confined space it became clear that the tramp clown took his disguise very seriously, right down to the smell. Standing close behind him, Miles was reminded of the smell that used to lurk behind the big dirty steam-cleaning machines in the Pinchbucket laundry, with a hint of old fish heads and a dash of ditch water thrown in. He wondered if the clown had been a Stinker when he was younger. Little nudged him. She was pinching her nose and squinting her eyes. Miles laughed before he could stop himself, and he saw Silverpoint glance at Little in surprise before turning his face away.

Floor after floor slid up past them, and sometimes coils of thick steel cable looped up outside the elevator like snakes seeking the higher branches of a tree, and still the elevator continued its descent.

Little stood on her toes and whispered in Miles's ear, "Is this what you meant by getting to the bottom of this?"

"Not exactly," said Miles.

Down and down they went, and still the tramp clown shuffled and stank, and Silverpoint's dark eyes stared at something distant that only he could see.

CHAPTER TWENTY-FIVE

A BOX OF STARS

Miles Wednesday, underfed, underground and undeterred, sat beside his four-hundred-year-old friend on a wooden bench, deep beneath the Palace of Laughter. The room they were in had once been a dressing room of some sort. There were faded blue stars painted on the crumbling ceiling. On the wall opposite him was a cracked and fly-spotted mirror, surrounded by singed light sockets. All but three of the sockets were empty, and of the three remaining bulbs only one worked. The room had a sad, abandoned feel.

"You'll get food and water later," Silverpoint had said as he showed them into their makeshift cell.

"What will happen to us?" said Miles.

"Nothing at all, little mouses," said the tramp clown, finding his tongue again. "You'll just get front-row seats to a nice show. Maybe you'll even get popcorn!" He sniggered and wiped his nose on his sleeve as he left the room. Silverpoint said nothing. Without another glance at his captives he locked the door, leaving them with the silence and the dim yellow light from the lone bulb.

They sat on the bench, listening to the fading footsteps of the tramp clown (only now did Miles notice that Silverpoint's feet made no sound). Little stared at the painted stars on the ceiling.

"Why would people make a box underground, then paint the sky on it?" she asked. Looking away from the fading stars, she reached into her pocket and carefully took out the flower that she had picked beside the stream while the tiger was fishing for trout. It was still as bright and fresh as the moment it was picked, despite all it must have been through in the pocket of her jacket. She twirled the stem in her hands and looked thoughtfully into the heart of the flower. "I thought when we found Silverpoint everything would be okay," she said.

Miles could think of nothing to say at that moment that would make their situation seem brighter. “We'll just have to see what happens next,” he said. It did not sound like much of a plan. He began emptying his pockets onto the bench. This is what he found:

- The end of a piece of sausage, soaked in slimy moat water
- A brass lighter
- A ticket to the Palace of Laughter, which seemed unharmed by its soaking
- An empty bottle of Dr. Tau-Tau's Restorative Tonic
- The long coil of rope that he had cut from around Little's waist when they reached his barrel
- No Tangerine

It was not much of an escape kit. He had given away his pocketknife, and had long since lost the heavy bunch of keys he had stolen from the Great Cortado's wagon. He pulled out an old hairpin that was wedged behind a corner of the mirror, and went to the door to see if he could pick the lock. A brass plate had been screwed over the keyhole on the inside, and without his pocketknife he had no way to try and loosen the screws. Under its flaking pink paint the wooden door was solid.

Little was looking at the bottle that he had fished from the stream. "What do the words say?" she asked. Miles read the label aloud, and Little shook her head sadly.

"This is not good," she said. "Laughter is a strand of the One Song. It's one of the strongest and brightest, but it lives in harmony with the others. If you tear it out and put it in a bottle, it becomes something else."

She put the bottle down and stared up again at the bogus sky. "That can't be the real Silverpoint." She turned to look at Miles. "Silverpoint is a longfeather. He commands the clouds and drives the wind before him. How could he become a clownmaster's lackey?"

"I don't know," said Miles. He searched for something he could say that would offer a glimmer of hope. "Perhaps he just couldn't show that he knew you in front of the other clown."

Little shook her head. "You were right, in the tunnel. He doesn't even know me."

Miles sat down beside her on the bench. There was nothing they could do, locked in a room far underground. He searched for something to distract her. "Tell me more about what it's like where you come from," he said.

Little closed her eyes again, and leaned back against the wall. "I don't have the words to tell it," she said. "But I'll try."

Miles began to clean the mixture of dirt and moat slime from under his fingernails with the hairpin. This is probably not the politest thing you can do when someone is about to tell you about a world of harsh beauty that is almost beyond your imagination, but Miles had never had much training in manners at Pinchbucket House. Little, at any rate, did not seem to mind. As Miles scraped and flicked, she spoke of her home in the sky.

"I come from a place called the Realm," she began. "It's a place that is never still. Our palaces and halls rise and fall, they grow and move and melt away with the turning of the Earth and with the flow of the wind. You could think of them as ships, but even ships don't join together and break apart as they sail."

"You're talking about clouds!" said Miles. "Are your palaces clouds?"

"That's how they appear to you," said Little.

"If I could go up inside a cloud in a hot-air balloon, would I see more people like you?"

Little shook her head. "You would see nothing but gray mist and half-light."

"Why wouldn't I see them, if they're there?"

Little leaned forward and put her chin in her hands. "Remember the water we saw on the road, walking out of Larde?"

"You mean the mirage?" said Miles.

"We saw water," said Little firmly, "but when we reached it, we saw nothing. It's the same thing with the cloud palaces. Some things are only seen when they want to be."

Miles thought about this for a minute. He could see no point in discussing the nature of mirages again with Little. Besides, he had another question, one that had been lurking at the back of his mind for some time. He was almost reluctant to raise the subject, but the question would not go away.

"Little," he said, "who was that . . . person who followed us in the city?"

"I don't know, exactly," said Little quietly.

"Was it the same person who we saw in the circus field?" asked Miles.

"Yes," said Little. "I mean no." She sighed. "It's hard to explain."

Miles tried a different tack. "Why did I feel so tired when we saw him?" he asked.

Little looked about her, as though someone else might be listening in the tiny, bare room.

"What you saw," she said, "was a Sleep Angel."

"A Sleep Angel?" echoed Miles. "Is that bad?"

Little nodded. "Most people will meet a Sleep Angel only once, and that's a meeting you shouldn't be in a hurry to keep. It's a Sleep Angel who will carry your last breath from you and release it on the wind."

Miles was silent. The room seemed strangely still. He pulled his jacket around him, although the air was stuffy and warm.

"Why was he following us?" asked Miles. He was not sure he wanted to know.

"I don't know why," said Little. "I shouldn't even speak of this—it's not allowed. I'm in enough trouble already." Their meeting with Silverpoint seemed to have washed away her confidence. She looked small and frightened again, as he had first seen her in the locked trailer. "He must be looking for Silverpoint."

"Why did we run from him, then? Maybe he could have helped us."

Little looked at him as though he were crazy.

"Sleep Angels are the highest caste there is. At least the highest I know of. Sleep Angels look after Life and Death. They don't normally make up search parties." She stared unseeingly at the floor between her feet. "If he's looking for Silverpoint, something is wrong."

"Maybe he's a friend," said Miles.

Little laughed. In the tiny room the shine seemed to have gone from her laughter, and somehow it just made Miles feel sad.

"Friendship is an idea that lives down here," she said. "Where I come from there is duty and loyalty. I suppose loyalty is a friendship of sorts, but everyone knows their place in the Realm. It's not a Sleep Angel's place to concern himself with someone from a lower caste."

Miles thought about this for a moment. "Are there many castes of Angels?" he asked.

"Of course! There are Wind Angels, Whitefire Angels, and many others." She seemed glad to leave the topic of the Sleep Angel.

"Whitefire Angels?" said Miles. "What do they do?"

"They draw a map of the One Song on the dome of the night. The map grows and changes as each Song Angel's part is sung. Without it, the Song Angels would lose their way, and the One Song would eventually come undone and all life would be scattered to the darkness. The stars are the crossing points of the Whitefire Map, where the strands of the One Song join each other."

"But the stars are billions of miles away," said Miles. "You couldn't reach them in a hundred lifetimes!"

Little smiled. "The stars are a living map on the dome of the night. I know this because I have helped to sing them into place for as long as I can remember."

Miles's head was beginning to swim. He was not sure whether it was from hunger or the strange notions that Little was releasing in the dimness of the small room.

"I got all my schooling from Lady Partridge," he said. "She has books full of the knowledge of men who have studied these things for centuries. Clouds are made of water vapor. The stars are suns like ours, so far away that their light is millions of years old when it reaches us. Are you telling me all these things are wrong?"

"No," said Little. She twirled the flower she had taken from her pocket, then held it out for Miles to take a closer look. The petals were yellow at the center, merging to a deep scarlet at their pointed tips.

"Look at this," she said. "What would you call it?"

"I don't know the name of it," said Miles. "It's a yellow flower with red tips."

"Isn't it a red flower with a yellow center?" asked Little.

"I suppose so. You could call it either."

"Then just because something is one thing doesn't mean it can't be another," said Little.

Miles thought about this for a while. It was hard to get his head around it all. He closed his eyes, which made things a little easier. Fat galleons of cloud began to sail through the blue night of his mind's eye. He could see stars winking between them, some closer than the clouds, some farther away. The picture gave him a feeling that everything was working as it should be in the universe, like a well-made clock with many parts. It made him smile.

He dozed fitfully on the hard bench. How long he slept he could not tell, but he was almost sorry when his dreams were interrupted by the muffled jingle of keys outside the door of their makeshift cell.

His stomach, however, was not a bit sorry. As far as he could tell, it was early morning by now, which made it nearly twenty-four hours since they had eaten. "I hope this is food," he said to Little.

A key turned in the lock with a soft click, and before he had time to wonder who might be outside, the door began to swing open.

CHAPTER TWENTY-SIX
THE ELECTRIC BOY

Silverpoint, pale-faced and long-feathered, stepped into the room in the early hours of the morning, his tall hat sweeping the faded stars. He closed the door softly behind him, took his hat off carefully and placed it behind the door. Little stared at the ground, as though she did not want to meet his eye again and see no sign of recognition. Miles looked at the hat in the corner, wondering if there might be food hidden inside it. Silverpoint walked across the room and stood in front of Little, his hands on his hips.

"And just where do you think you've been, little softwing?" he said sternly.

Little looked up at him, and her eyes widened. "Silverpoint?" she whispered. His cool face broke into a smile. Little jumped up onto the bench and threw her arms around him. Silverpoint squeezed Little tightly, and the lone bulb on the wall glowed brighter, as though extra power had surged through the crumbling wires.

He stepped back and held her face in his hands. "I am glad to see you," he said. "How on earth did you get here?"

"Miles helped me. We came on a tiger. We slept up a tree. He stole the keys from under Cortado's nose. Are you all right? A crow told us the way. Didn't you recognize me? Why are you helping them?"

Silverpoint put his finger to his lips and glanced briefly at Miles. "I'm sorry, Little," he said. "When you fell from the ceiling last night I had to pretend not to know you. If that sniveling clown had realized who you were he would have run straight to Cortado himself, and then we would really have had trouble. The Great Cortado has a redder soul than I first realized."

Little laughed with delight and hugged him around the waist. Silverpoint looked at Miles over her blond head. His face was serious again, and his dark eyes searched into Miles's face as before, but this time his gaze was more curious than unfriendly.

"I am in your debt," he said. He looked at Miles a moment longer, then suddenly held out his hand, as though he had just remembered this was the right thing to do. Miles took his hand. Silverpoint's skin was cool and smooth, but there was a strange tingle in his touch, like the tingle you feel if you are foolish or bored enough to put your tongue on the terminals of a battery. Silverpoint squeezed his hand. Miles squeezed back. It felt like an odd thing to do, particularly with someone who felt like a distant cousin of the electric eel.

Miles took his hand back. Enough was enough. "Actually neither of us could have got here alone," he said.

For a moment they stared at each other silently, then Miles cleared his throat. "I don't suppose you brought any food with you?" he asked hopefully.

"I'm sorry," said Silverpoint. "You must be very hungry. Your breakfast is on its way, but I'm afraid the chefs are a little"—he searched for the right word—"disorganized," he said finally. He disentangled himself gently from Little's arms. "How did you get into the Palace of Laughter without being seen?" he asked.

"We came in through the ear," said Little. "It was Miles's idea. Then we crawled through tunnels for ages. We could hear people laughing, but we couldn't find the show until it was almost over, and we couldn't see properly even then."

"Then you were very lucky. If you had seen the entire show you would have been lost for good. I have never seen anyone who can resist the power of Cortado's show."

"But *you* can," said Little.

"That's because I take the antidote. All of us who work here are given an antidote before every show. It makes you immune."

"Immune from what?" asked Miles. "What exactly is the Great Cortado doing to all those people?"

"It's a sort of hypnosis," said Silverpoint. "He sucks the laughter out of their souls. After the show they are given a small bottle of liquid and sent on their way. . . ."

Miles felt for the empty bottle of Dr. Tau-Tau's Restorative Tonic and took it out of his pocket. "Like this one?" he said.

Silverpoint looked at him suspiciously. "Where did you get that?" he asked.

"I found it," said Miles. "It was already empty."

Silverpoint nodded. "The tonic brings people back to their normal selves after they've been 'laughtered,' as Genghis calls it, but it only lasts a few hours and people soon develop a craving for more. Only the Palace of Laughter produces the tonic, and it has made the Great Cortado a very wealthy man. The more demand he creates for the tonic, the richer he gets."

"But why are you going along with it?" asked Little.

"I had no choice until now, Little. After we were given that sleeping potion at the Circus Oscuro I woke up in the back of a van. I was tied with ropes, bumping about for a day and a night and into the following day. I had no idea where you were. When we got here they said that I would have to do what they told me, or you would be killed."

"Couldn't you have tried to escape?" Little asked Silverpoint. He shook his head.

"I couldn't risk it. Genghis and Cortado go back and forth from here to the circus all the time. It's always on the move, and if I went missing from here they might have got to you before I could find it."

"Did they tell you that I had escaped from the circus?"

"No, of course not," said Silverpoint. "But I knew you were coming anyhow, and when that sandbag got loose I was pretty sure it was your doing. That was a very dangerous thing to do. Cortado was spitting mad. Once the audience had been put back on the train, we were all sent to look for you. It's lucky I was there when you were caught, or you would have been brought straight to the Great Cortado tonight."

"Actually it was me who released the sandbag," said Miles. "I was sure it would hit him. But how did you know we were coming?"

"I knew as soon as I saw that little dancing bear."

Miles almost dropped the bottle that he was turning over between his fingers. "You've *seen* Tangerine?" he said.

"If you mean the bear, of course I've seen him, and I knew at once he was Little's work." He fixed Little with a hard stare, and she lowered her eyes to the floor. "Cortado put him into the act as soon as he set eyes on him," said Silverpoint.

"Tangerine is in the show?" asked Miles in amazement. "I didn't see him. What does he do?"

"He can't be made to do anything, of course, because he's brainless. He just stumbles around and gets in the way. The other clowns fall over him. Why are you so interested in the bear?"

Miles felt slightly insulted on Tangerine's behalf, even though he knew the bear's head was stuffed with sawdust. The idea of Tangerine stumbling around with hundreds of people laughing at him made Miles feel slightly sick. "Tangerine is mine," he said. "I came here to get him back."

Silverpoint turned his dark eyes on Miles, as though searching for something too faint for the human eye to see. "How long have you had him?"

"As long as I can remember," said Miles.

"It will be difficult enough to find a way for the three of us to escape," said Silverpoint after a pause. "We can't jeopardize our chances looking for a stuffed bear."

"You can do what you like," said Miles, "but I'm not leaving without Tangerine."

Silverpoint shrugged. "That's up to you," he said.

"What are they going to do with us?" asked Little. "That smelly clown said we'd be made to watch the show."

Silverpoint nodded, and his face clouded. "It was the only way I could dissuade Cortado from wanting to deal with you right away. I persuaded him that when we found the culprit he should be locked up until the next show. Then he could be put in the front row, and we would have no trouble with him after that. You've seen what the show does to its audience, I think."

"When is the next show?" asked Miles.

"Tonight. There are usually two or three in a row, then Cortado and Genghis go back to the circus."

"Why don't they just take the Palace of Laughter show on the road with the Circus Oscuro, instead of bringing people here?" asked Little.

"Cortado uses the Circus Oscuro to recruit and train performers for the Palace of Laughter," said Silverpoint. "He needs to be absolutely sure of everyone he brings to work for him here. I believe they also like to screen the audience at the circus before handing out the invitations. I don't know exactly how they decide who gets a silver ticket, but you won't find a policeman in the audience here, or a psychiatrist either."

"Then we'll have to escape before tonight's show," said Miles. "You have the keys to this door. If you leave it unlocked when you go, I can sneak out and look for Tangerine. Once I've found him we can go back out through the tunnels, and you can come with us."

"It's too late for that," said Silverpoint. "Cortado has had the trapdoor nailed shut. The only other way out is through the doors, and Baumella guards those night and day."

"She must sleep sometime," said Miles.

"She sleeps on a chair that she puts against the doors. You couldn't open them without waking her."

Miles pictured an elephant gently lifting the sleeping giantess, chair and all, out of the way of the doors. He doubted whether any elephant would be strong enough. "Maybe we can find some way to disrupt the show and escape during the confusion," he said. "Couldn't you knock the Great Cortado out with a firebolt?"

Silverpoint shook his head. "If I hit someone any harder with lightning than I do in the show it would probably kill them, and it is not permitted for a Storm Angel to release a soul. I'll have enough explaining to do as it is, when we get home." He turned another hard stare in Little's direction, but she seemed to be carefully examining her nails.

Miles closed his eyes and tried to rerun what they had seen of the show in his mind's eye, looking for any opportunity there might be to turn Cortado's method against him. He did not get very far before he was interrupted by the sound of someone approaching from the corridor outside. The sound became more puzzling as it got closer. It was hard to tell if there were two people or more, or one person bouncing a large beach ball. Sometimes the footsteps seemed to be running, or even hopping.

Sometimes they all marched in step. There was even what sounded like a brief outbreak of tap dancing. As they got nearer, Miles could hear voices chuckling and quietly singing. Another voice said, "Ssssshhh!" and the sounds stopped outside their door. There was a snort of laughter, followed by a sharp rap on the door.

"This will be your breakfast," said Silverpoint, and as he walked to the door Miles heard him mutter, " . . . with any luck."

CHAPTER TWENTY-SEVEN
PROVIDENCE

Miles Wednesday, unwashed and unbreakfasted, stared curiously at the door of the underground dressing room. He could smell food, he was sure of it. Someone out there had some soup. Or maybe a chicken. He pictured Haunch the butcher, standing apologetically with a plate of fat sizzling sausages. Silverpoint opened the door and three small men tumbled into the room as though released from an overcrowded jack-in-the-box. Even if their noses had not still worn traces of red, yellow and green paint, Miles would have recognized them at once. They had changed out of their undertaker outfits into baggy pants and vests, and they fidgeted and hopped as though the floor were burning their feet. Two of them carried plates of stew, and the other a large glass flagon of water.

Silverpoint introduced them as Fabio, Umor and Gila, the famous Bolsillo brothers. Gila, who had ridden the sandbag through the air, winked at Miles and pinched his own nose. He balanced a plate on the tip of his finger and set it spinning, stew and all. Specks of gravy flew from the plate and spattered around the room. Miles could not remember ever having had stew for breakfast, but he was far too hungry to care. A drop of gravy landed on his upper lip and he licked it off.

"That's no way to eat your food," said Gila.

"That's no way to serve it," said Umor.

"Give the boy his supper," said Fabio, cuffing Gila on the back of his head.

"Supper's a bit late, I'm afraid," said Gila.

He tossed the plate, still spinning, up in the air. It missed the ceiling by a whisker, and dropped neatly into Miles's hands.

"The boy's a natural," said Umor.

"Should be in a circus."

"Circus is in him, I'd say."

"Too skinny for that."

The Bolsillo brothers spoke so quickly that it was

hard to follow who was saying what. They had bushy hair that grew low on their foreheads, and small black eyes that glittered under thick eyebrows. When they smiled, their little teeth were pointed.

Umor handed the other plate to Little and bowed almost to the ground.

"Thank you," said Little.

"The pleasure is all mine," said Umor to the floor.

"Then give it back," said Fabio.

Umor straightened up. "Thank you," he said to Little.

"Fabio," said Silverpoint, "we don't have much time, and there are things I need to discuss with Little."

"Of course," said Fabio.

"Say no more," said Umor.

Gila rummaged in the pocket of his baggy trousers and produced a small gray mouse. He put it back, and rummaged again. This time a deck of cards appeared. He shuffled them with a loud snap, and the three little men settled themselves cross-legged in a circle in the corner of the room.

Miles began to devour his stew. He had never tasted anything so good, and it was some time before he could spare his mouth for speaking.

"Maybe," he said through a mouthful of food, "we should play the Great Cortado at his own game."

Silverpoint put his finger to his lips and rolled his eyes in the direction of the three little cardsharps in the corner. "They are on our side, more or less," he said in a low voice. "But I don't know how far they can be trusted."

"What do you mean?" whispered Miles.

"They look out for each other, and care about little else," said Silverpoint, "and they can be a bit light-fingered. They've tried to steal your dancing bear from Genghis at least twice."

Miles glanced over at the Bolsillo brothers. They appeared to be absorbed in their card game. Gila handed the deck to Umor.

"You deal," he said.

"No dice. You deal."

"You're faster."

"Yes, but whenever I deal, you get all the aces. I think you cheat."

"I swear on my grandmother's horse I never did."

"Your grandmother never had a horse. She was a lighthouse keeper."

"It was a sea horse."

"Just deal the cards."

Cards began flipping between the three men. Although Gila was dealing, the cards seemed to be going in all directions. Umor was looking at his and giving back the ones he didn't like, which Gila would pass straight on to Fabio, except for one that he hid in the back of his thick hair while pretending to scratch his head. Miles stared at them in fascination for a moment, then he turned back and spoke quietly to Silverpoint.

"How many times have you heard Cortado hypnotize an audience?"

The Storm Angel shrugged. "Thirty or more," he said.

"Do you think you could do it yourself?" asked Miles.

"I've been thinking of that," said Silverpoint. "If I could gain control of the crowd myself, I may be able to overturn Cortado's plan in some way, but I don't think it's possible."

"Why not?" asked Miles.

"I've watched very carefully what happens," said Silverpoint. "There's a certain point at the end of the show where the pace suddenly slows, and the audience is . . . left hanging in some way. That's when Cortado comes up through the floor. I don't think it would be possible to gain full control over the audience before then. It's all timed very precisely."

"Deuce," cried Gila from the corner of the room.

"Checkmate," countered Fabio.

"Game, set and halftime," said Umor. "Deal again, maestro."

"Maybe there's some way to prevent him from coming up through the floor," said Miles. "Couldn't you go down and sabotage the throne?"

Silverpoint shook his head. "Nobody's allowed below stage except Cortado and Genghis. That area is kept locked."

"I've been there," said Fabio from the corner. Umor was shuffling the cards, and the three little men were listening in to the conversation. You could almost see their ears wagging.

"You?" said Silverpoint. "What were you doing there?"

"Sleeping," chuckled Umor.

"Fixing," said Fabio. "The throne wasn't working properly. I was fixing it."

"He has a way with machines."

"They do as he says."

"He threatens them with his grease gun."

"How does the throne work?" asked Miles.

"Big electrical engine. Rubber rollers against the steel pole," said Fabio.

"Engine starts up," said Gila.

"Rollers turn."

"Pole goes up, trapdoor opens, Bob's your uncle."

Miles glanced at Silverpoint, then turned to Fabio. "Could you sabotage the throne?" he asked.

"Nope," said Fabio.

Gila clucked his tongue. "That would be treason," he said.

"Treason with a reason," said Umor.

"Why couldn't you? You know how it works," said Miles.

"Because I don't have a key, Master Miles. Genghis keeps the key."

Miles put his empty plate on the floor and scratched his head thoughtfully. There had to be a way around this. "If we can't get below the stage," he said, half to himself, "we'll have to sabotage it from above." He pictured the mayhem that he had glimpsed from his vantage point high above the show. Unicycles. Giant pies. Elephants and grease cans.

"The grease can," he said, jumping to his feet with a smile spreading across his face. "That's how we can do it. The throne is raised by rubber rollers that turn against the steel pole. If the rollers were greasy, the pole would slip and the weight of the throne would make it sink back into the floor."

Silverpoint regarded Miles with his dark eyes. "I'm listening," he said.

Little looked at the excitement shining in Miles's eyes. She didn't understand much about the world she was in. It was heavy and solid and seemed to be full of locks and machines and ugly noises. Nothing changed or moved unless it was pulled or pushed or dragged with a rope, yet Miles seemed to know the secrets of this world as instinctively as she knew the currents of the sky and the tides of the air. If anyone could make this plan work, she decided, it was this thin, coffee-skinned boy who had saved her from the Circus Oscuro.

"Look," said Miles. "Here's my plan. You said you couldn't gain control of the crowd until the final moment anyhow. When the Great Cortado begins to rise up from the floor in a cloud of smoke, we'll be sitting in the front row of the audience, pretending to be brain-fried. I'll jump into the ring—"

"But by then we *will* be brain-fried," interrupted Little.

"I hadn't thought of that," said Miles.

"I have," said Silverpoint. "I will bring you my

dose of antidote when I'm given it. We only get them minutes before the show, but if I'm quick I can get down here without being missed."

"But then you'll be unprotected, and we'll have only half a dose each," said Miles.

"I know what to expect, and I will be able to resist the effects of the show," said Silverpoint. He did not look at them as he said this, and Miles had the feeling he was not as confident as he sounded. "As for you, it will dilute the power of the show somewhat, but you'll have to use all your will to block it from your mind from the start. It's the best I can do for you."

"What about their portion?" said Miles, nodding at the Bolsillo brothers. "If we pooled yours and theirs, we'd have four portions between six of us. That would be . . . two-thirds each."

"No!" shouted the Bolsillo brothers in unison.

"No sharing!"

"No dice."

"Bad enough as it is."

"We don't want to be turned into vegetables."

"But if we are, I want to be a turnip."

The brothers looked genuinely frightened at the suggestion. Miles looked at Silverpoint, and he shook his head. "Let's hear the rest of it," he said.

Miles shrugged. "When the smoke goes up," he said, "I'll jump into the ring. Fabio can toss me the oil can, and I'll pour the lot down the steel pole just as the throne starts to rise. With all that smoke around, no one will even see me. The throne will slip back down, and you can take over."

"What about the Bolsillo brothers?" asked Little. "Couldn't they grease the throne themselves?"

Miles shook his head. "We'll need them to distract everyone else. As far as we know, all the other clowns are on the Great Cortado's side. Then there's Genghis, and Baumella if she hears that something's going on. We'll need all the help we can get."

Miles had another reason for wanting to get into the ring himself. He intended to keep a sharp eye on Tangerine throughout the performance, so that he could scoop him up from the smoke and the chaos on his way to sabotage the throne. After the reaction he had got from Silverpoint earlier, he preferred to keep the bear-retrieval part of his plan to himself.

In the corner of the room Fabio had picked up the two empty plates and the water carafe and was practicing his juggling. The plates were crossing and recrossing with a dizzying rhythm, and the water bottle spun so fast it was just a blur as it rose and fell, rose and fell from the little clown's busy hands.

Silverpoint stared at the faded stars on the ceiling, his arms folded and a slight frown on his pale forehead as he worked his way through Miles's plan. "What happens when the Great Cortado realizes his throne has sunk back down? He'll come up through the trapdoor anyway before we can achieve anything."

"We'll have to block the trapdoor in some way," said Miles. He watched the Bolsillo brothers, who had all joined in the juggling act, and were passing the crockery back and forth as though they were one creature with six arms. The contents of their pockets—a deck of cards, some brightly colored balls and even the gray mouse—joined the plates and the carafe in their intricate flight. The mouse did not seem to mind at all.

"They can bring their elephant to stand on the trapdoor," said Miles, nodding at the juggling brothers, "and you can climb on her back. That way you'll be better able to get the crowd's attention, and the Great Cortado will have to go the long way to get up from underground. You'll just have to get control of the audience before he can return. If we can get them on our side they'll outnumber Cortado's men forty to one."

"Sun's coming up, Silverpoint," said Umor. He had produced an egg timer from his pocket, and the last few grains of sand were whispering through its narrow waist. Gila was feeding crumbs to the mouse, who now sat on his shoulder. Fabio continued to juggle alone.

"We must go," said Silverpoint. "We've been here too long already."

"Wait a moment," said Miles. He was not entirely happy with all the details of his plan, and there would be no second chance to get it right. "How are you going to gain control of anyone if you've given us all your antidote?" he said. "Couldn't you steal some for us instead?"

"I don't know where it's kept," said Silverpoint. "I've been trying to find out since I got here. It's always Genghis who hands it out. He only gives one dose per person, and he never brings anyone with him when he collects it. I offered to help him once, and he became very suspicious."

The crockery spun above Fabio's head with increasing speed. Umor had produced a harmonica and was playing a sad, soft tune. Gila lifted his mouse gently from his shoulder and dropped it into a trouser pocket.

"Ask him!" said Miles.

"None of them know where it is, I've already asked them," said Silverpoint.

"Not the brothers, the mouse," said Miles. He turned to Little. "You could ask the mouse if he knows where the antidote is kept. I'm sure he's done plenty of snooping about in places others can't get to."

"Snooping?" said Gila.

"Investigating, I mean," said Miles.

Gila shook his head. "Too dangerous," he sniffed.

"Please, let me ask him," said Little. "If we don't get some more antidote our brains will be turned to mush. What's his name?"

"Susan."

"Oh! She's a girl. That's much better," said Little.

Gila looked at her suspiciously from under his tufty eyebrows. "Why better?"

"Curiosity, of course," said Little. "Girls like to know everything that's going on. I bet she knows this place inside out."

"Well . . . ," said Gila, "you can ask." He didn't seem to think it strange that Little would be able to speak to a mouse. Perhaps Silverpoint had already told them about her, thought Miles. Gila produced Susan from his pocket and held her out on the palm of his hand. She looked up at Little. Her whiskers twitched. Little leaned forward and squeaked something. Susan squeaked back. Miles tried to remember how he had managed to tune in to the voices of the cats in the garden of Partridge Manor, but he was too worried and excited now to allow the meaning of the mouse's tiny voice to reach him. "What did she say?" he asked.

"Ssh," said Little. She conversed with Susan for another minute, then smiled. Gila and his brothers were watching her intently with their glittering black eyes. "She's done plenty of exploring while you've been snoring, and she thinks she knows where the antidote is kept," said Little. "She saw Genghis filling lots of little glass tubes from a giant bottle in a sort of laboratory. She says it's on the floor below this one."

"I was afraid of that," said Silverpoint. "This floor is the last stop on the lift. The only possible way down is through the iron door at the other side of this corridor, but it's always locked. I saw Genghis go through there once, but I didn't know where it led to."

"Can you ask her how she got into the laboratory herself?" said Miles. "Maybe there's another way."

Little and the mouse sqeaked back and forth for a minute. Unlike her conversation with the crow, the sentences were brief, as though mice did not have time in their short lives for wasting words.

"There's a chimney," said Little. "It runs all the

way up from the laboratory, through one of the pillars, and comes out at the top of the hill. They have some kind of a fire in a box down there—I don't know the word for it."

"A furnace," said Miles, who had got as far as "N" in Lady Partridge's encyclopedia, and therefore knew more than most boys of his age about things whose initial letter fell in the first half of the alphabet. He scratched the itchy stubble of his half-shaved head. "How can we use a chimney that comes out at the top of the head," he wondered. "To get into it, we'd first have to get out of the Palace of Laughter, and we can't do that, which is why we need to get into the laboratory in the first place."

"Susan says there are little doors into the chimney every couple of floors. She doesn't know what they're for, as they're too small for most people and she's never come across anyone in a chimney anyhow."

"I suppose they'll be hatches of some kind, so it can be cleaned out if it gets blocked," said Miles.

"If there's one at this level I don't remember ever seeing it," said Silverpoint. "There are dozens of dressing rooms and all the sleeping quarters on this floor, and even supposing we could get into them all, we're fast running out of time."

"Don't worry," said Fabio, who was still juggling

with the crockery. "Providence will step in when all else fails."

"What's Providence?" asked Miles, who had not yet reached "P" in the encyclopedia.

"Not sure," said Fabio. "But my mother always said that Providence looks after the foolish, and from the sound of your plan, you would qualify without difficulty." He winked at Miles, taking his eye off the flying plates and the spinning bottle for an instant. An instant was enough. The plates glanced off each other in midair and wobbled in their orbits. The juggling Bolsillo brother said something that sounded like "Hup!" He caught a plate between his pointed teeth and the other under his left arm, but he was too late to catch the spinning bottle, which sailed right over his head and met its own reflection in the yellowed mirror with a splintering crash.

Now the sound of a bottle shattering a mirror can be a strangely satisfying thing, but to the boy, the clowns and the angels it just sounded like very bad timing. They stared, frozen, as the bottle exploded on the floor amid the crashing shards of glass. The sound seemed to go on forever, filling the room and echoing down the empty corridor outside. But it was not the splintered glass that made them stare. Right in the center of the pale rectangle where the mirror had been, there was a small iron hatch set into the plaster. It stood slightly ajar from the impact of the bottle.

"Well, Master Miles," said Fabio when the last glass splinter had fallen. "Now we know what Providence looks like."

CHAPTER TWENTY-EIGHT
CHIEF GENGHIS

Miles Wednesday, black-faced and burn-fingered, hung from a thin rope in a sooty chimney deep in a giant stone head. The fine black soot had been stirred up by the flapping of Little's wings, and it was making him cough like a seal. The sound echoed and boomed through the metal tube of the chimney, until he was sure that everyone in the Palace of Laughter could hear him. His shoulders felt bruised from squeezing his way through the small iron hatch, and his eyes were smarting from the soot. He managed to force a few words out between coughs. "Go down . . . making . . . me cough," he barked.

"Oh, sorry," said Little. She fluttered downward and vanished into the darkness. The soot began to settle, and Miles could dimly see Gila's head poking through the hatch above him.

"You all right?" asked Gila.

"Sort of," said Miles.

"Rather you than me," said Gila. "We have to go now. 'Bye!" His head disappeared like a jack going back into its box.

Miles began to inch his way down the rope. It was the one he had cut from Little's waist when he rescued her from the circus, and had been in his pocket ever since. He wondered if it was long enough to get him to the bottom of the chimney. He could get no foothold in the soot, and his fingers burned from sliding down the rope. In the darkness it was easy to imagine a variety of horrible fates awaiting them below. He pictured a huge set of metal jaws like a bear trap poised to bite them in half, or a pool of acid that would eat them from toe to crown with a loud hiss. "Little?" he whispered. "What's down there?"

"Just me," said Little.

The end of the rope came without warning. One moment he was holding on with two hands, then with one, then his aching fingers gave way and he dropped into blackness. The tunnel began to curve a short way down, and he found himself sliding on his backside until he tumbled into the filthy furnace at the chimney's end with a clatter.

"Shhhh!" said Little from the darkness beside him. "Not so loud!"

"I'll try and remember that next time I'm falling down a chimney," said Miles.

They were in a small, dark iron box, crouched on a thick layer of crunchy ash, still slightly warm from the last time the fire had been lit. The furnace was just big enough to allow Little to sit upright, but Miles's head was pressed against the dusty ceiling. It made the dim dressing room they had come from seem like a room in a five-star hotel. In front of them was the thick glass plate of the furnace door. Miles shuffled forward and looked out through the glass.

The laboratory reminded him a little of the inside of Lady Partridge's tree house, but without the branches growing up through it. There were shelves from floor to ceiling, crammed with beakers, bell jars, boxes, calipers, tinctures, tonics, touchstones, brass scales, sulphur nuggets, rubber tubes, leather-bound books, dried herbs, candles, stirring rods, steam distillers, talismans, tusks, quartz toning vessels, assorted bones, rolled charts, Bunsen burners, pipettes, gold and silver colloids, powdered roots, and on a high shelf, a shrunken head with its hair tied in a knot and a crescent of bone passed through its nose.

In the corner was a wooden cabinet with gargoyle faces carved on each corner, and on top a pile of dusty books and a bust of Hermes Trismegistos, the father of alchemy. A large solid table with a clean-scrubbed surface stood in the center of the room. Among the flagons and boxes and stoppered jars on the table, Miles spotted a wooden stand with a row of thirty-six identical vials, each one half filled with a colorless liquid.

"Look," he whispered to Little. "That must be the antidote."

He moved aside so that she could look out through the glass. "There on the table," he said, "in the glass vials."

"I see it," she whispered. "How do we get out there?"

Miles fumbled with the catch on the furnace door. It was difficult to see in the semidarkness, but it was a simple catch and it did not take him long to open. The door swung outward. It was smaller than the hatch through which they had entered the chimney. "I don't think I can get through there," said Miles. "I'm not even sure you will."

Little tucked her wings away and poked her head out into the laboratory. There was no one there. She squeezed through the tiny doorway like a cat through a drainpipe, and dropped to the floor. In a moment she was back with two of the glass vials.

"Well done," said Miles. She smiled and passed one in to him, pulling the stopper from the other.

"Wait!" he said. "How do we know for sure that this is the antidote? It might be some deadly poison."

"Or it might make us twenty feet tall, like Baumella," said Little.

"You might grow a beard," said Miles.

"You might grow wings and turn purple," laughed Little.

"Well, here goes," said Miles. He put the vial to his mouth and swallowed the contents in one gulp. He expected it to taste horrible, or to burn his throat or make his ears hot, but it did nothing of the sort. In fact it didn't taste of anything much, apart from being cooler than he expected in that stuffy room. He could feel it slipping down his throat, and all his muscles relaxed as it passed down through him. In some strange way he thought it tasted blue, and he felt as though he had been holding his breath all his life without realizing it, and had only just let it go. Little was looking at him through the open door of the furnace.

"You have turned purple"—she giggled—"and you look a lot better!"

Miles looked down at his hands. They were the same color they had always been. He turned them over, but they were no different on the other side. "I suppose that was a joke," he said to himself. Out loud he said, "It's safe to drink."

As Little swallowed her dose, it occurred to him that it might have a completely different effect on her. He was not sure what was inside an angel, or whether their insides worked in the same way as his. It might be anything but safe for her. He shrugged. "It seems to work for Silverpoint," he thought, "and anyway it's too late now."

He handed his empty vial back out to Little. She was licking her lips and looking rather disappointed. "It doesn't taste of much," she said.

"You'd better put the vials back quickly," said Miles.

She held them up and looked at them. "But they're empty. They'll know someone has stolen them," she said.

"I hadn't thought of that," said Miles. He was annoyed with himself. It was an important detail to have overlooked. If two doses were missed, suspicion would be bound to fall on them, or more likely on Silverpoint himself. "Have a look around the room," he said to Little, "and see if you can find the big bottle that he filled them from."

Little placed the two empty vials back in their slots and began searching the clutter on the table, being careful to replace everything where she found it. "Nothing here," she said. She did a slow circuit of the room, examining the items on the shelves. There were bottles and jars with liquids of all colors, and some with clear liquids in which a variety of snakes and lizards were suspended, but they were covered in dust and obviously seldom disturbed.

She came to the wooden cabinet in the corner and tried the doors. They were locked. She rattled them a couple of times to make sure, then moved on to the next set of shelves, wedged between the cabinet and a large porcelain sink. The rattling sound continued, as though someone inside the cabinet were trying to get out. Miles poked his head through the furnace door with difficulty. "Little!" he hissed urgently. "I think there's someone in the cabinet."

Little was trying the brass tap on the sink. She looked over her shoulder at the cabinet and frowned. "Not there," she whispered back. "It's the door."

Miles looked at the dark wooden door in the far corner and realized she was right. A key was rattling in the lock, and now he could hear muffled voices from the other side. "It's too late," he hissed. "Get back in here, quickly!" He shuffled back to make room for her, but instead of heading for the furnace she ran lightly back to the table and lifted the two empty vials from their rack. He heard the key turn in the lock. Little was back at the sink, holding the vials under the brass tap. The tap squeaked as she turned it on, but as luck would have it, the sound was masked by the creaky hinges of the door in the corner, which opened at the same moment. The voices were clearer now. "Is that really as far as your ambitions stretch?" said the Great Cortado's voice.

Little ran back to the table, her feet making no sound, and dropped the vials back into place. They were half full of water, and looked no different from the rest.

"That all depends," came Genghis's reedy voice, sounding slightly defensive. Little ducked down behind the table. The Great Cortado stepped into the room, holding the door open for his big-bellied companion. Miles held his breath. A condescending smirk lurked under Cortado's magnificent mustache. Little reached up from her hiding place and stoppered the second vial just as Genghis came through the door, and at the same moment Miles realized that the furnace door was still wide open. He inched backward, trying to hide himself in darkness without the thick layer of ash beneath him crunching loudly. As he retreated from the furnace hatch he caught a last glimpse of Little crawling into the tight space under the table, before his view of the room was reduced to a small square of cluttered shelving.

"So you would like to be Mayor Genghis of Smallville," said the Great Cortado's voice.

"Oh no, not me," said Genghis. "You'd be the mayor. I was thinking more of . . . well . . . chief of police."

"I see," said Cortado. "And what town do you feel would be a worthy candidate, Chief Genghis?"

"Well," said Genghis enthusiastically, "I reckon somewhere like Larde would be ripe for the picking. With the money that's been pouring in from Tau-Tau's laugh juice, you could prob'ly buy the whole place, lock, stock and . . . whatever. We could set ourselves up in that big mansion just outside the town. It's a lot fancier than that pokey little town hall, and I reckon nobody'd be sorry if we gave the old loony that lives there her marching orders." He sniggered. "They wouldn't have no choice anyhow, not once you was mayor."

"I'm intrigued," said Cortado in a tone of mock sincerity that Genghis obviously took as genuine. "And what exactly would we do with this small population of peasant half-wits?"

"What would we do?" Genghis sounded a little confused. He began picking up the glass vials and placing them carefully in a worn leather doctor's bag. "Well . . . I could think of lots of things. For starters they would have to supply us all year round with the finest cigars and the best beers available. None of your yellow cat's pee, I mean real beer, with a big frothy head."

The Great Cortado suddenly appeared just outside the doorway of the furnace. Miles froze, afraid that he would look inside, but the mustachioed man just muttered under his breath, "Not the only thing around here with a big frothy head," and closed the furnace door. A momentary updraft lifted the fine ash from the floor and swirled it around the inside of the cramped iron box. Miles pinched his nose to stifle a sneeze, which made his eyes water. The voices in the laboratory were more muffled now, and he had to strain his ears to catch the drift of the conversation.

" . . . bear baiting, for instance," Genghis was saying. "They shouldn't never have banned that—it's just a bit of harmless fun. I used to go with me dad, God rest his soul, when I was no more than a kid. We had a dog ourselves. Snap, his name was. A good fighter, least he was until his back got broken. Eleven fights he made, and we always got ice cream afterward. And cockfights. Used to be two cockpits in Bunkrabble where I grew up. One at the canal dock, and the other in the priest's back garden. We could make 'em legal again, and have an arena built with a bear pit and cockpits, and fifty slot machines in each stand. That fancy church of theirs has a copper roof too, if you don't mind. That would pay for the whole lot if you stripped it down. And then we could have—"

"You'd have not much more than you've got now, but with the wheels taken off," interrupted the Great Cortado. "Genghis, you're a useful fellow at times, I'll grant you that, but I think you should leave the broader picture to me. It's not exactly your forte."

"I was just getting to the best bit . . . ," said Genghis, his voice trailing off. The itch in Miles's nose grew stronger. He could feel that sneeze hanging around, waiting for its chance. He pinched his nose again, wishing they would finish their conversation and leave.

"I can scarcely wait," said the Great Cortado, "but I'm afraid I shall have to. The performance starts in less than an hour, and we have some antidote to distribute, among other things. Have you counted the doses?"

"Thirty-six, Mr. Cortado. Got 'em right here in the bag," said Genghis.

"Good," said Cortado. "Then let's not waste any more time."

Miles allowed himself a small sigh of relief as he heard the door hinges creak again. His legs were cramped under him, and his neck ached from bending his head in the small space. He shifted his position slightly, kicking up another small cloud of ash, and that was when his sneeze chose to ambush him. It was a prize-winning sneeze, and when it came out it sounded like a donkey who had swallowed a large dog. It boomed around the metal furnace and echoed up the chimney and out into the evening sky, where it startled a passing tawny owl who had just set out for his night's hunting. A slightly more muffled version echoed around the laboratory just as the door slammed shut.

Miles bit his lip. The door of the laboratory looked solid and heavy, and with the creaking hinges and the loud slam he was pretty sure they would not have heard his sneeze. He debated whether to try and hide himself in the chimney, or to risk a quick look through the yellowed glass of the furnace door to make sure the two men had gone. He wiped his nose on the back of his sleeve and listened. He could hear no sound from the laboratory. Finally he leaned forward to look out through the window in the furnace door, pressing his forehead against the grimy glass.

He could just see Little's foot beneath the table in the center of the floor. There was no other sign of life, so he was taken completely by surprise when the furnace door was jerked open. It seemed to have grown bigger, and he almost tumbled out onto the floor. A large hand grabbed his collar, and he caught the flash of bright yellow socks and the smell of stale cigar smoke. A moment later he was hoisted through the air and held, dangling like a kitten, in front of Genghis's disbelieving face.

"Hello, Chief Genghis," he said.

CHAPTER TWENTY-NINE
FISH TO FRY

Genghis Big-belly, slack-jawed and dumb-struck, stared at the skinny boy dangling from his fist. The cigar stub detached itself slowly from his lower lip and dropped to the floor unnoticed.

"Can you put me down now please?" said Miles. Genghis let go of his collar, and Miles dropped to the floor. His legs, numb from being curled up in the dusty furnace, almost gave way under him, but he knew that if he fell he might draw attention to Little's hiding place, and he managed to remain standing. He returned the big man's bug-eyed stare steadily.

"It's him," said Genghis in his broken-whistle wheeze. "It's that little weasel *again*. I swear there must be ten of him."

"So I see," said Cortado, who was standing quietly in the open doorway. His face was white behind his luxurious mustache, and he spoke carefully, as though holding his anger back with some effort. He closed the door softly behind him and walked around the laboratory table, pushing Genghis aside. He grasped Miles's chin and tilted his face up to look at him, although in truth he didn't need to tilt it far.

"Well, Selim," he said, "your little vanishing trick did take me by surprise, I must confess. I was surprised that anyone would be so stupid"—he brought his face closer to Miles and measured out his words like ice cubes dropping into a glass—"as to . . . steal . . . my . . . property . . . from under . . . my . . . nose."

"She's not your property. People aren't anyone's property," said Miles. His legs were shaking now, more from fear of the Great Cortado's anger than from cramp, but he felt that somehow it would be worse for him if he let his fear show.

"Circus freaks," said the Great Cortado, "are not people. You stole her. Now you will tell me where she is."

"I don't know where she is," said Miles. "She left when I cut the rope from her wrists, and I haven't seen her since."

"He's lying, the little snake," said Genghis. He gave Miles a sharp clout on the ear with his bandaged and bitten fist.

"Save it for later, Genghis," said Cortado. "You won't rattle anything out of this boy's head like that." He turned to Miles and dusted some ash from the shoulders of his filthy jacket. The normal color had returned to Cortado's face, but the smile that lurked beneath his mustache was not matched in his eyes.

"Time enough to return to the subject of the freak later," he said. "As for you, Selim, your disappearing act seems to be surpassed only by your appearing act. Exactly what were you doing in my furnace, and how did you get in here in the first place?"

"I have a ticket," said Miles, producing the silver ticket from his inside pocket. He glanced at the furnace. He could see now that the small hatch through which Little had wriggled was set into a larger door that comprised most of the front of the furnace. It was this door that Genghis had opened in order to haul him out.

"So you do," said the Great Cortado. "But the ticket grants admisson to the auditorium, not to the furnace. And you are wasting my time, Selim."

"I got in through the chimney," said Miles. "I climbed on top of the hill because I didn't want to come in through the front door, and I found the chimney mouth up there. When I tried to climb down it, I fell, and got stuck in this dirty furnace. You should get Genghis to clean it out more often."

"I'll clean *you* out, little snake," wheezed Genghis. He raised his fist again, but stopped himself. "Can I hit him?" he said to the Great Cortado in a wheedling voice. "Just once?"

"I think not," said the Great Cortado. "If you knock him out now he might miss the show, and that would be a shame. After all, he does indeed have a ticket this time, and I'm sure once he sees what a fabulous entertainment we have put together he'll be much more open with us. His story doesn't explain such things as runaway sandbags and tunnel-crawling expeditions, and I am very keen to hear a more accurate version when we've cured him of his stubbornness."

"I could punch him in the kidneys," said Genghis hopefully. "That wouldn't knock him out, as such."

"After I'm finished with him you can do what

you like," said Cortado. "From what he tells me, nobody will be sending out a search party. But first I want to find out what he's done with my circus freak, and I don't want him spitting blood onto my clean shirt while he's telling me." He took Miles by the elbow and steered him toward the door. Genghis followed, carrying his doctor's bag and sulking.

The passage outside was short, and ended in a flight of steps that spiraled upward and out of sight. The Great Cortado was in a hurry, and he took the stairs two at a time, keeping his grip on Miles's elbow. Genghis puffed and panted several steps behind them. At the top of the stairs was a heavy iron door such as you might see in a bank vault, assuming of course that you were wealthy enough to have any business at all in the basement of a bank. Miles and the Great Cortado reached the door, and waited for Genghis to catch up.

The larger man was gasping for breath by the time he arrived. He rummaged in his pocket for the key and fumbled it into the lock, beads of sweat trickling down his forehead. He leaned his weight against the door, and it opened onto a curving corridor. Gas lamps hissed quietly in their ghostly globes between the many closed doors, and beside each door was a small wire basket screwed to the wall. "I suppose," panted Genghis, dropping a vial of antidote into each basket as he passed, "that you'd have something grander in mind than a small town like Larde. Maybe like Sevenbridge, or even Turmeric."

The Great Cortado sighed deeply and shook his head. "Did I ever show you the scar that tiger left me before I killed it, Genghis?" he said. Miles pricked up his ears.

"Nasty business," panted Genghis. "What of it?"

"What of it, he asks," muttered Cortado, half to himself. They reached the elevator, which stood with its gates open at the far end, and squeezed in. Genghis pulled the rattling iron gate closed and punched the button, and the elevator creaked slowly into motion. He opened his doctor's bag and took out the two remaining vials.

"I'll tell you what of it, my boneheaded friend. I came within a whisker of losing my life to that tiger, and once you have stared into the mouth of death you will never look at life in the same way again. The tiger taught me a lesson that I would never forget, even if it were not indelibly written into my flesh. Do you know what that lesson is, Genghis?"

"Stay away from tigers?"

The Great Cortado laughed. He uncorked his vial and swallowed its contents. His laughter ceased at once and a frown took its place.

"I know," said Genghis. "It's 'Never tie your blunderbuss to the wall with wire.' If you'd just hung it on a couple of them big hooks, you'd have—"

"Shut up, Genghis," said Cortado. "If you spent less time blabbering and more time listening, you might learn something."

"But you asked—"

"It was a rhetorical question, Genghis. The lesson the tiger taught me was this. We arrive on this Earth as feeble, mewling bags of spit, and most of us remain little more than that until the day we die. The only thing that makes a real man is power. Without power over other people, and over the dumb beasts themselves, you are nothing." He smoothed the ends of his mustache thoughtfully. "That tiger was left to me by a good friend of mine. He was a man with heart and energy and humor, but none of these qualities were worth a rat's whisker when it came down to it, because he didn't have the power to avert the cruel trick that fate had in store for him."

"Blimey," said Genghis. "That's a bit bleak, ain't it?" He swallowed his dose of antidote and replaced the two empty vials in the bag, belching loudly as he snapped it shut.

"Bleak? It's reality. Before I looked death in the eye, my ambition was simply to own the biggest and most successful circus in the land. I wanted fame and money, but I knew nothing of the importance of power. Power is the only thing that counts, Genghis."

The elevator continued to grind slowly upward through its stone shaft. The Great Cortado's face grew pensive. "I spent years researching the power of laughter, and devoted many more to devising the tools with which to control it. You don't think I spent all that effort just to become an unofficial civil servant in a godforsaken cluster of stone huts like Larde."

"Er, no. Of course not," said Genghis. He frowned for a moment, then said, "Why did you?"

"Because I have bigger fish to fry," said the Great Cortado. Miles paid close attention. The two men seemed almost to have forgotten he was there, but he had listened with interest as the Great Cortado listed what was not included in his ambitions, and now he was curious to know what was.

"Tau-Tau's tonic is more addictive than any amount of beer and bear baiting to someone who's been processed by our little show. More even than those steamed ginger puddings you stuff into your fat face as though there was no tomorrow." There was no sign of a smile on the Great Cortado's face as he said this. Genghis licked his lips thoughtfully.

"Being the only people who know how to make the stuff puts us in a position of considerable power, and that power grows greater with every godforsaken village we put through the mangle. If we were to cut off the supply of Tau-Tau's for a week, we'd have the whole country out in riots. But this is just a start, Genghis. Once I have enough—"

Genghis cleared his throat loudly and jerked his head at Miles.

"What is it, Genghis?" sighed Cortado.

"The boy," said Genghis from the corner of his mouth. "He'll hear you."

The elevator ground to a halt, and the Great Cortado waited for Genghis to open the gates. "What of it?" he said. "By the time he has seen our fabulous show he'll be hard-pressed to remember his own name, and I'm sure this conversation will have slipped his mind altogether." He smiled coldly at Miles. "Open the gates, Genghis," he said.

"Once we have the peasantry hooked, it will be time to reel in the bigger fish," he continued, as he stepped out of the elevator. "We will have a season of gala spectaculars at the Palace of Laughter. They will be by invitation only, and we will round up every duke and marchioness and government minister, every bishop and rabbi and general, the prime minister and the chancellor and the entire royal family and God Almighty himself, if we can find his postal address, and we will lay on a show that outshines our most hilarious performances by a factor of three. We will entice everyone with power and influence in the land to spend an unforgettable night under our roof, and before the week is out they will be back in their town halls and palaces, and the power and influence will all be in my pocket."

Genghis let out a whooshing sound that was meant to be a low whistle. "Well I'd have to say that your plan makes mine look like kid's stuff, and no mistake," he said. "You've certainly got the breadth of vision there, that was lacking in my little scenario."

"Elegantly put," said the Great Cortado. "Now let's get our guest down to the auditorium before the show begins." They walked along another curving corridor. There was only one door in this one. It was painted midnight blue, and the words "Master of Ceremonies" were carefully stenciled onto it with silver paint. The Great Cortado stopped outside the door and turned to Miles. "This is where we part for now, Selim. We'll have another little chat after the show, and I have no doubt you will be more cooperative then. Genghis, make sure he has a ringside seat." He closed the door after him, leaving Miles and Genghis alone.

They stepped into the gloom of the entrance hall, Genghis gripping Miles's elbow with his unpleasant pinch. Between the tall pillars Miles could dimly see the outline of Baumella the giantess seated, just as Silverpoint had said, with her back against the huge double doors. He could not tell if she was awake or sleeping. They marched toward the smaller doors that led into the theater itself, neither of them noticing the wiry, blackfaced figure of String, who watched from the shadows behind one of the pillars. His recaptured bone was tucked into the belt of his trousers, and there was a glint of malice in his eye.

"Now," said Genghis, tightening his grip on Miles's elbow, "what was that you said about making me clean out the furnace?"

"That was just a little joke," said Miles.

"I'm not laughing," said Genghis.

It was on the tip of Miles's tongue to say "That'll be the antidote," but for once he kept his mouth shut. In their hurry they almost bumped into a sour-looking man hobbling on a pair of wooden crutches, his leg plastered from toe to knee.

"What happened to you, Bobo?" wheezed Genghis. "Slipped on the soap, I suppose."

The hobbling man gave off a smell that was every bit as sour as his face, a smell that Miles recognized from the night before, when he and Little had been brought down in the elevator to their temporary prison. It was the tramp clown, unpainted today, and certainly still unwashed.

"Very funny," he grunted. "Matter of fact I fell off the high wire, broke me friggin' ankle. I see you're babysittin' one of them little jokers. Who got lumbered with the other one?"

"The other one?" said Genghis. He twisted Miles's arm up behind his back and brought his face down until the burning tip of his cigar was an inch from the boy's nose. "So you weren't alone in that lab, you little weasel. "Here, Bobogeek . . . ," he said to the tramp clown. "You just got yourself a new job. Take this one in and make sure he gets a seat in the front row. If he tries anything funny you can hit him with your crutches. You can call it self defense, you being a cripple and all. I've got another one to catch."

"Right so," said Bobogeek, "and try not to let her outsmart you this time, eh?" He let out a nasty whinnying laugh.

Genghis gave no answer. He let go Miles's arm and aimed a clout at his head. Miles ducked, and the big man's fist landed a hard punch on Bobogeek's arm.

"Oy!" said the tramp clown. "What was that for?"

"For the little weasel," wheezed Genghis. "You can owe it to him." He turned on his heel and hurried back toward the elevator.

CHAPTER THIRTY
MANY A SLIP

Miles Wednesday, filthy, front-rowed and (shhh!) antidoted, sat wedged into a narrow space right at the ringside. On his left sat Bobogeek, his plastered foot stretched out in front and a couple of small but persistent flies buzzing around his head, and to his right sat none other than Haunch the butcher of Larde. Haunch had looked at Miles in surprise as he sat down beside him. "Well well, Master Miles," he said, craning his thick neck to get a better look at the boy. "I didn't see you on the train, nor in the hotel neither, and I thought I'd seen everyone. You was hiding in a luggage rack, I'll wager."

"Not me," said Miles. "I wasn't even on the train. I walked here."

Haunch the butcher guffawed. "That's a good 'un, boy. There must have been something special in them bones I gave you. Reckon I'll double the price on them in future—too good for dogs they are." He chuckled again.

"What on earth is he laughing at?" Miles thought to himself, but then he remembered the stolen antidote he had taken, and he forced a small laugh out of himself for Bobogeek's benefit. It felt like a strange noise to be making.

"Not sure I'd have recognized you, mind, with that funny hairstyle," Haunch went on. "Must be all the fashion, eh? You're the second lad I've seen with a funny hairdo since I came in here. Tell you what," he said, leaning close and tapping his nose with a thick finger, "come round and clean my yard next week, and I'll keep some sausages by for you this time. You're a good little worker, lad." His breath smelled of the brandy that he had had the foresight to bring with him on the journey, which no doubt also accounted for his mood being lighter than usual.

Miles wondered for a moment who it could have been that Haunch saw with an odd hairstyle, and decided that it must have been himself, as Bobogeek steered him down through the seats to the front row. The other seats had been filling up steadily, and the circus band had taken their places among the strange assortment of pipes, horns and gongs in the pit at the far side of the ring. Miles could spot many other faces that were familiar to him from his hometown: Piven the baker and his wife sat opposite him, and behind him was Flifford the bicycle mechanic, difficult to recognize without smears of gray axle grease decorating his face. Father Soutane sat over to the right, listening earnestly to the stream of gossip that Lily the florist poured into his ear. There was not much that Lily did not know about what went on in Larde, and where there were gaps in her knowledge she was happy to fill them in with details that she made up herself.

The boom of an enormous gong signaled the arrival of the clowns, who trotted and cartwheeled down among the seats and spilled out onto the clean sawdust of the ring. The band struck up the same crazy music that Miles and Little had heard from the tunnels the night before. The music looped and squealed, but it did not sound at all funny this time. Miles watched the rest of the audience, some of whom were already beginning to chuckle, and he took his cue from them. When the clowns began an exercise routine that looked like a chaotic kind of tai chi, Miles made himself laugh along with the rest.

He could see Silverpoint, in his tall chef's hat, directing the exercise routine with graceful movements that the other clowns were failing miserably to mimic. Silverpoint glanced over at him, and Miles could see his eyes searching the benches for Little. His face remained expressionless, and after a moment he looked away.

Haunch's shoulders were shaking now with laughter. Miles couldn't remember if his own shoulders shook when he laughed—he had never thought to check. He tried shaking them, but it just felt silly, so he contented himself with producing laughter of the non-shaking variety. Bobogeek was scanning the rest of the audience, his arms folded and his crutches parked by his side. His face wore a miserable scowl.

All of a sudden the music stopped, and the clowns froze with it. In the center of the ring stood the Great Cortado, his hair slicked back and curling behind his ears, the huge mustache on his small round face perfectly waxed and pointed. He had changed into a dark blue suit with silver buttons, and he spoke without trumpet or megaphone, his voice booming around the packed theater as though it belonged to a man four times his size. **"Ladies and Gentlemen, welcome to the Palace of Laughter,"** he began. **"Tonight it is your Immense Privilege to witness the most spec-tac-u-lar, the most Fan-tas-tical, the most Hil-larious Ex-trava-ganza of Laughter . . . ,"** and on he went, word for rolling word, with the opening speech that Miles had heard from the tunnels the night before. The audience listened a trifle impatiently, eager to get past the introduction and on with the promised hilarity. Some tittered at the sight of the Bolsillo brothers, who were not having as much success as the other clowns at staying still, and were having a little spat with much rib digging and eye poking. Fabio was picking the Great Cortado's pocket as he spoke, pulling out a large handkerchief and looking at it with an expression of disgust.

Silverpoint was staring Miles in the eye, as though he could find some clue there as to the whereabouts of Little, and how they had become separated, but Miles could give no kind of signal without making Bobogeek suspicious. The Great Cortado was approaching the end of his speech.

" . . . be prepared to be entertained as you have never been entertained before!" he boomed. **"Tonight the greatest comics in the Wide World will take you Beyond Laughter, and your Lives will be Transformed, FOREVER!"**

The people clapped and cheered. "Didn't they hear what he just said?" Miles thought to himself. "What do they think he meant?" It seemed so obvious to him, squeezed into his seat and waiting for disaster to befall him in one guise or another.

A cloud of blue smoke enveloped the Great Cortado, and when it dispersed he was gone. Miles felt pretty sure he had not disappeared through the trapdoor. He searched in the dimness of the banked seating and spotted Cortado after a moment, slipping out through one of the exits at the back, unnoticed by the mesmerized audience. The band had struck up as he finished speaking and was in full flight again. The music seemed a meaningless babble. In the middle of the ring lay a clown, dressed in a tramp costume and with a downturned white mouth painted on a blackened face, who Miles guessed must be a stand-in for the injured Bobogeek. He was trying to sleep under an open newspaper. Between his feet lay a small white dog, who kept snatching the newspaper in his teeth and pulling it over himself. Each time he did this the clown gave a violent shiver and grabbed it back.

The tramp clown finally got the upper hand. He began to snore like an ox, the band counting out his snores with booms and clashes of their gongs. The Bolsillo brothers, meanwhile, were wobbling at breakneck speed around the ring on their unicycle. While Fabio pedaled, Gila and Umor perched on his shoulders. Umor whistled, and the elephant ambled down through the startled audience and began to chase the unicycle. The people of Larde laughed until they cried, and the music squealed on.

Miles listened to the harsh, ugly laughter and he began to understand now what Little had said about the One Song. The hysterical braying of the audience was not real laughter. It had been torn from the One Song like a single filament from a rope, and without the harmony of the other strands it could cut through the soul like a taut wire cuts through cheese. He tried to block out the sound and concentrate on the show, searching among the flapping boots and rainbow trousers for any sign of Tangerine. As he forced out a noise that he hoped would suffice for laughter, he worried too about Little. He hoped that she would have wasted no time in escaping up the chimney once they had closed the door behind them. If she delayed too long Genghis would surely find her still there on his return, and without Cortado to control him there was no knowing what he might do. Miles pictured her flying up the length of the chimney and out into the night sky, and holding on to that thought, he forced his attention back to the antics in the ring.

If you have ever had to wait in the wings for your part in a play or a show, you may have some idea how Miles felt as he sat wedged between a large butcher and a smelly clown and watched for his moment. The antidote he had taken certainly quenched laughter, but it did not have the same effect on nerves. His stomach was full of knots, and half of him wished that something would happen that would prevent him from having to leap up on the stage at all. His timing would have to be perfect, and there would be no second chance.

He stole a glance at Bobogeek. The smelly clown was staring at his snoring substitute with a look of sour boredom on his unwashed face. In the ring, the snoring clown was having a dream. Another clown, dressed like a clean and colorful version of himself, perched behind him on a large boulder, holding a small fishing rod. He whistled loudly as he fished, a broad white smile painted on his face. Behind him Miles could see Fabio Bolsillo attempting to oil the elephant's knees. His two brothers were proving more of a hindrance than a help. A lot of oil ended up underfoot, and there was a great deal of slipping and sliding.

The fishing clown suddenly caught a bite, and after a brief struggle a sea lion appeared from behind the rock, the end of the fishing line in her whiskered mouth. The sea lion was dressed in a lime green tutu, and the fishing clown lost his heart to her at first sight. He tumbled off the rock and landed on one knee, clasping his hands and serenading the sea lion with a wordless barking song. The band played on, and the audience howled with laughter.

The tutu-wearing sea lion turned tail and fled, the fishing clown hot on her tail. His hat fell from his head and began to run around the ring as though it had a life of its own. Miles watched it curiously. Suddenly the hat came to rest, and a small orange bear climbed out. Tangerine!

Miles almost leaped from his seat at once. The newly washed bear had regained some of his bright orange color, but there was no mistaking his floppy legs and his slightly crossed eyes. Besides, there were not many stuffed bears who could stumble about a circus ring on their own, waving at the audience and tripping up the performers. The people of Larde, purple faced from laughter, clutched their sides and pointed at Tangerine. So much was going on at one time that many of them seemed unable to decide which way to turn. A look of bewilderment began to mix itself with the laughter in their eyes. The music raced ever faster, and the action in the ring became a whirlwind. The fishing clown seemed somehow to have died. The Bolsillo brothers ran out from behind a screen in their undertaker suits, carrying a coffin. It was shorter than the clown, but they wedged him into it. They lifted the coffin, and the bottom fell out, corpse and all. The Bolsillo brothers threw away the coffin and buried the fishing clown in a mound of sawdust. A giant daisy pushed its way up through the mound.

Miles was distracted briefly by a light from the back of the auditorium, and he saw Genghis slipping in from the hallway outside. His face was black with soot and with anger, but he appeared to be alone. Miles looked back at the ring. The elephant had reached over Fabio's shoulder and grasped the daisy with his trunk. He pulled, and the clown came up from the mound, stiff as a board and still clutching the daisy in his intertwined fingers. Miles could no longer see Tangerine. He searched the ring, but the bear was nowhere to be found. The Bolsillo brothers were chasing the resurrected clown, who had stolen their unicycle and ridden it straight through Silverpoint's pie. Silverpoint was shooting firebolts in all directions. His face wore its usual calm expression, but the firebolts seemed to be coming thick and fast, and there was barely a clown in the ring whose trousers, hat or wig wasn't smoldering. The band was playing like a party of dervishes, and the booming, clanging and squealing made Miles feel as though his head itself were one of the gongs.

Genghis was making his way toward him now, pushing the stupefied Lardespeople aside as he clambered over the benches. Miles looked back into the ring in desperation. Silverpoint was pointing straight at him, his cool eyes fixed on Miles's face. A firebolt crackled through the air toward him, finding its mark just above him and to his left. Bobogeek let out a howl of surprise. His eyebrows had disappeared and his tufty hair was smoking. "Oy!" he roared. In the center of the ring the trapdoor was opening, and from it poured a thick cloud of purple and green smoke. Beside the trapdoor

Silverpoint was shouting something at Miles that he couldn't catch. The Storm Angel cupped his hands around his mouth. "You're on!" he yelled.

Miles felt as though he had suddenly been unglued from his seat. He leaped into the ring as the shape of the throne began to emerge from the colored smoke. The three Bolsillo brothers were leading the elephant around the back of the throne, ready to park her on the trapdoor. Fabio tossed the oil can into the air as Miles ran toward the pillar of smoke. "Mind the holes," shouted Fabio. What holes? The floor was flat and smooth beneath the sawdust. The ring seemed twice as large now that he was in it. A blur of open-mouthed faces filled the surrounding darkness. He caught the oil can and almost dropped it straight through his fingers. The outside of the can was slippery as a fish, and more oil was pouring from at least three different places. *Those* holes! The throne continued to rise. He reached the smoke cloud, still searching for Tangerine, and tried to stop, but the floor was already slick with oil, and though his feet stopped, Miles kept going. He collided with something hard and fell backward into the greasy sawdust.

As the smoke began to clear, he could see he had hit the edge of the open trapdoor. He scrambled to his feet with difficulty, oil still pouring from the holes in the can. The dark shape of the throne loomed above him, already nearly at its full height. He had lost precious seconds, but it was not too late. The narrow spout would not pour quickly enough, so he grasped the slippery can with both hands, leaned out over the yawning hole, and turned it upside down. For a long second nothing happened, then the last few drops of oil dribbled from the can and began to trickle slowly down the steel pillar.

Miles held his breath. The can was empty. The smoke was dispersing, and he squinted up at the throne that towered above him. It had not slipped downward by so much as an inch. Time seemed to have slowed to a crawl. He could see the Great Cortado high above him, framed in the glare of the lights. "Now you have felt . . . ," the Great Cortado began, and stopped. "Now you . . . " He leaned out from his throne and stared down at Miles, who was suddenly aware of how funny he must look: a failed, half-shaved saboteur coated in oil, soot and sawdust.

He expected to see a look of thunder on the Great Cortado's face, but to Mile's surprise it looked as though two people were fighting for control of his features. Cortado seemed to be struggling not to laugh. Suddenly it dawned on Miles what must have happened. The Great Cortado had not had any antidote! Standing in the creaking elevator earlier that evening, he had unknowingly swallowed nothing more than a mouthful of plain water from the brass tap in the laboratory. Now a thousand nights of concentrated laughter were welling up behind his reddening face, looking for a way out, and only Miles could understand what was happening.

He glanced quickly about him. Silverpoint and the Bolsillo brothers were looking at him expectantly. The audience's laughter had begun to falter, and a number of clowns were advancing on him menacingly. He thought of Little, hiding somewhere below, far from the world of light and freedom where she belonged, and the tiger's words echoed in his head: "A friendship should be judged by its depth, not by its length." Miles nodded to himself. It was time to set her free.

He picked up the empty oil can and threw it at Bobogeek's stand-in, who was getting too close for comfort. The can bounced off his head with a loud *toink*, and the tramp clown slithered comically in the grease before losing his balance altogether and landing heavily on his padded backside. "On with the show!" shouted Miles. The Bolsillo brothers exchanged puzzled glances, then sprang into action as though Miles's words had released their overwound clockwork. Gila, rolled into a ball, came careering across the ring and bowled over three of Cortado's clowns like skittles. Umor grabbed the crutches from Bobogeek, who was slithering across the ring on one plastered foot. He hopped up onto the crutches like a pair of makeshift stilts and tottered over to the fishing clown, now the same height as him. "Look at me, I'm normal!" Umor hollered. The audience laughed. He grabbed the fishing clown's nose and tweaked it hard. The clown gave a yelp of pain.

The band, confused, struck up again, and their insane music rattled around the theater, bringing more laughter in its wake. A clown's curly green wig burst suddenly into flames, and another found the seat of his pants on fire and began to run around the ring shouting for a fire hose. A burly clown with a long red nose like a carrot grabbed Silverpoint from behind. There was a loud crack, and the man staggered backward with blue sparks flying from his ears. Miles expected to be confronted with an irate Genghis at any moment, but he seemed to have vanished into thin air, yellow socks and all. A strangled sound came from above him, and he looked up to see the Great Cortado pointing at him with a quivering finger.

"This boy . . ." He choked, the words barely escaping his throat. "This boy . . . has ruined . . . my . . . show."

And he began to laugh.

CHAPTER THIRTY-ONE
TIN CAN'T

The Great Cortado, clownmaster and laughter-tamer, stood on his throne high above the people of Larde, and laughed. He threw back his head and opened his throat wide and a volcano of laughter roared up into the Palace of Laughter's domed ceiling. It bounced off the pillars and echoed around the walls until it filled the entire theater. He doubled over and clutched his stomach, he bellowed and hooted as the tears ran down his cheeks. Year upon year and show upon show, joke after joke after gag after pratfall came back to him in an irresistible rush, and with no antidote to protect him his face turned pink, then purple, and the veins stood out on his forehead like knotted string. His face-painted henchmen stared, openmouthed, as he crumpled to his knees and tumbled slowly from his perch, falling twelve feet to the floor below and landing with a clang, his head wedged tightly in the empty oil can.

There was a moment's stunned silence, then Silverpoint stepped in front of the Great Crumpled Cortado. He raised his arms as he had seen the Great Cortado do every other night for months. "Ladies and Gentlemen," he shouted, but before he could get any further he was interrupted by a growl from Bobogeek, who had struggled to his feet and was standing unsteadily on his good leg. He pointed at Silverpoint and Miles. "Saboteurs!" he yelled in his nasal whine. "Hypnotists! Subversives! They're trying to take over your minds. Don't listen to a word!"

"Ladies and Gentlemen," began Silverpoint again, shouting louder this time. "Now you have seen the true power of laughter. Elemental laughter that can restore your souls to—"

"Don't listen to him!" yelled Bobogeek. "He'll turn yiz into baboons."

At this, Silverpoint's calm expression cracked slightly. He sent a firebolt flying at Bobogeek's chest, knocking him backward into another clown.

Behind them the faces in the crowd were looking confused and angry. They were muttering to one another, and some were shouting, "Saboteurs! Hypnotists! Baboons!" Somewhere in the middle of the crowd a man was still laughing uncontrollably. It sounded like Genghis.

Silverpoint tried a different tack. "We're on your side. *They* are the hypnotists. You will be safe with us." But without the height of the throne he was just one of a gaggle of clowns trying to shout one another down.

Cortado's henchmen had picked themselves up, and extinguished their wigs and trousers. "Get them," they shouted to the crowd. "Hold them down! String 'em up!"

"He's one of them," shrieked a woman in the audience. Several men, and a little old woman with a sharp green umbrella, had left their seats and were climbing into the ring.

Silverpoint stepped back from the advancing clowns and the irate audience. "What now, plan man?" he muttered to Miles. "And where's Little?"

"She's hiding," said Miles.

"Where?" hissed Silverpoint, but Miles was saved from having to answer. At that moment the main double doors at the back of the theater burst open and a loud voice said, "That's ENOUGH!"

The audience, the clowns and the saboteurs turned as one and stared up at the double doors. Even Genghis, the unlucky winner of the second vial of plain water, twisted his head and gazed up through streaming eyes from where he sat in the aisle, giggling like a large, fat hyena.

Lady Partridge stood framed in the doorway, her hands on her hips and the red dragons flaming in her coal-black dressing gown. "SETTLE DOWN, ALL OF YOU," she boomed, and she began to march down the sloping aisle toward the ring, stepping over Genghis as though he were a bag of rubbish. A stream of cats followed in her wake.

The big clown with the carrot nose stepped in front of her as she approached the end of the aisle. "Authorized personnel only," he said, raising his palm like a policeman stopping a truck.

Lady Partridge paused and stepped to one side. "Gulliver!" she said, and to Miles's astonishment Baltinglass of Araby popped out from behind Lady Partridge's large silhouette. His woolly hat was still on his head, and several days' white stubble bristled from his chin.

"That's no way to speak to a lady," he barked at the clown, and dealt him a sharp crack on the shin with his cane. The clown let out a yelp and hopped backward.

"Who on earth are they?" said Silverpoint.

"It's okay," beamed Miles. "They're friends of mine." He had never been so pleased to see anyone in his life. Lady Partridge swept toward him across the ring like a monument on wheels. Baltinglass followed in the path that her long dressing gown made through the sawdust. Bobogeek, the only one who wasn't glued to the spot by this unexpected interruption, hop-clunked toward them on the one crutch he had managed to retrieve. Baltinglass of Araby stopped and turned toward the sound.

"You got a wooden leg, lad?"

"No, ye blind fossil," sneered Bobogeek.

"Would you like one?" shouted Baltinglass, and he whipped a sword stick from the center of his cane. Bobogeek stepped backward sharply.

Baltinglass wrinkled his nose. "What happened, did you slip on the soap?"

There was a howl of laughter from the aisle. "That's exactly what I said," spluttered Genghis, and he collapsed into giggles again.

The audience had given up trying to make heads or tails of what was going on. They slumped back in their seats with their jaws hanging open, some of them still breaking into fits of laughter.

"Hello, Miles dear," said Lady Partridge as she reached the foot of the throne, and she gave him a wink that only he could see. She looked over at the Bolsillo brothers and their elephant. "Well don't just stand there, boys," she said. "Ask Jumbo to lift me up on this thing." She waved up at the empty throne, as though it had been raised specifically for her arrival.

"The name's Tembo, ma'am."

"Well, Tembo, ask your elephant to give me a lift."

"Tembo's the elephant, ma'am. He's Gila. Hup!"

"Lucky she's been in training," said Gila.

"Manners, Gila," said Fabio, pulling Gila's hat down over his eyes.

Tembo curled her trunk and Lady Partridge stepped onto it. The elephant raised her high into the air. "Hup," said Gila again, and Tembo stood on her hind legs. Lady Partridge wobbled slightly, but if she was nervous she didn't show it. She stepped onto the platform and sat herself on the throne, her untidy pile of gray hair obscuring the manic clown's face painted on its high back.

"Now," she boomed, "would someone please tell me what is going on here? You all look like you've spent a month in the asylum."

"Who are you?" shouted Bobogeek, trying to shake a cat from his leg without falling over. "And why should we tell you anything?"

Lady Partridge glared down at the smelly man. "A gentleman would wait his turn," she said. "However, since you ask, I am Lady Partridge of Larde. In fact, you could say that I'm now a Partridge in a Bare Tree." Some of the audience groaned at Lady Partridge's terrible joke, and even Genghis stopped laughing for a moment.

"Well?" said Lady Partridge, looking down at Miles.

"This man is the Great Cortado," said Miles, pointing at the crumpled heap with his head in an oil can. "He's devised a way of hypnotizing people with laughter, so he can get them hooked on a tonic that only he knows how to produce. He plans to gain control over the whole country."

"Is that so?" said Lady Partridge. She sat straight-backed on the throne and swept the audience with a stern gaze, like a schoolmistress with a class full of naughty pupils. "You were about to let this half-pint with a tin can on his head take over the country?" She gave a healthy guffaw that seemed to sweep the remnants of stale laughter from the air. "Tin can't, more like," she boomed.

The audience groaned. Lady Partridge's awful sense of humor was swiftly taking the edge off their hysteria, and only Genghis, who like Cortado had suffered from a massive overdose of Palace of Laughter performances, chuckled on helplessly.

"Well well," said Lady Partridge, searching the gloom beyond the ring. "Hilda Scratch, is that you? Your mascara has all run down to your chin, girl. You look like a badger. And Spivey, your wife has fallen off her chair. Pick her up for goodness' sake, man. What on earth's the matter with you all? One day trip and you go completely gaga. You all plainly need to get out more."

As she spoke, some of Cortado's clowns began to sneak out of the spotlit ring and up through the dumbstruck audience toward the exit doors. It seemed as though the tables had well and truly turned on their leader. They did not know what kind of treatment this formidable woman would have in mind for them, and they did not want to stay around and find out.

"They're getting away," whispered Miles to Baltinglass.

"No they're not, Master Miles," Baltinglass whispered back. "My nephew Radovan and his constabulary have the place surrounded. At least thirty pairs of good boots I heard, and a great deal of whistle blowing, although that had to be stopped when we got near the place. Had to take the whistles off a couple of the younger lads. Excitable chaps, but keen."

"Taking over the country indeed!" continued Lady Partridge from her throne. "I can scarcely believe you could all fall for this mind-control mumbo jumbo. You should be ashamed of yourselves! I don't doubt that you could all do with cheering up, but there are better ways to brighten your lives than the sort of quackery that these charlatans are trying to sell you. You could start by not cheating your customers out of their change, Piven. Everyone knows they come out of your shop a little light in the pocket. And you, Lily Green, why don't you set up a town newspaper so everyone can read your gossip in black and white, and with the same details to boot? You could get that sister of yours to run the florist shop for you."

She scanned the faces in the gloom, and their owners began to straighten themselves up, as though waking from a bad dream. Many were dimly aware that they had seen this lady in the dressing gown somewhere before. They took out handkerchiefs and wiped their chins. They straightened their hair and their ties in case they were next in line to be singled out.

"And you, Father Soutane," said Lady Partridge, "you should be running a choir in that church of yours, instead of cranking out the same dismal tunes week after week from that wheezy old organ. From the sound of the braying I heard on my way in here, you'd have plenty of strong voices to choose from. Maybe if you all got together three times a week to sing a few stirring songs, you wouldn't get so overexcited when you do get out for a day trip."

The Great Cortado began to stir in the shadow of the throne. Miles caught the movement out of the corner of his eye, and watched him closely. He sat up shakily and reached his hand up to feel his head. His fingers walked around the slippery outside of the oil can, then knocked on it once or twice. "Anyone home?" came a muffled voice from inside the can. "Nope," replied the same voice after a pause. "Got a new head then," said the Not-So-Great Cortado to himself, and he began to laugh in a muffled, metallic way.

Lady Partridge peered down at him. "Help him up, there's a good fellow," she said to Silverpoint. The Great Cortado's legs buckled under him a couple of times, but eventually Miles and

Silverpoint succeeded in getting him to his feet. The tinny laughter that echoed from inside the can was answered by fits of giggling from Genghis, slumped in the darkness of the aisle. As he lay there helplessly, a small figure with a topknot slipped out unnoticed from behind the seats and rifled through his pockets before disappearing through the double doors at the back of the theater.

"Take a good look at these two fellows," said Lady Partridge to the people of Larde. "I think we can safely say that they're out of the World Domination business for the foreseeable future. Now perhaps we can all forget about this nonsense, and make our way back home." She looked down at Baltinglass of Araby. "Gulliver, please lead these people back to the Station Hotel, where they can have a good night's rest before making the journey home. Tell the landlord that the Circus Oscuro will be footing the bill."

And so the people of Larde began to gather themselves—butcher and baker, horse doctor and seamstress and librarian and priest, like a crowd of revelers waking from a party that had gone on for far too long. They helped one another into their coats, picked up their neighbors who were still wobbly on their feet, and made their way to the exit doors, herded by the blind explorer, who was not above dishing out the odd rap with his stick to keep things moving at a brisk pace.

At a word from Gila, Tembo lifted Lady Partridge down from the Great Cortado's throne, and with the help of the elephant the Bolsillo brothers joined Baltinglass in rounding up the stragglers and leading them out of the theater. As the last few Lardespeople left, Sergeant Bramley made his way into the theater. His uniform was rumpled and he had lost his hat, but he looked pleased with himself.

"Thirty-four assorted villains and one huge tattooed lady apprehended, Lady P," he reported as he marched down toward the ring. "The suspects have been placed under arrest and an agreement has been reached with the city constabulary. Cheeky bleeders, begging your pardon, ma'am, wanted to take credit for the whole operation, but we settled on taking the ringleaders back to Larde to be tried by the district judge, while the lower-ranking scoundrels get locked up here in Smelt North Central."

"Congratulations, Sergeant Bramley," said Lady Partridge. "An excellent day's policing without a doubt."

"Nice of you to say so, Lady P," said the sergeant. "I take it this here is the criminal mastermind?" he added a little doubtfully, eyeing the Great Cortado with his tin-can head.

"He's called the Great Cortado," said Miles. "He's been hypnotizing the whole country, bit by bit."

"Is that so?" said Sergeant Bramley, wondering where he had seen this boy with the strange hair-style before. "Well he won't be doing no more hypnotizing once we've got him under lock and key." He took the disoriented Cortado by the arm. "You're under arrest," he said for the tenth time that evening. He had smashed his previous arrest record, which was two vagrants in the same summer, and he was very pleased with himself. "Now," he said, addressing Lady Partridge, "if you wouldn't mind taking these two young lads and vacating these here premises, I'll send in my boys to seal them off for further investigation."

"You go on ahead," said Lady Partridge. "We'll be leaving shortly, and we'll make sure to seal off after us."

"Well . . . ," said Sergeant Bramley, but Lady Partridge fixed him with a hard stare, and he said no more. He marched the Great Giggling Cortado up the aisle to where Genghis lay in a sniggering heap. With the practiced use of his truncheon, the sergeant managed to prod him to his feet and arrest him too, and out through the double doors he went, an archvillain in each hand and a beam of satisfaction on his doughy face.

"Well indeed," said Lady Partridge when he had gone. "I'm delighted to see you safe and sound, Miles, but where is Little, and who is this young man?"

"This is Silverpoint," said Miles. "And I left Little hiding in the laboratory, down in the basement."

"A pleasure to meet you, Silverpoint," said Lady Partridge. "And now we had better fetch Little at once. She must be frightened down there on her own."

"Genghis has the key," said Miles, suddenly remembering the locked iron door to the basement.

"Which one is Genghis?" asked Lady Partridge.

"The big man with the yellow socks, who sergeant Bramley just arrested."

"Then we shall go outside at once and have the sergeant search his pockets for the keys, and while we're about it I shall persuade him to lend us a van and a driver so we can all repair to Gulliver Baltinglass's house for the night, as soon as we have rescued Little. I can't wait to hear how you managed to storm the Palace of Laughter and tin the

Great Cortado all by yourselves."

"I'm staying here," said Miles as a wave of tiredness swept over him. "I can't leave until I've found Tangerine."

CHAPTER THIRTY-TWO
STRING

String the ex-Halfhead, revenge-bent and armed with a reclaimed bone and a dozen keys, crept through the deserted corridors deep below the rapidly emptying theater. He had sneaked into the Palace of Laughter with the crowd of peasants, wrinkling his nose at the unfamiliar smells they wore, which he imagined must be the smells of cows and sheep and other country things that he had never seen. He had hidden himself behind a pillar in the entrance hall as the audience filed into the theater. From his hiding place he had watched as Genghis appeared, dragging Miles by the elbow. He saw them meet the man with the broken leg, and overheard enough of their conversation to guess that the winged girl was still hidden somewhere. He had seen Genghis take the creaking elevator to a lower floor, and after a while he had seen him reappear, his face as black as thunder, tucking into his pocket a large ring of keys as he entered the auditorium.

It was clear to String what he had to do. He would sneak into the theater itself and steal the big man's keys while his attention was distracted by the show. He was no stranger to picking pockets, and he felt confident that the hysterical laughter and crazy music he could hear through the doors would provide him with good cover. The real problem lay in getting to the double doors that led into the theater in the first place. The entrance hall was deserted except for String himself, a giant tattooed lady, and a number of tall pillars. He could dart from one pillar to another if the giantess would just look away, but she sat on her chair against the huge wooden doors, and stared straight ahead of herself until he began to think she might be a statue that had been placed there while he wasn't looking. He was about to risk a quick dash to the theater doors right under her very nose, when there came a hammering on the main door, and muffled shouts from outside. The giantess stood slowly, and lifted her heavy chair aside as though it were doll's house furniture.

When she swung the great doors open she was confronted by a woman as impressively large in width as she was in height. The woman was backed by a number of police, and String instinctively pulled back farther into the shadows. "Kindly let us in," said the broad woman in a stern voice.

The giantess shook her head. "No admission without a ticket," she said. The two large women stared at each other, hands on their hips.

A policeman with a pasty white face stepped up beside the broad woman. "Open in the name of the law," he said.

The giantess answered without even looking at him. "No admission without a warrant," she said.

Suddenly a cat appeared at her feet—a large ginger cat who strolled into the Palace of Laughter with neither ticket nor warrant, followed by a black cat with white patches, and a white cat with black patches. The giantess, caught off guard, stared down at them in surprise, and a moment later she was surrounded by disheveled-looking police with misbuttoned tunics and stubbly chins—and one even wearing pajama bottoms—like an eagle being harried by starlings. They overpowered the giantess by sheer weight of numbers and dragged her outside, while the large lady and a wrinkly old man with a white stick marched on into the theater, leaving the doors wide-open and unguarded behind them.

Stealing the keys had been easier than he had expected. There was chaos of some kind going on in the big ring at the center of the theater. The entire audience seemed to be drunk, and the big man with the keys was lying right in the middle of the aisle, laughing like a loon, and did not even notice being relieved of his property.

String had taken the elevator down to the lowest level, and was now opening each door in turn and searching the rooms for the winged girl. He needed to find her as quickly as possible so that he could make her show him the way out through the clown's ear, since the main entrance was crawling with police. All the doors he had found so far were unlocked, and he chuckled to himself at the stupidity of their occupants. It was true that there wasn't a great deal of value to be stolen, but his pockets had been steadily filling with a fair haul of loose change nonetheless, and a couple of pocket watches to boot. He had found no trace of the girl, however, and he was just beginning to worry that he would not find her in time, when he came to a heavy wooden door and found it locked.

"Bingo," said String to himself. "Now all I have to do is find the right key." He began to try the keys one at a time. Most fit the lock but would not turn. One turned a fraction and got stuck fast, and he tugged and rattled it impatiently. Time was running out, and there was a nasty smell of rotten bananas from the room he was trying to open that was making him feel slightly sick. Suddenly the key turned, and the lock opened with a click. String smiled. He pictured the girl sitting frightened and alone in the corner of the room. She was small, maybe five or six, and she may even already be tied up. He did not think he would have much trouble with her one way or another.

It would have been better for String if he had pictured an enormous black beast, with eyes like holes in the darkness itself, crouched on the other side of the door and filled with a howling madness, for that was what was waiting for him as he chuckled to himself and rattled the keys in the lock.

He turned the handle to open the door, but as he did so it burst outward and sent him flying across the corridor. He slammed into the opposite wall, knocking himself out cold, and slid to the floor, as the nameless hairy beast barged out of its cell with a barking cackle and loped away toward the elevator.

Miles Wednesday, tired, triumphant, but still Tangerine-less, searched the empty theater for his missing bear. He looked in the discarded clown's hat from which Tangerine had emerged in the first place, and he searched among the other props that littered the ring, but he could find no sign of him. Silverpoint had remained to help him, while Lady Partridge went outside to look for Genghis's keys.

The boy and the angel picked their way slowly around the ring, turning over everything they could find. Miles called Tangerine's name, but the vast empty building seemed to answer with a forlorn cackling, as though the crazy laughter were still leaking from the stone walls themselves. He called again, and the cackle answered. It sounded louder this time, and it made the hair stand up on his neck. He had heard that sound before.

"Silverpoint," he said. Silverpoint straightened up, tucking something quickly into his pocket, and turned to him.

"I think The Null is in this building," said Miles.

"You think what?" asked Silverpoint, frowning. "What do you mean?"

"That," said Miles, pointing over Silverpoint's shoulder with a trembling finger, "is The Null."

The creature crouched there, almost filling the doorway. Its red mouth hung open in the hairy blackness. Silverpoint turned and stared. The Null launched itself down the aisle suddenly, heading straight for him. Silverpoint stepped backward, sending a bolt of lightning toward the beast, which howled with pain but did not stop its headlong charge. There was a rustling sound like someone shaking out a starched sheet, and Silverpoint's magnificent wings spread from his shoulders, tearing through his chef's jacket as though it were wet tissue. The creature bowled into him before he could get off the ground, and they rolled over and over across the floodlit ring, an angel and a demon in a ball of sparks and fury. There was another crackle of blue fire and a roar of rage, and a moment later The Null was charging on toward Miles on its feet and knuckles, smoke rising from its burnt hair, and Silverpoint lay motionless on the floor, his eyes closed and his wings outstretched in the greasy sawdust.

CHAPTER THIRTY-THREE
LITTLE

Miles Wednesday, upside-down and oil-coated, hung by his jacket from The Null's ebony fist, high above the empty ring in the Palace of Laughter. After knocking Silverpoint out, the black beast had come straight at him, grabbing him without slackening its pace, and had begun to climb one of the ornately carved pillars that circled the ring. It climbed swiftly, and Miles dangled by a handful of cloth, hoping at first that the jacket would rip and let him drop, and then that the jacket would hold so he wouldn't fall. He held his breath against the smell of rotten bananas and singed hair. He could see Silverpoint, far below and stretched out still on the floor like a drawing of an angel in flight. He saw a small orange dot clamber from the pocket of Silverpoint's destroyed jacket, and even in the grip of the nameless beast he felt a moment of relief that Tangerine had been found.

At the top of the pillar was a carved capital, with laughing stone faces peering from between curling leaves. With a grunt The Null climbed onto the flat ledge above the capital and hauled Miles up after it. The ring was like a saucer far below. Miles looked at The Null's mighty jaws, and remembered the splintering sound as they demolished the bone it had swiped from him back at the Circus Oscuro. The beast let go of his jacket and grabbed him tightly around the chest with its hairy arms. The breath left his lungs with a whoosh.

Miles felt like a marshmallow in a nutcracker. He pushed against The Null's chest with all his strength, and found himself looking straight into the blackness of its eyes. As the beast squeezed tighter, it seemed that the eyes sucked him into a fathomless universe of pain and howling darkness that was trapped inside its bony skull. He could not bear to look any longer, and he squirmed and wriggled, as much to get away from that terrible void as to try and free himself from the beast's bear hug.

He was becoming dizzy from lack of air, and still the beast squeezed tighter. He could hear vague sounds of shouting from below, but he could not look down. As his vision began to fog over he looked across at the laughing stone faces on the next pillar, as though they could somehow help him. He imagined that one of the faces swung open, and he felt an odd desire to laugh. "Now I'm seeing things," he thought.

He saw the face of Little appear where the stone face had been a moment before. The Null squeezed tighter. Little's face was followed by her hands gripping the stonework, and she seemed to pop from the hole in the pillar, wings fluttering in a cloud of soot, and glide through the air toward him. She was calling something to him, but he could not hear her over the sound of his blood roaring in his ears. The Null let out a howl and swiped at Little as she came close, still gripping Miles with its other arm. She dodged the blow, and swooped around to land on the ledge behind them. With the last of his strength Miles tried to free himself from the monster's hold, but his struggling did not loosen The Null's grip in the slightest. He could feel his ribs cracking, and he saw the beast lash out again at Little. It felt as though he were watching from somewhere far away.

She tumbled from the ledge, then recovered herself and flew back toward them, hovering just out of reach of The Null's hairy arm. He could feel his consciousness slipping away, but before the blackness could overtake him he had the strange notion that he could hear the sound of singing.

It began like a single voice from a half-remembered dream, and grew stronger and fuller until it swept right through him like a flowing river of light, a sweet blend of birdsong and breeze, of bells and rushing riverwater, and a thousand other sounds of warmth and life and sunlight. It was the most beautiful song he had ever heard, and his pain and fear melted away before it. All the dreams and hopes, the sorrow and simple joy that he had ever felt seemed to be woven into the music as it swirled through him and around him, and the brightest thread of all, the shining sound that held it all together, was the sound of laughter—real, warm laughter glinting through the weave of life and friendship like a thread of gold.

Miles realized that he was breathing again. The Null's deathly grip around his chest had loosened. It let him go, and in his dizziness he almost fell forward into space. He saw Little smiling at him, still just out of reach, as she came to the end of her song.

He knew that the beautiful sound that had quieted the beast and saved him from death must be her real name, the name that she could never utter without binding herself to Earth, but still he did not want the music to end. As the last few notes died away, Little's wings melted into her skin and sadness overtook her smile. Miles watched helplessly as she fell toward the ring far below, just a small girl tumbling over and over with no magic, no wings, no song left to lift her.

The ring was crowded now with people, looking up toward them. He could see Lady Partridge standing there among the blue-uniformed policemen, and the three tiny figures of the Bolsillo brothers, holding between them something that looked no bigger than a coin. Little fell straight toward them, and they shuffled first to one side, then to the other, never taking their eyes off her. After what seemed like forever she landed right in the middle of the trampoline, for that is what they were holding, and bounced high into the air. The assembled policemen broke into applause, and suddenly the whole scene transformed itself into a simple circus act. A troupe of fools dressed in pajamas and misbuttoned uniforms ran in circles around a fat lady, while a tiny acrobat bounced gracefully on a trampoline held by three tiny clowns, and Miles was struck by the strangest of feelings. Perched high above the floodlit circus ring like a trapeze artist awaiting his cue, he felt truly at home for the first time in his life. It was as though he had always belonged here, and the circus had just been waiting patiently for his return.

Miles turned to look at The Null, sitting slumped against the pillar, its fearful eyes closed and its huge jaw slackened into something that looked almost like a smile. He leaned back against the pillar beside the stupefied beast. His cracked ribs began to ache. "And where do you fit in, I wonder?" he asked, as tiredness swept over him and he slipped from consciousness.

Miles Wednesday, monster-squeezed and song-saved, awoke on a lumpy sofa in a firelit room. He could dimly see people sitting around a fire that blazed in the hearth, talking in low voices. He tried to sit up, but a sharp pain shot through his bruised ribs. "Ow!" he hissed.

The talk around the fire stopped, and everyone turned to look at him. "So you're back from the uncharted regions, Master Miles," barked Baltinglass's voice. "I hope you planted a few flags along the way!"

"Sit up carefully, my dear," said Lady Partridge, "and I'll get you a mug of cocoa."

Miles eased himself into a sitting position. He had been bandaged tightly around the ribs and propped on soft cushions, and the bones had been removed from his hair. He could see now that he was in Baltinglass's living room, dimly lit by a couple of candles that the old man had managed to dig out of his supply depot, and the flickering light of the fire in the hearth. Baltinglass of Araby sat in a leather armchair by the fire, a large gin and tonic in his hand in case the malaria chose that moment to ambush him. Lady Partridge rose from another armchair, cats spilling from her lap as she made for the kitchen. Fabio, Gila and Umor perched on an assortment of stools, and Little sat on the rug in front of the stone hearth, smiling at him for all she was worth and looking none the worse for her fall from the ceiling of the Palace of Laughter.

"Where's Silverpoint?" asked Miles.

"Resting in the bunk room," said Baltinglass. "Had a tussle with a yeti, so they tell me. Could've sworn he had a couple of broken bones when I looked him over at the Palace of Laughter, but when we brought him back here to set 'em, I couldn't find so much as a fracture. Tough as a Magyar, that lad. Hasn't come round yet, though, so we've left him in his cot."

"And Henry!" said Miles, feeling a sudden stab of guilt at the thought of the small boy suspended in the night sky. "We have to go back for Henry. I promised!"

"It's all right," said Little. "The policeman rescued Henry."

"My own nephew, Radovan Flap, rescued the boy," shouted Baltinglass. "Climbed up in the dark with a lantern hanging from his belt and brought the lad down single-handedly. No shortage of pluck, that young Radovan. Gets it from his mother's side, may the gods play a happy tune on her old bones. Would've gone up myself, but the lad wouldn't hear of it."

Little came and sat on the end of the sofa, shooing a couple of cats out of the way. The soot had been cleaned from her hair, and she was wearing an old dressing gown many sizes too big for her.

"How are you feeling?" she asked.

"A bit bruised, but I'll be fine. But what about you? What about—"

Little put her finger to her lips. Miles lowered his voice to a whisper. "Why did you have to sing your name?" he asked. "You can never go home now, can you?"

Little shook her head.

"Couldn't you . . . couldn't you have found The Null's own name to sing to it, and kept yours to yourself?" whispered Miles.

"I looked for its name," she said, "and I found the place where it should be, but there was only a black hole in the One Song itself, as though the name had been torn out and stolen." She winced at the memory, then smiled at Miles. "Besides, I want to stay here with you. You need a little sister."

Miles searched her face, but could see no sign of regret. He felt a warm feeling spreading from his stomach.

"Won't you miss it? The Realm, and . . . and flying?"

"Of course," said Little, "but I've found something better."

"What could be better than flying, and that beautiful music?" He could still hear an echo of Little's Song in his ear, and he hoped it would never fade away.

"The One Song is beautiful," agreed Little, "But . . ." She searched for the words. "But up there, I only got to sing it. Down here I can live it. Down here I can have real friends." A smile lit up her face. "And that reminds me . . ."

She reached in her pocket and took out

Tangerine. She handed him to Miles. The small bear wriggled out of his hand and climbed to his shoulder, where he snuggled against Miles's ear. The familiar feel of his worn fur seemed to ease the ache in Miles's ribs, and the smile of contentment on his face stretched even wider.

"Thank you," he whispered.

"Told you so," said Umor from the edge of the fireplace.

"It's really his," said Gila.

"Then it must be him," said Fabio.

"Has to be," said Umor.

"He doesn't look very dead," said Gila. Fabio shushed him with a frown.

"Where did you grow up, Master Miles?" asked Fabio.

"In Pinchbucket House," said Miles. "It's an orphanage. Why?"

"Can you remember where you got that bear?"

Miles shook his head. "I've had him all my life. I know I had him when I came to the orphanage, because the Pinchbuckets never gave us anything."

"We can remember," said Gila.

"Eleven years ago to the day," said Fabio.

"Which makes it your birthday."

"Happy birthday, Master Miles."

Miles looked at the three tiny men, wondering what kind of game they were playing. "What do you mean?" he said. "Even I don't know when my birthday is."

"It's a long story," said Fabio.

"We thought you were lost, a long time since," said Umor.

"Or dead," said Gila. He rummaged in his pocket for a handkerchief, and finding none, blew his nose on the corner of Fabio's jacket.

"But I've never met you before I came to the Palace of Laughter. How could you know about me?" asked Miles in bewilderment.

"We were there the night you were born," said Fabio.

"We gave you that bear when you were only hours old."

"Before you even had a name."

"Your father, Barty Fumble, was our boss, Master Miles."

"He was like an uncle to us."

"Or an aunt."

"Not really. He was big and strong, with a beard."

"So was the bearded lady."

"Whatever happened to her?"

"I heard she opened a barber shop in Nape."

Miles stared at them with his mouth open. "Barty Fumble was my father?" he said. "Of Barty Fumble's Big Top?"

"Ah, you've heard of Barty Fumble's Big Top?" said Umor.

"Of course," said Miles. "A ti . . . a friend told me the story. But Barty left the circus and took his son with him." He tried to picture the big bearded man in the dead of night, leaving the circus that was his life, stricken with grief and carrying his infant son in his arms. "Me," thought Miles. "Barty Fumble's boy."

"Then . . . what happened to Barty . . . to my father? Where did he go?"

Fabio sighed. "I wish I could tell you the answer to that, Master Miles."

"He left in the dead of night," sniffed Gila.

"And we never heard from him again," added Umor.

"Nor of you, neither, until yesterday."

Miles could scarcely grasp this astonishing news. In the space of a minute he had gained a little sister, and learned that the father he had always believed to be dead was none other than Barty Fumble himself, and that he might still be alive. He was surprised to find tears welling in his eyes as he realized, too, that there was no such hope for his mother. An entire family history had stepped into place behind him. It was a history he already knew something about, and it certainly explained why he had felt so at home perched high above the circus ring in the Palace of Laughter.

Little echoed his thoughts. "That's why the tiger said you had the circus in you," she said, smiling. "I told you tigers never lie."

Miles nodded. It was all too much to take in, and his head swam with the details. Was it just coincidence that Barty Fumble too had counted a tiger as his friend? And why did he leave his child to grow up in the mean grasp of the Pinchbuckets? Suddenly he had answers to questions that he had always carried at the back of his mind, but they brought more questions in their wake, and he was not sure that he wanted them. He had always told himself that both his parents were dead. It was a simple story and a hard one, but knowing the truth seemed to make things much more complicated.

"Don't hold it against your father, my dear," said Lady Partridge. She sat on the arm of the sofa (which creaked in protest) and handed him a mug of steaming cocoa. "We can never understand the decisions people have to face without knowing all the details, and sometimes not even then. In time you may learn more about your parents, and their story will become clearer."

Miles nodded. There were too many things spinning around in his head, and he still had more questions to ask. The Bolsillo brothers dragged the heavy sofa closer to the fire, and there they all sat in comfortable silence, each with their own thoughts: the boy, the lady, three tiny clowns, a blind explorer and a four-hundred-year-old girl with the faint outline of a lost pair of wings etched into the skin of her back.

Silverpoint, marble-skinned and straight-winged, took his leave the following night in Baltinglass's moonlit orchard. He had recovered with remarkable speed from his encounter with The Null, and said that it was time for him to return home and explain his absence, and how he had managed to lose a Song Angel to the hungry Earth. Before he left he had tried to persuade Miles to let him restore Tangerine to his former self. He pointed out that Little was not permitted to give life to any inanimate object, and that the walking, dancing bear was a grave offense against nature. If its existence was discovered, he said, it would make matters even worse. At this, Little flew into a rare temper and refused point-blank to let Silverpoint near Tangerine, and eventually he was forced to let the matter drop.

Silverpoint shook Miles's hand as he had when they first met, and though Miles was ready for the tingling sensation it still made his hair stand on end. The Storm Angel's dark eyes looked searchingly into his for what seemed a long time, then he turned and embraced Little, lifting her off her feet. As he did so he whispered something in her ear, and his eyes flickered in Miles's direction. Little seemed to stiffen slightly. "Take care, little softwing," said Silverpoint.

"Good-bye," said Little as he put her gently down, and behind the tears that glinted in the light of the moon, Miles thought he heard indignation in her voice.

Silverpoint stood in the stillness of the autumn night among the rows of apple trees, and with a frown of concentration on his pale face he conjured up a storm to cover his departure. Black clouds rolled in from nowhere like pirate ships, covering the moon and throwing the small town of Cnoc into darkness. A sudden torrent of hailstones lashed the roofs and clattered in the leaves of the apple trees.

"Will you be in a lot of trouble?" shouted Miles above the noise.

Silverpoint nodded. "I expect so," he said. "They'll probably have me making drizzle for a century."

The winged boy walked backward through the trees until he had placed a distance between himself and the others. He looked up into the blackness above. A twisted rope of blue lightning split the sky with a deafening crash and struck the spot where he stood, leaving Miles and Little momentarily as blind as Baltinglass himself. When their sight returned, the black clouds were dissolving like dreams. One of Baltinglass's apple trees was split clean in two, and Silverpoint was no longer there.

The morning after Silverpoint's departure Miles woke late, with the sunlight slanting in through his window. The sky was washed clean by the storm that the angel had created, and the rich smell of damp earth drifted in through the open windows. He found Baltinglass, Lady Partridge and the three Bolsillo brothers deep in conversation on the sun-dappled patio. They were discussing a plan to devise an entirely new show from the remnants of the Circus Oscuro, under the ownership of the

Bolsillo brothers themselves, which would reverse the Great Cortado's sinister hypnosis, and wean those people who had been "laughtered" off Dr. Tau-Tau's Tonic for good. Miles thought he heard Little's name mentioned, but the subject seemed to change when he arrived.

He sat himself at the table and listened with his chin resting on his hands, but no one paid him any further attention, and after a while he took an apple from the wooden bowl in the center of the table and went to look for Little. He found her eventually, after an extensive search of Baltinglass's rambling house, sitting in the window of a small tower room in the roof. She was gazing through the dusty pane at the lightning-split tree in the orchard, and when he asked her if she was all right, she nodded, but did not say a word or turn her head to look at him.

Miles sighed and closed the door softly behind him. He wandered down through the house and out into the orchard, feeling slightly left out. He made his way toward the far end of the walled garden, where the orderly apple trees gave way to a jumbled undergrowth of strange foreign plants with enormous dark leaves, as though some far-off patch of jungle had been unable to part company with Baltinglass and had followed him home. Miles scuffed his feet through the first fallen leaves, and when his toes met the weight of an apple in the grass he gave it a sharp kick, sending it sailing into the undergrowth. There was a low growl, and a tiger's head appeared from the bushes. Miles felt his heart leap.

"Tub boy," grunted the tiger. "I might have guessed. Your manners haven't improved since we last met." He turned and disappeared into the undergrowth, and Miles almost ran to catch up, half afraid that the tiger would vanish as he had before. He found the tiger stretched out in a small clearing in the center of the miniature jungle. Miles sat down in the grass nearby.

"You found what you were looking for, I take it?" said the tiger.

Miles nodded. He hardly knew where to start.

"I got Tangerine back," he said, "and we found Silverpoint." He picked up the bruised apple and twirled it on its stem. "Lots of other stuff happened too, after you left. We could have done with your help in the Palace of Laughter."

"You still insist on thinking you can call me up like a plumber, I see," rumbled the tiger. "In any case, you seem to have managed all right by yourselves."

"I barely escaped with my life," said Miles. "It was Little who saved me."

The tiger looked at him. "I told you she would prove a valuable companion," he said. "And I am not often wrong. How did she manage to snatch you from the jaws of death?"

"It's a long story," said Miles.

"Then you had better put it in a nutshell for me," yawned the tiger. "They say patience is a virtue, but it's not one of mine."

"She gave up her name for me," said Miles, "and now she can never go home."

"More riddles," said the tiger. "I won't waste time trying to solve it, but it sounds like a noble sacrifice. You had better make sure she never regrets it."

"I'll do my best," said Miles.

"I should hope so," said the tiger. He stretched out in the grass and flicked his tail idly. "Of course, I may have played a small part in your rescue myself," he said.

"You did?" said Miles. "But I thought you wouldn't go near the city."

"You thought right," said the tiger. "But I'm surprised you haven't wondered about the fortuitous timing of your rescue party's arrival."

Miles frowned in puzzlement. "You mean you told Lady Partridge?"

The tiger chuckled. "You should know I am not

in the habit of popping up in people's living rooms, especially if they happen to be perched in a tree. Your ample friend, however, has the good sense to listen to her cats, even if she has little understanding of their speech. It was enough to inform them where you were, and that you were stepping into deep waters. They are resourceful little midgets you know, and plucky too."

Miles considered what the tiger had told him. "Why did you do that for us?" he asked.

The tiger sighed. "Questions, questions," he said. "Life follows its course like a river runs in its bed, tub boy. Perhaps you should just be grateful that things have worked out for you, and leave the chattering to the monkeys."

"I am grateful," said Miles. "Thank you."

"Think nothing of it," said the tiger. "Now I must be on my way, and it's time you went to cheer up your little friend in the attic. She has been moping at that window since before sunrise, and she has probably had enough of being alone by now."

Miles looked up at the window. He could just see Little's pale face in the gloom, and he wondered if she could see the tiger. A chilly breeze rustled through the bushes, making him shiver as he got to his feet. "Will we see you again?" he asked.

"It's my experience," said the tiger, "that once you have crossed someone's path a couple of times you are bound to cross it again in the future. Unless, of course, you have eaten them," he added.

"So long then," said Miles. He took a last look at the tiger, stretched out and striped in the jungle shade, and pushed his way through the bushes into the cold wind of the autumn day.

CHAPTER THIRTY-FOUR
THE LARDE WEEKLY HERALD

Miles Wednesday, villain tamer and hero of Larde, sat in an old armchair in the rebuilt gazebo by Lady Partridge's pond, and read aloud to The Null from a newspaper. He did not imagine for one moment that the creature could understand what he was reading, but it was still subject to frequent fits of madness, and the sound of his voice seemed to have a calming effect. In any case Lady Partridge had set him the task of reading the paper from cover to cover each week as part of his education, and he found it easiest to concentrate in the peace and quiet of the early morning when he brought The Null its breakfast.

The gazebo had been converted into a sort of fortified residence for the beast, after a lengthy and boisterous town meeting had debated its fate well into the night. Mayor Doggett was all for having The Null put down at once. He said it was a menace to society, and should be stuffed and mounted and displayed in a prominent place, such as the lobby of the town hall, where it might become a renowned attraction for visitors. This idea had earned him a sharp kick under the table from Mrs. Doggett, who suggested that the beast should be presented to the Smelt city zoo, where it could be reunited with "others of its kind," although she was as vague as anyone on what that kind might be. After many other suggestions had been shouted by the Lardespeople, from harnessing The Null to a plough to training it as a game warden, Miles had stepped up to the podium and the people had fallen silent to hear what he had to say.

He began, in a hesitant voice, by saying that he of all people would have good reason to want The Null stuffed and mounted, or locked away in a far-off zoo. The townspeople nodded as one. Yet despite having been throttled to within an inch of his life by the beast, Miles went on, he could not help thinking that somewhere deep inside its fearsome exterior there lay something like a soul. The townspeople began to look more doubtful at this, but Miles would not elaborate. He was thinking of what Little had told him about the creature's missing name, and he wondered privately how it could be that any creature could be left unnamed in the tongues of both men and of angels, but this was not something he felt he could explain to the people of Larde. At this point Lady Partridge stood and boomed that if it was Miles's wish to try and befriend the creature, that was good enough for her, and she would have her gazebo converted to provide suitable accommodation. If there was anyone in Larde who had the nerve to try and obstruct Lady Partridge's wishes, that person was certainly absent from the meeting that night.

Now The Null sat brooding in a corner of the straw-carpeted room, separated by a set of stout bars from the small lobby with the armchair where Miles sat. The newspaper from which he was reading was *The Larde Weekly Herald*, which Lily the florist had set up on her return from the Palace of Laughter. Like most of the people who had made the trip, her memory of that night's momentous events was dim and confused, but she had returned to Larde with a strange urge to leave the flower business to her sister Maggie, and go into the newspaper business instead. Taking full advantage of the town's collective amnesia she produced a first issue that was so fat with outlandish stories that it sold out in a matter of hours, and a second edition had to be hastily printed, followed by a third.

The exploits of Miles Wednesday had featured heavily in the first few issues of the paper, making him something of a local hero. Stories of the Boy from the Barrel who had fought savage tribes in the city and brought down a notorious villain almost single-handedly had been read and reread, until many people were surprised, when they met him, to find that he was not ten feet tall.

Lady Partridge's dramatic rescue mission to the Palace of Laughter had also been covered in some detail. Though she had refused to be interviewed personally (far too busy for that sort of thing) a riveting story had been pieced together from the accounts of various policemen and other witnesses. Apparently Lady Partridge's cats had somehow alerted her to the danger in which Miles and Little had found themselves. How the cats could have known, far less made their anxieties clear to Lady Partridge, no one could say. In any case she had grasped the seriousness of the situation at once. She had intercepted Sergeant Bramley just as he was locking up the police station for the night, and harangued him into rounding up his two constables and setting off for the surrounding villages to collect a rescue party. The half-pajamaed task force had taken to the highway in a small fleet of battered police vans, and since half the population of Larde had taken a train to the Palace of Laughter the day before, the policemen reasoned as Miles and Little had done, and followed the railway tracks.

If the policemen felt disgruntled at their rude awakening, their tiredness soon turned to excitement as they hurtled through the dawn at breakneck speed. Sometime before midday they had roared into the sleepy town of Cnoc, their whistles and sirens blowing, and screeched to a halt outside the house of Constable Flap's uncle and Lady Partridge's old friend, the famous explorer Gulliver P. Baltinglass. There were many dry throats and full bladders to be dealt with, but to their surprise they found that Baltinglass of Araby had not only met Miles Wednesday, but had provisioned him and sent him on his way two days before. When Baltinglass in turn learned of Lady Partridge's mission, he had torn off his apron and clambered into the lead van, leaving a relieved Rufus Weedle to escape the third and last day of his hard labor, at least for the time being.

There were so many conflicting accounts of what had happened when the rescue party reached the Palace of Laughter, and about how it was that the Boy from the Barrel had already managed to dethrone the Great Cortado and subdue him with a tin can, that Lily had decided they should all be published in the interests of balanced reporting.

As for The Null itself, the exact nature of the beast continued to be the topic of much debate, which led to it being described both as a previously unknown species of hyena, and as a cross between a giant Ivory Coast Baboon and a Tibetan Yeti, in the same issue of the paper. Several policemen from Larde and the surrounding villages claimed that the beast had been attacked by angels as it attempted to strangle the Boy from the Barrel, and that the boy's little sister herself had been one of them, and was over five thousand years old.

These last stories were of course dismissed as complete fantasy. Most people put them down to the long journey the brave constables had undertaken at great speed, which might have rattled their brains somewhat, but they enjoyed reading them all the same. As for the girl herself, there was always a smile on her face and music in her laughter, and the Lardespeople had grown so fond of her that they would not have cared if she had come from the planet Neptune.

The second issue of the *Herald* also featured a detailed account of the mysterious disappearance of Mr. and Mrs. Fowler Pinchbucket from the town orphanage. The paper reported that Miles Wednesday, the Boy from the Barrel, had paid a visit to Pinchbucket House the day after his return from his adventures in Smelt, accompanied by Sergeant Bramley and his two constables. They had a warrant to search the premises on suspicion that the Pinchbuckets had been stealing the property of the orphans and using the children themselves for slave labor.

To their surprise they had found the orphanage in an uproar. A party had been going on for most of the night, and there was not a sign of an adult in the whole building. None of the children were sure what had happened to the Pinchbuckets, except for two small boys, Ruben Monday and Lawrence Friday. Their outlandish statement told of a huge tiger that had appeared in the orphanage hall in the dead of night. The terrified boys, who had been paying a secret visit to the orphanage kitchen, claimed that the tiger had bounded up the stairs and made his way straight past them to the Pinchbuckets' bedroom. A moment later, the *Herald* said, the Pinchbuckets had emerged shrieking from their room and had stumbled down the stairs and out through the front door of the orphanage, with the tiger in hot pursuit. They had not been seen or heard from since. In the absence of any more reliable witness accounts, the sergeant had filed the incident under Missing Persons, and the case had been closed.

Lady Partridge had been appointed the new director of the town orphanage by Mayor Doggett himself. She had found herself unexpectedly wealthy once more thanks to a miracle cure produced by an obscure factory that her late husband had owned. The chemical in question, which was meant to be a weed killer but had had no effect whatsoever on the gardens of the nation, was discovered by accident to be an excellent cure for insomnia, halitosis, pessimism and nose-drip. It was now selling like hotcakes all over the land, and with the money that had been pouring into Lady Partridge's coffers she had hired a team of skilled craftsmen to restore her mansion to its former glory. Once the restoration work was completed she planned to move the orphanage lock, stock and barrel from its grim municipal building to her newly refurbished stately home.

The *Herald* had reported the appearance of the Once Great Cortado and his accomplice Genghis in court, to answer charages of Attempted Despotism and Accessory to Mind Control Offenses respectively. The two men had been assessed by a leading psychiatrist from Shallowford, who decided they were unshackled from their wits and unfit to answer the charges. They had been committed to the secure wing of Saint Bonifacio's Hospital for the Unhinged, where Cortado would refuse to emerge from his cell for days on end, lurking in the darkness with nothing for company but his own hollow laughter. Genghis, by contrast, had found a use for himself tending the hospital's vegetable garden, between fits of helpless giggling. Inside his Wellington boots he still wore lemon yellow socks.

And so the winter wore on. Lady Partridge's new orphanage took shape steadily. In the mornings the children were schooled by Lady Partridge herself in what used to be the ballroom. Baltinglass of Araby would make the occasional surprise visit to give them a vigorously shouted geography lesson, filled with crocodiles and canyons and endless oceans of white sand, and afterward he would stomp off to have lunch with his nephew, Radovan, who had adopted Henry once all attempts to trace his family had failed.

In the afternoons the children played in the rambling gardens, and the sound of their laughter, like a genie which had finally been released from the gray bottle of Pinchbucket House, filled the grounds and the rooms of the mansion itself, which the Lardespeople had begun to refer to as "The Real Palace of Laughter." By night the grand bedrooms of Partridge Manor, filled now with brand-new bunk beds and warmed with real log fires, whispered with the soft breathing and the night sighs of its new occupants, mingled with the purring of the cats who curled up at the childrens' feet.

In the crisp winter nights Miles would often dream of his father, Barty Fumble, the barrel-chested man with the huge beard and the laugh that could rattle windows. He would see him on a lone horse in the mapless canyons of the South, or sunken-cheeked in an eastern opium den, with nothing for company but a burden of sorrow that none could help him carry. In these dreams Miles came to understand why his father had left him in the orphanage on that distant night. He had lost the wife he loved to a fate he was powerless to control, and the fear that someday this might happen to his son was more than his broken heart could bear. Miles would wake from these dreams with an empty feeling. He knew how it felt to face losing someone he loved, but he longed to tell his father what he had learned himself: that a hundred hours of friendship was worth more than a hundred years with a padlocked heart. Lying in his bed he promised himself that one day soon he would follow his father's trail and bring him back, man or bones, to the only family he had left, even if that trail led to the gates of hell itself.

As he waited for sleep to return Miles would think over the adventures he and Little had shared. He pictured them riding on the tiger's back, or crawling through tunnels in a giant clown's head, almost as if it they had been people in a story. He would look at the sleeping face of Little, her skin still glowing faintly when moonlight touched her, and wonder if she dreamed still of soaring through the magnificent realm in the skies, the world that she had given up to save his life. He would think then of the promise that he had made to the tiger at the end of an orchard on a chilly autumn day, the promise that whatever the future might bring, he would do everything in his power to make her life on earth as magical as the one she had left behind.

ACKNOWLEDGMENTS

Thank you, Mary Waugh,
for the peace and quiet of your yellow boat,
and Eunice McMullen
for your masterful hat trick.

The Julie Andrews Collection
encompasses books for young readers of all ages that nurture the imagination and celebrate a sense of wonder.

For more information about
The Julie Andrews Collection, visit
www.julieandrewscollection.com.

Words. Wisdom. Wonder.

Did you like this book? Julie Andrews would love to read your review of THE PALACE OF LAUGHTER, or any of the books in the Julie Andrews Collection. Write to her at:

JULIE ANDREWS
THE JULIE ANDREWS COLLECTION
HARPERCOLLINS CHILDREN'S BOOKS
1350 AVENUE OF THE AMERICAS
NEW YORK, NY 10019
or
INFO@JULIEANDREWSCOLLECTION.COM

From time to time we will post reader reviews on the Julie Andrews Collection website. Please include permission to quote your review and include your name and location when you submit it.

Other books you might enjoy in the Julie Andrews Collection:

BLUE WOLF by Catherine Creedon

DRAGON: *Hound of Honor* by Julie Andrews Edwards and Emma Walton Hamilton

DUMPY AND THE FIREFIGHTERS by Julie Andrews Edwards and Emma Walton Hamilton, illustrated by Tony Walton

DUMPY'S APPLE SHOP by Julie Andrews Edwards and Emma Walton Hamilton, illustrated by Tony Walton

DUMPY'S EXTRA-BUSY DAY by Julie Andrews Edwards and Emma Walton Hamilton, illustrated by Tony Walton

DUMPY'S HAPPY HOLIDAY by Julie Andrews Edwards and Emma Walton Hamilton, illustrated by Tony Walton

DUMPY'S VALENTINE by Julie Andrews Edwards and Emma Walton Hamilton, illustrated by Tony Walton

DUMPY TO THE RESCUE! by Julie Andrews Edwards and Emma Walton Hamilton, illustrated by Tony Walton

GRATEFUL: *A Song of Giving Thanks* by John Bucchino, illustrated by Anna-Liisa Hakkarainen

THE GREAT AMERICAN MOUSICAL by Julie Andrews Edwards and Emma Walton Hamilton, illustrated by Tony Walton

THE LAST OF THE REALLY GREAT WHANGDOODLES by Julie Andrews Edwards

THE LEGEND OF HOLLY CLAUS by Brittney Ryan

THE LITTLE GREY MEN by BB, illustrated by Denys Watkins-Pitchford

LITTLE KISSES by Jolie Jones, illustrated by Julie Downing

MANDY by Julie Andrews Edwards

SIMEON'S GIFT by Julie Andrews Edwards and Emma Walton Hamilton, illustrated by Gennady Spirin